BUBBLES

Genc Xërxa

April 2017-January 2018

Rekuiem

Burn me with the cold ice water, which only Ibri knows how to do, powder me in the Serpent who knows how to confuse many black things, reveal all the secrets that except Lushta no one can cook, with the weight of being present, the blade of the word, oh sword of falconry. Send me where the lullaby of the last years, the first lines speak, I didn't run away from the pain, I was angry with the future, hurt in the head, Yes! I didn't mention it, with open eyes I have often laid my forehead on this earth that gave me, name, life, fate and everything that I am now.

A plate in me, a mark even for those that I never managed to be. Burn me, pulverize me or scatter me so that my smell from now on has a name.

With the sounds of Satch's guitar crying, the dusty wind blows like it speaks that it is not the last breath, but a new beginning, where I will never be consumed... forever!

To The Father

Prof. Besim Xërxa

In memory of all sexual victims in the wars of the former Yugoslavia, especially those that occurred in Kosovo, with the aim of empathizing with them, where the state and the country's institutions are doing very little in this regard for this social category.

Table of Contents

I

As soon as she woke up, Shpresa looked up at the roof, wet from the rain that had been falling for hours. Throughout the night, she looked around the entire room, which was choked by the smell of humidity and the walls that only manifested jinx. She looked at Arbër, her brother, who was still sleeping. He had grown up and it was evident from the size of the sheet that no longer fit him. There was her brother, her mother, her father, …Arber was her whole life. For a moment she watched an insect on the wall, trying to find some prey to eat, crawling around the rickety dresser and sometimes the furniture that creaked if you touched it, finding its way through the cracked wall.

The concentration on the work, the effort that the wandering creature was doing, made Shpresa stand up for a moment, frightened. She looked at her body, her nightclothes and saw that she was covered in blood, her period was bothering her. With the fluid flowing from her body, her soul felt relieved for a moment. She ran to change her clothes while her brother was still sleeping and he still had time to go to class, it was seven o'clock. Shpresa, trying to wake up, rubbed her eyes with both hands until she stood in front of the mirror in the bathroom, which was colder than outside. The house was ruined like she was from sleep, which was more tiring than it was restful. She splashed her eyes with cold water, faced her face, the image that seemed fragile through the cracks in the glass. Those cracks resembled her soul that had been broken and shattered many times. Her face now seemed to be mistakenly mosaiced by pieces of glass that never made up the entirety of her face, it was detached and broken into pieces where each piece didn't match the other, didn't resemble herself. As if she was afraid. Suddenly she quickly moved away from looking him and glanced once more at her brother whom she was looking at with a pain, melancholy like something that was tearing her apart, tearing her away from the vision that had remained in the previous glass. She had to get ready for her daily work. She wore of pants that she had ready as a uniform. She often wore them with a blouse that had lost its shine and looked at her hand bag and the shoes that didn't fit at all, didn't tie together in a way. But these were all the best things she had at the moment. She put some cream on her face since she didn't have the makeup assortment that matched her makeup, combed her hair and approached the kitchen, if you could call it that. There was a hotplate and a small refrigerator next to some cupboards that held the food items reduced by the budget that this household could afford. She took a piece of bread, heated some water to prepare some tea for herself and her brother, placed some pieces of cheese on a plate. She placed them on the table for Arbër and herself on a wooden tray, before they left the house. Arbër woke up from the noise or movements of his sister in the alcove they called the kitchen, which was an integral part of the single room and the bathroom that was located as an annex in the adjacent part of the house. He opened his eyes, saw his sister doing the same thing she did every morning, addressing his brother, calling:

-Honey, are you awake? Come on, wake up and we'll have breakfast together because we're leaving, don't be late, - said the sister in a sweet voice, trying to lighten his view, his sad gaze, from the eyes that were fixed by the raindrops that had fallen on the corner of the wall.

- What are we having for breakfast? Don't say cheese with tea, please, as if jokingly, - said the brother, knowing what awaited him as a morning awakening.

Shpresa, with a friendly look, approved of his joke and silently arranged the table where he would sit. The two of them thoughtfully finished a few bites of bread, with linden tea, which she had taken from her garden. Shpresa ate very little, something was not chewing, she didn't like the food, it didn't go well. She drank the tea and got up. The two left the house, one for school and the sister for the Danaj couple who were older, where she took care of cleaning and was a household help. Arbër was in the ninth grade of the city's primary school. They had to use transportation to get to their destinations since they lived on the outskirts of the city. Shpresa, looking at the house that looked like a log cabin, quickly walked along the yard and remembered how her uncle had sheltered them there after the war, and even today, they had been there for ten years. She remembered a lot of things in the meantime and a cold current ran through her body, she shivered but she stopped at the van stop that would take her to Danaj. She hugged Arbër who continued towards the school and they parted ways. The van in which she was sitting was humming with patriotic folk songs. The voice was so loud that it pierced her ears. The van was enveloped in all sorts of food aromas and humidity carried by the other passengers, were crowded together. From the window she saw her childhood friend Liria, whose name seemed to suit her lifestyle. Dressed beautifully, she shone in her walk with full self-confidence, her beautifully combed, golden hair with an artist's hat, with a beautifully twisted scarf spoke of a modern lady.

Suddenly, an international car approached her. She got in after it stopped. They were her work colleagues, who had come to pick her up for work. She had been working for an international organization since after war. It had been going quite well for her. Without taking her eyes off her, Shpresa remembered the time when they were children and the games they had played together. They had been classmates, inseparable until the war and divided entire families, men and women, of course and friends. There was also talk of newlyweds or lovers who had promised each other an eternity together, but the black plague had taken its toll. The war had intervened and stolen the next days of loving fidelity. She remembered the whole time and it seemed to her that very soon she reached the family where she worked.

After getting off, she left the van with the cheerfulness of a broken and monotonous tile, the fresh air was very welcome compared to what had reigned until a moment ago. She took a deep breath, glanced towards the largest house in the neighborhood that was not far from where she stopped. The closer she got, the bigger the house became, it stood out in terms of its plan, appearance, and beauty, there was no comparison in that neighborhood. The house itself spoke of the owners being financially well-off and having good welfare and considerable capital, which they had actually accumulated over the years during their work in Switzerland. Shpresa got ready and went into the house.

II

Liria just escorted the bidder to the procurement office regarding a contract at the international office where she worked. She received the bid before the application deadline, stamped the time and date on the hermetically sealed envelope, and before handing it over, she signed for the receipt of the document in a register book, wrote down the details and time of the bidding business. On the way to her office on the second floor, she chose the stairs instead of the elevator. As she walked the stairs, she seemed to regret it, even though the elevator was full of previous people, she took it. She still looked tired from the party last night, when together with her work friends and some other international colleagues she had stayed in various bars until the early hours of the morning. As she approached her office, she remembered that from excessive drinking it seemed that she had ended up in bed with a colleague who had been attracting her for a long time.

No, it wasn't the drink, it hadn't done it, it was just the catalyst that had sped up the process by suppressing her emotions and euphoric feelings, the alcohol had only created an atmosphere and canceled the prejudices and excessive thoughts that go around in your head when you are sober.

She hadn't been drunk, just happy, she told herself. She laughed to herself with that guilty cynical smile when she remembered last night, she seemed to have liked John's fiery bed. Maybe she should repeat it again, she thought to herself. All these thoughts were shattered when some photos from last night started coming to her smartphone. Some she remembered and some very little. Browsing through Facebook applications, she noticed a notification in her post that intrigued her attention. She read that an invitation had been made by the high school generation who wanted to gather for the tenth anniversary of their graduation. Invitations, organizations and proposals had been made about where they would gather on the virtual application that had recently become more than necessary for this type of social communication. All the information, movements, innovations and events around the globe were summarized in that device that was more than ten centimeters long.

An entire world was inside it. Many of the users thought that privacy and intimacy died with the arrival of this smart device. Holding the phone with one hand and the other hand resting on the table and with the palm of her hand stretched out on her head, a state in which she was trying to somehow hold it up due to the heaviness of her head as the headache had begun to do its job, as if sleepily she began to remember those days of her high school life that had left deep impressions on her life. She remembered Shpresa, Besa, Driton, Besim who had been the company with whom she had spent the most time. She had not seen them for a long time. They contacted here and there through these types of social medias with those who had them in their possession. Shpresa had experienced horrors during the war, she was not doing well even though she had been one of the most beautiful and polite students and girls of her generation. It was said that life had abandoned her. Dashuria or Besa, as her friends called her, had married immediately after finishing high school. It was said that she was happy and had two children, a girl and a boy, and they lived in Prishtina in one of the downtown neighborhoods. She had not seen her for a long time.

Driton had continued his postgraduate studies and was doing well in the philosophical world. He had always been shy, but very polite, she remembered Dritoni's handsome and innocent face, unlike Besim who had joined his brother in Switzerland immediately after the war and very little had been heard of him since then. It was said that he had run a family business well, earning quite well. She thought she laughed out loud when she remembered Besim's spiritual soul, which was very vibrant and energetic. He was interested about women and openly said it everywhere. The thought flashed through her mind that they had once played those love games with him since high school. He was always well dressed, perfumed and loved life.

A hedonist in his own. He drank alcohol to be the center of attention, to impress girls, but there had been times when he had rolled a three-leaf cigarette, in an attempt to show that he was an adult and a bohemian who knew how to live. The whole society knew Besim as such, unlike his other friends. Maybe now he has calmed down - Liria said to herself and in the meantime, photographs of memories and moments with society flashed through her. Through all these analyses and premonitions, she tried to describe herself, but something was stopping her, almost as if she was afraid, going crazy. She couldn't turn her head back to those years that were full of passionate kisses from the most beautiful boys in the neighborhood she remembered, hugs and the warm nights in the back seats of the cars of her friends' fathers, or the various excursions where she was the first, she remembered more than that. Now she had a well-paid job, she had a luxury car, an apartment she owned, clothes from the most famous and extravagant world brands.

She frequented all the places where the most important people in public life in the country stayed, but something seemed to be missing. She was lonely even though she was always surrounded by friends, if you could say so, especially in the center of the male world, but sometimes she felt depressed. She lived alone in the apartment, she had separated from her parents in order to continue her life as she wanted, despite the fact that she was not married and didn't seem to be close to that act, unlike what most women dream of, she had turned thirty and was still single. She was sad when she saw women her age in the company of their husbands walking as a couple with their children, who gave her a sense of happiness, belonging, and the loving devotion of being a wife or mother. She had not experienced these feelings. Perhaps they would make her feel fulfilled.

Other women, in contrast, envied the life she led, immersed in the endless luxury that came from the fat salaries she received or the countless gifts from admirers and society who wanted to have her around. Most of the gifts came from care, the offering of nights that only she knew how to do. She was not that beautiful, but charming and always smiling, with a slender figure like a cypress, medium height, puffy lips that often teased her if she had had surgical interventions or were filled with silicone or botox. "No, no, don't tire me out," she often said. Her two blue eyes, often penetrating, made the look through them at the whole world of blueness, escaping from herself in search of other unexplored horizons where curiosity does not find infinity in the full sense of being free from fear, pain and uncertainty. Their lack of feeling made her more insecure, cowardly and suffering. Thoughts stopped when her officemates Andi and Drita turned to her:

-Lirie, shall we go to the coffee bar? Let's have a coffee together, we've worked hard and you look tired. Is this one of those sleepless nights? - she said, laughing. Leaning on Lirie's desk, she suggested they leave the office. Andi, short, with big eyes, was always standing next to her.

- Okay, I need some air. Andi, will you bring me my jacket from the hanger? - she said, waving in it direction and getting up from the chair, they got ready to leave.

-Where are we going? We won't be going far from the office, we don't need a car, if we do... tell me, I'll take mine - said the short man, looking at his two office mates, who, walking thoughtfully, seemed to want to tell him that they would be staying somewhere nearby. In silence, she realized that they didn't need transportation. The chubby Drita was trailing behind them, as she couldn't keep up with their fast pace, which made her gasp for breath several times while walking.

It had started to rain outside. As shadows of the day, they hurriedly entered one of the nearby corners of the bars, trying to avoid the raindrops that suddenly began to fall to the ground.

III

Danaj's woman escorted Shpresa to the door after she finished her work hours. She could barely walk, she had disc problems and limped on one side, to avoid the pain that irritated her sciatic nerve, a pain that radiated from the bottom of her back to the soles of her feet. She was overweight and with a chubby face she looked like the most beautiful pandas of the North Pole in appearance, similar to a white face with a few black spots, with her characteristic walk, once on one side and then the other.

-Shpresa, just a moment, I almost forgot, take some of the lunch we had today, I'll send it to Arbër. He really likes my pies, - she said with a charming smile and an altruistic halo. She entered the kitchen with her usual panda-like steps, while Shpresa stood speechless in the doorway. She took the bag full of food, thanked and greeted her employer and headed home.

- Say hello to Uncle Bedri, since we didn't meet today, - said Shpresa as she closed the courtyard door on her way out. Aunt Myrvet nodded her approval and they both left in opposite directions. Uncle Bedri, as Shpresa called him, had a group of friends with whom they met almost every day in one of their so-called places, the chess players' place. There Bedriu would spend time, feelings, problems and all, and could stay for days and nights, without knowing. When the weather was good, they would stay outside, if it was rainy they had their own nooks that resembled pensioners' spaces.

-Make two moves with the pawn, or someone else don't touch the officer, or I'll attack you with the queen, - numerous suggestions were heard that were more like shouts than advice from the many who stood above the heads of the two players and waited their turn to join the game. Bedri enjoyed quite good health even though he was in his seventies. He was thin, with an appearance that didn't give him even half a century of age. Because of his physique and passion, he often went hunting with friends and walked for kilometers. Usually they hunted partridges, rabbits and sometimes a wild boar.

Shpresa didn't get to see Uncle Bedri for almost the entire day. She spent the whole way home in thought. She remembered Arbër as she approached the neighborhood. It was four in the afternoon, she was in a hurry to get to her brother as soon as possible. Arbër usually finished school around one in the afternoon, returned home with his neighborhood friends, and waited for his sister until she got home from work. He was good at his studies, he usually liked natural sciences and foreign languages, but less so social sciences. He was one of the standouts in the class.

After getting off one of the city vans, she entered the alley that led to another alley that extended and right on the corner was the house where she had lived for several years. On the way, she saw her friend Besa who was taking care of her children who she had just picked up from the city kindergarten. She was in a hurry to get to her parents' house to see them after the work she did in one of the state institutions. She worked at the Ministry of Education, in the sector of plans and strategies for primary and secondary education. It was going well. She complained that they were not working at all, most of the time they were sitting or had no work at all, while they were paid regularly, their salaries were averagely good.

-Shpresa, I barely knew you, how are you? I'm in a hurry, here with these children, carrying them up and down. I just picked them up from kindergarten and want to visit my parents in the meantime, until Bekim gets back from work. How are you? How are you doing? - she spoke in a half-breath while trying to hold on to the children who were four and five years old, the girl and the boy who wanted to be free from their mother, and if they ran away, it seemed like she would never catch them again. From the constant attempts to untie their hands from those of their mother who was holding them tightly, Besa ignored her children's movements and looked Shpresa in the eyes.

-How much your children have grown, how beautiful they are! I just finished work, I'm hurrying home too, - Shpresa spoke warmly. It's been a while since we've seen each other, we haven't been together, I miss being together, but these troubles of today are not leaving us, - Besa replied while she forcefully pulled the children towards her, who seemed to calm down for a while. We'll meet anyway, - Shpresa spoke with a kind smile full of positivity conveyed to her friend.

-I heard after talking to Liria that this year we had the tenth anniversary of our graduation, maybe our generation will get together, but anyway you and I will see each other these days, we will have a coffee. - she said, moving away from the dragging of her hyperactive children. She made a sign that she had to leave, since these little guys were still not leaving her alone. She headed towards her parents' apartment.

On the way to her brother, Shpresa was full of thoughts, most of which were difficult. She seemed to laugh to herself at times and to be saddened by the many memories that weighed on her head. She didn't even notice that she was already close to home. She saw Arbër in the yard trying to repair a bicycle that had been worn down by time and the abuse of a turbulent boy. The bicycle, if you looked at it, showed more than time, desire, the past and the challenges that those wheels had passed through the hands of a child.

-Arbër, I brought you spinach pie, Aunt Myrvet sent it for you, let's go inside so your food doesn't get cold, - Shpresa said while running, after opening the door of the house. With a nod of approval of admiration and innocence, the brother followed his sister behind.

- Blessed are her hands! She melted it all! Aunt Myrvet cooks very well, but do you, sister, ever know how to cook for us like her? Wow, very tasty! - Arber said while devouring the food and sometimes made sounds of pleasure, which his sister didn't hear because she had her head resting on her hands and pretended to be present. It was noticeable that she, who had not been there for a while, seemed to have the whole burden of the world on her shoulders. From time to time, she would just nod in agreement with what her brother said, so as not to seem ignorant towards him or to not feel insulted. She didn't eat because she had kept Aunt

Myrvet company, they had eaten together in the absence of Uncle Bedri at her insistence.

Besa's words about the meeting with the generation came to her mind. As much as there was joy, there was also concern about the event that would follow, the organization long-awaited by the vast majority.

While her mind was half-formed, she got up from the table where she was sitting, even though it was the first days of spring, a coldness spread through her entire body. She went out into the yard to get some bushes and wood, to light the stove and to finish some housework that was left over from last day. Meanwhile, Arbër licked his fingers and sighed from the delirium of devouring his favorite food. Dusk soon arrived and the day for the brother and sister ended those moments. Only beautiful dreams could save that evening that were rare since they were dominated by nightmares that were frequent, they came almost every time it got dark, it was like an unwritten rule.

IV

Driton and Besim had met in one of the city's restaurants while waiting for Fitim to join them. While they were talking to each other, they had not seen each other for some time, a luxury car with official license plates approached in front of them and suddenly Fitim came out of the back doors. Two bodyguards followed him, until the official signaled them that they could leave him alone. He walked proudly and with a pronounced self-confidence, although short, with a large nose, sparse hair and round eyes as if hanging on his cheeks, and shining from the beautiful suit and scarf that wandered while walking, where its flew and as if he was pointing with his finger to his friends "here I am, you didn't believe that I would reach this state." The reprimand was accompanied by the sharp eyes of the friend who had just approached his friends of the generation.

-Look what an official Fitim has become! What a luxurious car, plus an escort, look how important you have become, boss Fitim! - Driton greeted him with a smile until he approached their table.

-Can I join you gentlemen? I'm on duty, so I don't have much time, I have a meeting later. Look at you Besim! What are you doing like this, what is this beard, this style, these pants, does it seem to me that Besim...? No, it's not possible, you who have been drinking alcohol, smoking, running after women... You... you... No, it's not true, it's not possible, - surprised, he didn't take his big eyes off Besim. - That's why we are gathered in this bar, without alcohol! Now I understand everything.... you have evolved or devalued, you have become a mujja or an imam, - Fitim mocked his childhood friend, laughing.

-Suphanallah o Fitim, what I saw, I see big changes in you too, we haven't seen each other for a long time. I proposed Driton to meet in this place. Yes, I have changed, you can see it, a little late but I have returned to the right path, the path of God, thanks God, - Besim stood up from his seat. Fitim, I remember very well when you joined us in the eighth grade, after you moved with your family from the village. You evolved too, you are well with work, with position. Who would have thought that Fitim, whom we used to take with us, to not get lost on the streets, we would accompany him to the door of the house... look now, he has become an important person, a decision-maker! - he would ironically joke with his friend and in the meantime he would speak words of praise from the Quran about the achievements he saw in Fitim. He would congratulate him, he would make a gesture of congratulations in his direction, until he was barely noticeable from the glasses he wore and his long beard with clothes as if he had worn several sizes larger. He seemed completely covered or wrapped as if with a sheet, only if he were given a guitar he would resemble one of the brothers of the well-known rock band ZZ Top.

Driton saw both of them. He was the only one who had not changed in appearance, style, mind and perception towards what surrounds him or things whether they are in relation to the world, its meaning, its connection with the social and the influences it makes between people. He looked at Fitim who from a poor, unrefined boy, without a pedigree or tribal social status had transformed into a very important personality, dressed in a suit with a famous Italian brand, the perfume that was felt from the entrance, fragrant from a distance, special American glasses, always in the company of two people who seemed as if they had been torn off a steep and large rock especially for him. If you saw them up close you would be terrified by the sight, while the luxury car had black windows, in the discretion that Fitim was inside, yes yes.... . had become one of the most unique in our society today.

The long hair of a thinker falling on Driton's forehead suddenly made him turn his attention to his eyes, which seemed to be somewhere between a piercing longing and sting, which suited his face, which was accompanied by intelligent features, which revealed more about him than if he spoke himself.

On the other hand, there was Besim, who as a high school student had never left two stones unturned. How many problems, how many incidents, jokes, he had caused between his high school days and society. How many times had he left the teacher because he had disturbed the peace in the math class, when he had not answered the questions regarding the multiplication of numbers, saying "prof, I have the calculator, it don't tire my head," or the little loves he had by chasing after all the pretty girls in school. He had taken his father's car without his knowledge, he had gathered his friends, there were almost ten people in the car, they had barely gotten in and after drinking in one of the city's cafes they had an accident somewhere, but luckily no one had been hurt, except for his father's car, who had sentenced him to not go out it for weeks, except school-home. Now he stood with the image of an imam, completely transformed from a vandal, a bohemian soul into a saint. What could have happened to these two? How can people change so much?

Surely there is something, a reason that pushes them to undergo so many changes. In our case, we have a movement from one extreme to the other, - the philosopher thought to himself until the other two friends joined the conversation, where one of them tried to reveal his entire religious discursive arsenal to the interlocutor, who seemed not to be very interested and from time to time moved his foot nervously and looked at his watch to see if he was late for the agenda he had revealed to his friends.

-"If you gather in a restaurant where alcohol is served, I will not come, I will not participate in the graduation anniversary," Besimi said firmly, trying to get on topic, about why they had gathered here today.

-Listen, we gathered to discuss how we will do it, where we will gather and have we informed everyone about the case in question, while you Besim, don't rush, I still can't believe these words are coming out of you. It would have been good for us all to gather and discuss, and for our personal positions not to be the cause of differences. If you refuse to join us, then there is something more precious, more important than our entire society, yours. If you are decisive, then it is up to us to submit to you and impose your desire on everyone about where to go. We will also have to talk to the others and see what they think, but I would have advised you as a friend, don't be a rejecter, but an integrator, a collaborator. When I think about who is speaking these words, I feel like laughing. Don't get me wrong, but maybe I'll get used to the new Besim, who I'm meeting today. We met in this place with your selection, but will we manage to convince everyone else with your suggestion, we'll see, - Driton spoke, trying to give direction to the conversation and the solution to the situation.

-I am only following the path of goodness, of God. Where there is alcohol, it is haram, to enter it is a sin, because only bad things come from consuming alcohol. On one occasion, the prophet, while walking, saw two people drinking alcohol and laughing and having fun, later on his way back, he saw the same people fighting and trying to kill each other, it is more than true, - the religious man spoke with deep conviction.

-Okay, okay Besim, no one is saying to overdo it, anything that is overdone is a sin, even bread or water if overdone will lead to stomach aches, not just alcohol. But we should be advised, to take the opinion of others, what they want, how they see this, we should not be absolute or imposing. We wait and see, we don't need to get angry, - Driton spoke, while

Besim was getting angry, almost as if he didn't like his friend's approach. Fitim approved what the philosopher said silently, with a nod of his head.

- Friends, I have to go. As I warned you, I have work to do; we will be in touch about everything, whatever you decide, let me know in time. I will join you wherever you decide, - he said as he left. He got up from the table, approached the waiter, paid for the drinks they had on the table and left. His friends gestured, why he was in a hurry to pay. Outside, rock people were waiting for him, who, equipped with all the security devices for escorting, quickly put him in the car through the back door. On the way, his scarf was still blowing in the wind, making he seem like he was still waving to his friends as he left. The escorts sat in front, one of them seemed to be driving. They briefly attracted the attention of passersby, but they were soon lost in the heavy traffic.

The friends who remained at the table stayed a little longer and after a while the two separated. Besim had time for prayer, while Driton headed towards the library. He was looking for a title that he had been looking for a long time and could not find in the various bookstores in the city.

V

It was a rainy day, as April can sometimes be. Brother and sister parted ways in the morning, each in their own direction, after a restless night of sleep that Shpresa had. They lost sight of each other, behind the alleys that led to the main road, in places an unpaved road, which called for shoes to embrace the mud that was abundant on those city streets. If by chance a car driven by a careless driver passed by, you could also be sprayed with mud or dust mixed with rain, which often resembled the dough of a chocolate-covered dessert, you could only distinguish the smell, even the taste. In a hurry, to reach the bus that would take her ..., Shpresa seemed to be fighting the wind, the rain, through her fragile umbrella that wandered sometimes to one side, sometimes to the other. Her image in that umbrella fight reminded you of Don Kishoti, but now in the form of a girl, a woman in transit to a destination where the road seems difficult.

Unable to see well ahead from her umbrella that tried to hold her in front and protect her body from the wind, her vision was not good, she walked only by instinct, mechanically. She knew that road while sleep. For a moment, she moved the umbrella away from her face, which was torn by the air currents. In passing, along an entrance to a house, she saw a tall person wearing a raincoat who, with his child by his hand, had taken shelter and were waiting for the right moment to go out into the rain. They seemed hesitant about the weather that awaited them outside the shelter, but it seemed that they had obligations. The child dressed as a chubby boy had a plastic tube in his hand that made soap bubbles through a stick that the wind carried so fast and burst that he could not possibly practice the game.

The curious child in the circumstances he found himself in, didn't want his father to hold his hand, he wanted to play. As soon as Shpresa saw the boy, she was stunned, her feet could not walk, no, they were stuck deep in the mud that she could not move. The ground began to collapse under her feet, or so it seemed to her... A thunderous shiver ran through her whole body with a deathly cold that suddenly, as if Gabriel (Xhebrail) would tease her from time to time. She could not move, she could not even control the umbrella, she was lost and confused. The rain was hitting her, but she still didn't wake up, she had her eyes fixed on that game of the boy who could no longer make balloons.

The man holding the child by the hand noticed Shpresa's confusion, from his gaze and movements he wanted to signal to her if everything was okay. But who to tell? She still looked distracted, as if she had almost seen a ghost with her eyes. She managed to pull herself together somehow and started walking. It seemed that now she was controlling herself as much as she could, but the tears didn't, she didn't manage at all, they were mixed with the rain and they didn't know which were the tears, since she was still subject to the rain. She walked, at that moment without knowing where she was going. A car door closed - bam! She hold her head and ran into a corner that was fortunately away from the rain. She was not herself, she didn't look well at all. She remembered the anxiety, the memory she often tried to forget, that she wanted to inflict on himself... because no, not me, it hasn't happened to me, it's always about someone else. Never about her. She tried to sell herself this reality or lie, but her subconscious often betrayed her, reminded her of how bad it was.

The slamming of the car door sounded like the boot of a uniformed Serbian policeman, when they forced open the door of the house in those March days of the war. The slamming reminded her of when four men armed to the teeth entered. The family had prepared to eat breakfast that day, if you can call it that, with a few foods, reduced to fill the stomach somehow. The mother had cooked a corn bread and they had laid out on the table the yogurt, what they had in the end. The father was holding a cigarette in his hand with a wierd look that seemed to want to absorb the whole world through swallowing a puff of tobacco. Shpresa was near her mother, helping her around the table, while little Arber was playing with the same soap bubbles that he had as that boy who was sitting by the rain and who seemed to be in the company of his father.

-"Ovamo svi, shiptarsko djubre jedno", (Everyone here is Albanian trash) shouted one of the policemen who forced his way into the house. One, who gestured, seemed to be their leader. Two rushed at the parents, grabbed the father by the arm and pushed him against the wall, the mother by the hair, and everything she had in her hand fell to the ground.

The third one stared at Shpresa with his mouth open like a hyena approaching a fragile zebra. He glared at her until she looked away, her eyes fixed on the floor and her back against the wall.

- Take whatever you want, just leave us alone, - the father said in a trembling voice, trying to protect his family with his hands and gather them close to him. He somehow put Shpresa and Arber behind his back, while the two policemen forcibly and with barrels in their mouths held them in front of him. The third one didn't take his eyes off Shpresa who was at the zenith of girlish beauty. She had just turned eighteen, she had a slender figure, wavy hair with braids that made every heart soften, weaken even the strongest or wildest ones who have no feelings. The fourth one was the superior. He only ordered, gave orders only with signs, with his eyes or his hand. He looked like an orchestra conductor whose notes were in front of him and knew how to play each part or score of the symphony that exuded gloom, sorrow, the scent of death.

-Nismo došli samo za novac, zlato ili šta posedujete, mi ćemo uzeti više nego što vi imate dati. Uzećemo sve, majku vam tursku! (We have not come just for money, gold or whatever you possess, we will take more than you are able to give, your Turkish mother!) - one of the two who were holding the mother and father spoke, taking out a bottle of alcohol with one hand from his many pockets. He drank a few sips as if it were water and offered it to the others. Two of them were served, one refused. Returning the bottle to the place from which he had taken it, with the other hand he fired a volley of bullets onto the roof, tearing himself apart like a rabid beast whose mouth was drooling with saliva and the poison it was releasing down below.

The superior gave a sign and the one who had set his eyes on Shpresa, grabbed her by the hand and hair and started dragging her. She screamed, calling for help. The father came closer to pull her out of the beast's clutches, but a hard blow from the butt of the machine gun threw her to the ground, bleeding. Mother and Arbër were crying, screaming, while Shpresa tried to somehow escape the hyena by holding on with her hands, nails, fingers, with everything she could to avoid being sent to the room. Suddenly, a hard blow came to her stomach from the superior policeman, which made her surrender and fall to the ground, huddled. They calmed her down somehow when the Serbian superior came closer, squeezing Shpresa's face, who reeked of alcohol.

-Sad ćes videti kako srbin pravi ljubav maco, sećaćes se ovog mo- menta dokle budes živela, ako…

(Now you will see how a Serbian makes love, little bird, you will remember these moments as long as you live)- with a bite of Shpresa's lips like a snake that releases poison with its hands, he threw her to the ground. He signaled that whoever wanted her could have her. The policeman who had his eye on her hurried to enter the room first. Shpresa somehow got up, ran, took what she found in that room to protect herself and went and stood behind the wall, resisting.

The policeman grabbed her by the hand, managed to shoot her in the face and jumped on her. He began to tear off the clothes she had on her body. She resisted, fought but was also hit by the thirsty vampire who was impatiently waiting to suck her noble blood. His colleagues saw that he was unable to control the prey he had inside him, one of them went to help him.

The bleeding father tried to pull himself together and go help his daughter. The mother begged God, bread, and humanity to spare them, to not harm them, especially Shpresa and Arbër. She fell to her knees, begged, cried, and kissed their feet, just to let the children go. They laughed, drank a few sips from a shared bottle, and with the tip of a knife, they tagged and caressed Arbër, who, although very small, held the tube of soap foam with both hands and cried without knowing what was happening. His young head could not understand what was happening in their house while they were thinking of having breakfast. His angel-like eyes didn't impress Lucifer or the war ravens that Satan had sent especially to them.

-Saćekajte gospodine i vi ćete ući unutra kod vase ćerke, samo po- lako, ćemu žurba?(Wait, sir, you will also go inside to your girl, slowly, why are you in such a hurry?) -

The superior spoke and grabbed the bleeding father and took him into the room where his daughter was being raped. One of them grabbed him by the hair, while the other held him..

-Gledaj gospodine ćerku kako se pretvara od devojke u lepu ženu, bas dobra za srpsku policiju, svaka vam ćast gospodine, u ime Srbije mi ze zahvaljume za ovakvo dobro gostoprimstvo, (Look at your daughter, sir, how she is turning into a beautiful woman, very good for the Serbian police, good job, sir, on behalf of Serbia, we thank you for the hospitality offered)- The superior spoke on father's face, rolling his eyes and sighing under his breath. His eyes were covered with blood.

The mother held her head, continued to pray, asking for mercy. She and Arber were held by the other two police officers, while the other two worked on Shpresa's still-wet body, right in front of her parents.

Shpresa, tight by the hands of one, cried out, wailed until the other entered it and took more than what could be taken from a house, a parent, a family, a homeland. Oceans, seas, mountains seemed to collapse, apocalyptic signs were called with the blood of lost maidenhood, where the hand and the brain were not in coordination. They took the saint by stepping into the next day, where even death does not work.

After the two policemen had done the devil's work, sent in his name, the other two approached to enter the same dance of Mephisto. One accepted, rushed like a noose on the prey that had now been hit by the teeth of the previous ones several times, she was bleeding, screaming... she was tired, tired even of death, it was not coming to save her even in these moments, when Shpresa was looking for her so much. She was covered in blood and it seemed that even the pieces of flesh were missing, they had torn her so badly that she no longer had either body or head, her soul had already been consumed. The family members, stunned, didn't look up, they had no strength. As if they had been blinded for a long time. They wanted not to see, not to be there at all. With the entrance to hell, the parents seemed to have already died, they were only there briefly, by chance...

One of the four policemen refused to tear Shpresa apart after his three friends had done so before. It was clear from his eyes that he had regretted everything that had happened to the poor family members at home. As he approached Shpresa, who was bleeding and bruised and lying on the ground, with regretful eyes, the superior gave a signal. With a small movement, they fired their weapons at the bodies of the mother and father. One of them approached Arbër with a knife in his hand. The policeman who hesitated to rape Shpresa spoke:

-Dosta je momci, mnogo smo preterali, pustite dećka, dete je,(Enough guys, we've gone too far, release the boy, he's just a child)- he signaled that they had done enough damage to this house, they could go. The superior teased the policeman like a coward, slapped him lightly on the face saying: "This is how you fight for the state, you milky-lips",

and waved his hand towards the exit. The remorseful policeman looked once more at Shpresa who lay there looking like she was about to die. He apologized with his eyes for everything that had happened to her and her family at home. It seemed as if Shpresa accepted the apology because at least Arbër was alive. She doesn't remember anything else except waking up and seeing herself in Arbër's embrace who had stayed with his sister for hours by her side, holding the soap tube.

She hadn't noticed that she had stepped out into the rain. She was completely soaked. She started screaming, thinking she was covered in blood. Driton passed by, who barely recognized Shpresa, seeing her condition.

-Shpresa, are you okay? Do you know me? I'm Driton, - he said, grabbing her hand and trying to get her to her feet, as she was huddled in a corner of the building where the rain beat down on her from time to time, depending on the wind and the direction it was blowing. She suddenly woke up from her friend's voice. She began to gather herself, to see where she was, what had happened to her.

-I am sorry! I got lost for a moment, I had a big headache, I was on my way to work, but look how I've fallen," she spoke wirdly, her face looking as if she had seen the horror of the world with her own eyes.

-I know a place near here, Shpresa, when I was in college I used to go with my friends. We go because they make good salep, they have natural tea, it will do you good. Shall we go? - Driton spoke humbly, wanting to calm his friend down. - But at work... it's not good for Aunt Myrvet and Uncle Bedri, - she spoke, worried in thought, as if the sky in her head had not yet cleared.

- Listen, Shpresa, we're going to let them know that you can't go today. Let's have a drink together, then I'll walk you home to change your clothes because you're still wet from the rain.

They agreed. As they walked together, she still thought she saw soap bubbles, and every time she heard a cacophonous noise, she would jump like a pig on a hot coal, stressed. Driton noticed that something was wrong with her.

They drank the famous salep together, talked about many things that belonged to the past and the present. It seemed that Shpresa was refreshed a little by the company of her friend whom she once sympathized with so much.

They went out together. On the way, walking, they didn't notice that the rain had stopped. The clouds began to move away. The sun tried to come out to break through the clouds, but it was difficult. Some flashes of rays reached the surface, but it seemed that immediately the clouds did their job and covered the entire atmosphere, becoming cloudy and losing their shine on the ground.

VI

All day the next day, Dritoni was thinking about Shpresa. He remembered her frowning face, her lost eyes. Something is wrong - he thought, pacing around the room. Since he had left her near the house, she had not left his mind for a moment. There is something, he talked to himself, sometimes even out loud. He had heard from his friends about the traumas, the events that had happened to her during the war, she had lost her parents, she had been left with her brother. Could it be that now those consequences are appearing, the absence of a mother and father from a young age, for both of them?! Life seems to have tired her. It is a heavy burden for her. Still, her spiritual beauty had taken its toll and had manifested itself in appearance. Regardless of the suffering, the graceful features of a girl who now seemed mature were still noticeable.

Maybe with a few small make-up or style interventions, she could become a model or a mannequin that would make even the most famous ones jealous. He had liked her for a while, but he never managed to tell her what he once felt for her. He had considered her a sister. He thought he would offend her if she took the bold step, so his sympathy had faded into the ether, but still, every time he saw her, he felt the same way about her. Apparently, time had not been able to change his heart. He had often been impressed by her views on life and her uncompromising commitment to her studies, for which she stood out among her friends.

Dritoni, in addition to her physical side, had also been lost in the spiritual world of Shpresa, who with a sophisticated tact and a calm voice, her mouth had only revealed sweet words. She was always pleasant to be around. Shpresa failed to find the love of her life, especially after the war and the horrors she experienced, she almost gave up looking. She also suffered trauma from the male world, sometimes she didn't feel comfortable around them. Her brother and his care kept her alive. Arbëri was everything to her, he was life itself.

Is there something I don't know? His words, kept ringing in Driton's mind. I know her, I know those eyes. Yesterday they seemed much different to me... I didn't know them, nor did they know me. A mystery in itself, why... how... I think I'm going crazy. Enpugh, i will not think about her anymore. I'll leave her because she had a severe headache, just like she said.

But how,.... Dritoni fought with himself for a while and finally gave in. He once had a girlfriend, they were almost engaged, but something had not worked out between them.

They were two different worlds. If one had loved the white, the other had always been for the black. If the desire for a walk had been expressed, the other one had asked to stay inside. There are some small things that often affect a relationship and very quickly know how to become big, if the couple does not manage to control them. He remembered that relationship for a moment and compared it with Shpresa in whom he always found understanding and compromise.

There had never been any misunderstanding between them. He thought, compared and always asked himself, but he could not get an answer. He did some psychological, social, post-traumatic analyses, but he could not forget the look and the way he remembered yesterday.

He left his room in the apartment, met his parents, since he still lived with them. His sister was married well into a generous family, while he had a brother who was in exile who was well off. He came from time to time, especially for summer holidays. He was married to a Swedish woman and have two children, a girl and a boy. The Swedish woman was very well integrated into the family, as was his brother who had adapted to the Swedish state.

He worked as a journalist for a well-known local newspaper, sometimes for a forcigner. Dritoni went out, went to the office where he worked, but he couldn't concentrate at all on his work. He had to compile a report on a political topic, but he couldn't do it while he was there, which was unusual for his commitment. He decided to get some fresh air and take a walk. Maybe he would find the focus he was looking for at this moment. He decided to call Liria. They agreed to meet at the city park. Liria promised not to be late, since lunchtime was approaching. During the one-hour break, he could sometimes go further because there was no strict control over the workers at the mission, even though the entrances and exits were digitalized and coded, recording every movement, not to mention the cameras that recorded every movement.

They met. Liria, as usual, with an extravagant appearance and a modern style that many girls coveted, stood out from afar.

Dritoni had no trouble noticing her approaching, as he had arrived at the dating place earlier.

- "Maybe I wasn't late even though I'm walking fast," Liria explained as she approached Dritoni.

- No, not at all, I just got here too, maybe I'm not disrupting your schedule, your lunch break, - the friend reasoned.

- Not at all, his friend reassured.

They started talking about the usual things that happen when friends meet. They both got to know each other with things that had been bothering them lately. But there was something else that had been bothering Driton lately. He decided to discuss it with Liria. He told her about Shpresa, whom he had met by chance the day before yesterday, and how he had found her. He tried to describe her emotional and spiritual state and the delirium in a coma station where he had found her. Liria just listened to the description of her interlocutor and tried to enter the world of the story and the feeling of compassion that her friend had for Shpresa.

-I heard around that she experienced terrible things during the war. I know that they killed her parents in front of her, her little brother barely escaped. Is there anything more terrible, for a girl, for a child, - Liria spoke in a suppressed voice, trying to get into her friend's head and reason about the events that her friend was going through, while they walked along the paths of the park. For a moment, while she was talking and imagining the scenes, the images in her mind, her legs began to no longer support her. She leaned against a park bench and immediately sat down, making Driton join her.

-Your eyes sparkle when you talk about her, it seems you still love her. You've always liked her, -Liria said with a light, affectionate laugh and looked into his eyes with curiosity, so that she could draw out from him what words often fail to say.

- I'm worried about her, there's something hidden here, something that drives me to search and investigate about her condition.

It seems that it's more than complicated, I don't know how to help her, how to approach her, - Dritoni spoke thoughtfully in a low tone, almost as if he was talking to himself and had forgotten that he was still in the company of the extravagant woman.

- Driton, i never had the courage to ask about her war experiences," Liria said compassionately, rubbing the edges of the seat with her hands, looking down at her feet.

-It's true, it's hard to ask someone who has suffered so much to go through the same thing again. Maybe they want to forget, or it's better to open up and let out all that burden, anger, and scream that is surely grinding them from the inside. Dritoni asked and answered himself, forgetting again that he wasn't alone. With a dry wooden stick, he made drawings, different lines, until at one point it seems he used too much force and the stick split in half. The painting he had made in the dust seemed to have remained unfinished. With his foot, he destroyed that entire creation.

They also talked about the meeting that was preparing to take place, that of their generation. They talked about Besim's suggestion and his approach to this meeting.

-Yes, I heard. I haven't seen Besim in a while. He's changed a lot. In the meeting we had by chance in the city, he didn't approach me like he used to, and he was hesitant to give me his hand. I was in a somewhat unenviable position, when I remember how many events we've been through together. Driton, you know that Besim and I are similar in nature, so I was very surprised when he was so cold towards me at that moment. I felt insulted and distant in relation to my best friend from high school. Yes, yes, everything is possible now, I'm not at all surprised by him now, not even by the proposal to get together in his own way, - she laughed and argued with herself when she remembered how many events they had experienced together, from the most deviant ones to problems with the law and breaking the rules and social codes of that time. Is it possible? - she asked herself. Driton listened to his friend's words, creating images in his head, some experienced and some heard from friends, as Liria did.

They continued walking along the streets paved with gravel and sometimes with concrete blocks, while they passed by the edge of the tall oak trees that were just beginning to come to life. April had arrived. The vegetation, dressed in its green robe, had entered as an express fact that tickled the bees nearby from the green branches, whose pipes resembled nettles that poke their heads out of the abyss, moment by moment. The pollen also seemed to have arrived. The dandelions provoked their noses so that they both sneezed until they approached the park exit. Each took his own way to work. Dritoni thought he could finish his journalistic report, while Liria hurried not to be late. On the way he thought of stopping somewhere and getting something to eat.

VII

Besimi woke up early to start the morning prayer, as was preached. He decided to pray the Fajr prayer at one of the mosques near his home. He remembered for a moment how far the mosque had been abroad, when he had to walk a long way to get there. Now it was very close, about several hundred meters. He always practiced whenever possible to perform the obligatory ritual as he called it in one of the city's shrines. Even though he woke up early in the morning, he would perform ablution at home and run to the shrine where he would meet a large number of people, which seemed to grow day by day. Most of them were unemployed and spent part of their time there, or exchanging lectures from different imams, modern scholars as the preachers called them. From time to time there were also misunderstandings and disagreements regarding the interpretation or the way religion was practiced.

Often the differences came through the generations in question, the way in which the faith was once dedicated and now with the development of knowledge and the transmission of information from the various schools of the Middle East it was thought that they had advanced in this direction. Each school or country where the Islamic religion was preached had its differences and ways of conceiving the practice of religion. It seemed that there were more perceptions or ways that needed to be cherished. Several branches or sects were created that differed from each other in the doctrine of piety. The stricter the regulations and requirements, the closer you were to the desired paradise. It was one of the radical concepts that challenged the social order and social interaction.

There was an influence between social roles, gender, identity, etc. They were more strict, rigid in the codes that had to be adhered to. Here lay the differences with previous generations who had been more liberal in relation to religion and had not been alienated or inculturated as they were now seen with the tendency that this spirit could lead in that direction. They had practiced religion in the service of human, the individual, with the aim of socialization, compassion, solidarity and help in need. It was not in substance that human should serve religion, but always the opposite.

Today it seemed to have slipped into some views or planes of some groups, which seemed to have closed in on themselves, had created asociality, didn't show solidarity if you didn't belong to that clan, that social group, and they never empathized with you, if you hadn't chosen "the right path, the only path that the Creator had determined" according to their interpretation.

After finishing his morning ritual, Besimi ran back to bed. He thought he would take advantage of a few more moments of sleep since it was not yet seven. He usually did this when he was at home and not at work. He slept until around nine o'clock while the other members prepared tea and breakfast to eat. His mother usually made delicious meals. Knowing that it was from the New Bazaar, his specialty was pastries, especially the famous toplijas that the Hasjans used to make on the Prizren side. They were usually cooked with cheese. His mother's accent itself showed the difficulties she had in speaking Albanian even though she had been married to an Albanian man, Besimi's father, for over forty years.

It was said that the influence of Besim's uncles had led him to take the path he was now on. One of his uncles had lived in Bosnia and had seen horrors with his own eyes during the nineties when the war between Bosniaks and Serbs broke out. Religious identification and religious discourse had taken its toll every time they met and discussed in the family circle, where Besim had received instruction and knowledge. Later, he had also entered several Islamic circles or groups outside the country where he had managed to nourish even more modern knowledge or an adequate interpretation of Islam, which until recently had not been done properly. He had entered deeply into these cells and his whole life, his lifestyle had changed in accordance with and dedication to religion.

His mother had supported him a lot on this path. My son will become restrained, disciplined with codes of decency and devotion to the Creator. He was lively by nature, he had caused many problems in the past, she was happy that he had calmed down, found himself and left all the bad things in the past. His father had been indifferent to this. His teaching profession had often not been adapted to his son's worldview, so he had often said jokingly that of the two antagonistic paths he was taking, it seemed to him that perhaps this obsession would save him from some evil that had once taken its course. He only recoiled when he remembered that night when the police came to his door looking for his son, after together with his friends

had broken into a liquor store after running out of alcohol at one of the many parties that were being organized at that time at friends' houses.

-It is better for him to pray, to follow the path of religion than to take the path of a criminal - he had told his family and friends. He thought that religious education would calm his mind and way of thinking and he would become more polite, more restrained, educated and always moralizing towards deeds and evils. The fear of God would probably make him calm down. Since his parents, teachers, family members, correctional centers seemed to be useless.

After breakfast, he put on his clothes, his pants that were shorter than usual, they looked like they were from the seventies, some kind of pop or hippie style, but these were different, they were wider at the bottom and shorter. He combed his beard a few times, although he didn't has it thick, but as long as he had it he tried to keep it clean, he sprayed it with a few drops of opium perfume, took a misbaha with him and on the way out he somehow guessed whether to take the Islamic hat, the takiyah, or not.

He had it since his visit to Mecca during the Eid holiday when he had received it as a gift. He decided not to take it. He quickly went out to meet with friends, like-minded brothers who were growing day by day. Most of them were hopeless and constantly prayed for a better day, a better life, for everyone, and especially for themselves and their families. They also sought salvation from evil, the evil that had gained momentum recently, as they had anticipated, with the changes that had occurred in the social order, especially in the narrower one, the family circle, with the opening up of society and the creation of a new reality after the war.

He met his friends and companions. They had a favorite place, which was run by a well-known imam of the city who had completed his studies in Saudi Arabia, and they often gathered to discuss many religious issues related to Islam and to explain them adequately, since no honest explanations had been given before. It was more improvised and never really explained things and their substantial meaning. The time for the truth had come, as the people said. All the tables looked the same because the men, seemingly synchronized, had the same appearance.

If there was a woman, she had to wear a hijab. Tea, coffee and all this spectrum were drunk, an image created to look like it was not in a city in Kosovo, but to give the impression that you were somewhere in a distant Middle Eastern country. But we quickly transformed from the older pants, the national clothes into alla-Turkish then alla-Franga now into clothes of Eastern cultures… What will we become, tomorrow… how will we dress…?! - thought those who were not part of that bar.

For a moment, while sitting at the table with friends, Besimi thought he saw Vesna. He was stunned. An electric shock ran through his entire short body. In front of him was a woman in a burqa. Her eyes so closely resembled his former girlfriend that he almost lost his temper. He took a sip to cool the fire inside, but the tea, which was still hot, seemed to make him feel even worse. He let out an unconscious sound that made everyone at the table turn their heads. He showed with his gaze that nothing was wrong, that he was fine. He no longer dared to look at the woman in front of him who was standing with two other women dressed similarly. His brain was confused for a moment.

Shpresa was still devastated, even though she was at Danaj's house, she was very quiet. The images of yesterday seemed to have no end. She remembered the quick burial of her parents under curfew; her uncle who took them in after the war offered them the house, since Shpresa could not stay in that house any longer. The house had become hell for her. Whenever she stood there, she constantly saw the policemen with sharp knives playing like a vampire dance, who with their tips caressed her brother, mother and father, while it seemed to her that they were sometimes stuck in her heart and sometimes in her womb and laughing until blood dripped, then with their drooling tongues they licked the sharp blade and foamed, like rabid dogs.

Her uncle didn't need a house at the moment as he was in Sweden with his family. He had moved during the famous exodus of millions in 1999, beyond the borders of Kosovo, an exodus that humanity had not seen since the Second World War. He was doing well there and had no intention of returning to Kosovo for a while, until the state was consolidated as he said and until it came into the hands of some good person, since the current ones seemed to work only for themselves.

As she cleaned Aunt Myrvet's living room, Shpresa remembered yesterday. She felt like crying and laughing, both sad and happy after being in Driton's presence. She had tried many times to raise a hand on herself whenever she remembered the horror, but she had not succeeded because she had thought about her brother, Arbër. On the day of the incident, she had almost thrown herself into a neighbor's well, but the owners of the yard had stopped her. She often cursed herself for not being able to do it and free herself from the pain and suffering, but sometimes she got over it and thought that maybe it was better that she stayed by her brother's side. Since then, she had not visited her parents' house and she thought that she would never have the strength to go. Deep in dark thoughts, her face changed depending on what came to her mind and you could easily see that she was in trouble. Her distraction caused her to do the same thing mechanically, unconsciously, almost two or three times. Aunt Myrvet noticed her, advised her, and begged her to take a break from work and have a coffee on the veranda in front of the house, which had now taken on a good shape from time and the tall flowers that had grown around it, creating an aromatic halo of a diverse spectrum of colors in her beautiful yard.

VIII

The news came that Besa had an accident and was lying in the city hospital. Her life was out of danger, she had only some minor injuries. While she was driving from the kindergarten, after dropping off the children, she had set off towards her parents to see them in the morning before starting work. Suddenly, a car that seemed to be in a hurry and had not kept the appropriate distance between the cars had hit her car from behind.

Besa had received light injuries to her neck, a slightly scratched forehead, and from the impact she had injured her head on one of the side windows of the car, since the impact of the collision was accompanied by a strong shaking of the car from behind. Besa was immediately given first aid, at the same time her husband was notified, who from his shop where he ran a profitable business, immediately went to the hospital to receive the news.

The parents were not notified because they were old enough not to worry until their daughter got better. Besa was the only daughter present in the city, since one sister and one brother were abroad. She had become a sacrifice for her parents who were old and in poor health. She had always been between two houses: hers and her parents'. Not a single day had passed without meeting them at least twice a day, on the way to work or when she returned, after picking up the children from daycare. Her care was worthy of every praise. Fortunately, they were also close by in terms of housing. We should not forget her husband who had always been understanding and supportive of Besa's devotion to her parents. It was often thought that it was a gesture of affection, since her husband had lost both parents early on, and he had irregular contact with his brothers.

After everyone was informed about Besa's case, they ran to see her. The next few days it had gotten better and the parents had been notified in time, as their daughter had not visited them as they had been accustomed to. They had begun to worry about her, feeling that something bad had happened to their Besa, who they compared to a houseboy, the dedication as sworn virgins did, but in her modern case, she was married.

Liria, along with Fitim and Besim, had taken the time to visit her. At the entrance of the hospital during the visit, Besa's husband had met them and led them to the ward where their friend was lying. As soon as they had accommodated, the visitors had met Besa and her father who was standing next to her. Wishing her a speedy recovery, (they had bought her light vitamin snacks that would refresh her and give her strength in her recovery), they hugged her one by one. While the visitors tried to find and position themselves near the bed, Dritoni entered and Shpresa who seemed better, having recovered in recent days. The room was filled with Besa's visitors. She was so happy that it seemed that she had recovered. She felt a hope, a motive that made her walk home at that very moment, healed by the care and closeness of her friends that she felt at that moment.

-May our sister be well! - everyone almost unanimously wished her recovery.

-God has seen you, our sister, with the good and care for others that you have shown, the Creator has rewarded you, for that purpose you didn't suffer. He is one and sees everything, the good and the bad of every sinner like us. May you be rewarded by Him and follow the path that the prophet has left for all us! -Besim began to fall into the spotlight with his religious discourse, trying to get support and approval for what he said, words that are usually used in such cases of misfortune that the injured very well accept and have an effect in such social circles.

-May God be with you, son, for the words you said! - Besa's father greeted him. - So be it, amen to your prayers and the wish that your friend recovers quickly without consequences! It seemed as if the father's eyes began to fill with tears.

Fitim approached and said that for anything they needed for Besa, he was ready to help.

-If there is a need for medication or further treatment, I have my connections in ministerial departments, I am always available, - he spoke with determination and dedication, addressing Besa's father and husband.

- Thank you, but there's no need! As you can see, it's not a serious injury, Besa is recovering and within a few days we hope they will release her for home care.

Just a few X-rays to be completed in case there is a fracture or deeper injury. - the husband spoke in respect for the care that his friend showed in public.

- No, there's no need, Fitim, my brother, don't worry, I'll be fine, - Besa spoke, excited about all the increased attention they had towards her.

Besim almost all the time tried to ignore Liria who looked more beautiful than ever before with her extravagance and the care she always showed for her appearance. Besim always looked at her with contempt and made a face as if his former close friend had committed some fault, a sin. His eyes spoke in a raving way and were preachy, shorter than the skirt she was wearing. Driton and Shpresa noticed Besim's approach to Liria.

-We hope to see you soon in a better place than the hospital and I don't see any reason why we should stay longer because you are tired. Of course you need a break. - Driton wished, signaling that they could leave. Shpresa approached Besa, hugged her tightly and pulled back. Everyone gathered around her to greet her on the way out, while Besim continued to secretly follow Liria out of the corner of his eye.

At the exit, after meeting Besa's father and husband, they continued towards the main exit of the hospital.

- A word of advice, my sister, this way of dressing does not correspond to the rules and ethics of etiquette, - Besim spoke reproachfully, addressing Liria.

-How do you have the right to address me like this? With what right do you preach? You even want to interfere in my life and advise me, how to behave, how to dress, or how to think? Do you think I should become like you, uniform in your attitudes and views? Only then will you be able to accept me, only when I accept your rules and codes, only then or not? - she spoke indignantly and irritated with the approach and suggestions that Besim made towards her.

-You! You don't even dare to speak to me like that for a moment, you who have tried to kiss my lips or touch my body so many times, and now you have become some kind of transformed moral preacher. I know you, I know you very well. Behind religion you try to hide greed, exaggerated lust, an attempt to dominate and impose thought in society, but no… I will never accept these traps of yours! - spoke Liria, irritated and touched, who seemed to be only increasing her bitterness and losing her temper.

- Okay, okay, calm down, please don't let anyone hear us, - Driton spoke, trying to calm the blood between the once inseparable friends. Fitim agreed with what his friend said.

- "Leave it, Driton said well, forget about these things. Let's go have a coffee together, I'll pay," the official friend tried to change the subject and distract the agitated conversation.

- Fitim, you always pay, today I'm want to. Today the drinks are on me, - Dritoni objected.

- If you'll excuse me, I would withdrawn because it's time for Asr and I have to fulfill my obligation, Besim said, taking steps back and heading in the opposite direction.

- Go and think about it, I hope that next time you will come adapting to all of us, and not all of us submitting to your desires and whims, or separate yourself from all of us. Pray, seek salvation for yourself, your ego. You don't need us! - Liria replied ironically. It seemed that the angry aroused by her friend who had now taken a few steps away from them had not yet passed.

Shpresa didn't speak, didn't connect, just watched in silence what was happening around her. She had other troubles, of a different nature, it seemed that she didn't fit into this topic, circle, world. She felt isolated in the most sanctioned way possible.

They quickly got organized, took Fitim's luxury car and together they ended up in one of the famous bars in the city. They stayed for a while, had a great time and after taking a few quick photos, they each went about their business. Only Driton accompanied Shpresa on the way home.

IX

Driton was in the office working on the usual reports of various political agendas, which often seemed imposed by various decision-making circles and never went in line with the basic demands and needs of citizens. Usually they were topics of a national, political character and of special importance for the country, but the problems that citizens faced in their daily lives seemed to be in second place.

While he browsed through various portals reading the news prepared by his colleagues, he spent time on his smartphone, checking for any news, messages from friends he had on social networks, who were very different from real friends. This type of virtual communication was created with the same meaning for this type of friends who often didn't even talk to you if you met them on the street, and maybe sometimes you spent the whole afternoon exchanging different conversations through this tool that is shaking up the world, all societies, yes... yes... this smart device. Suddenly, while reading, he saw a news item that immediately caught his attention. He couldn't believe his eyes. He read it two or three times, then closed the work laptop he used in the office. He started thinking to himself. How is it possible? No, no, it's not possible - he told himself.

He couldn't believe what he had just read. To clear up any doubts, he opened the computer again and started reading, once or twice. Yes, it's true! Fitim had been imprisoned on suspicion of mismanagement in the ministerial sector where he worked. International justice units have also been involved in this matter.

Fitim… is it possible?!- he was talking to himself. He turned back time and remembered how he had entered his first day in their elementary school classroom, wearing a pair of old clothes that he never took off for a full semester. His parents were from the village, but regardless, the whole class had welcomed him warmly. He had suffered a lot. He had not done well in school. He had worked any kind of job to give his family a boost. His father was involved in agricultural work. He had fields in the village and he had spent most of his time there. He brought various foods from the crops on their lands, dairy from the cattle.

They lived in a house they had recently bought in a suburb of the city. Their mother was a housewife and always took care of the housework, which was very abundant, since they had many children, three sisters and four brothers. Fitim was among the younger ones. The older boys helped their father in the fields and cattle work, while the girls took care of the housework and helped their mother. With the beginning of the unrest in the country and the persecution by the Serbian state, some of the older children illegally fled the country. There they worked and financially supported the large family in Kosovo. When the war broke out, two of the oldest had joined the ranks of the KLA.

They had come from abroad. They had entered through illegal mountain border crossings. One had also been the commander of a well-known brigade in an operational area, so they had prepared the entire organization and logistics from exile. With the intensification of fighting in different areas of the country between the Serbian state and the Kosovo Liberation Army, the two brothers had fallen martyrs in close combat with the enemy. One died in border mines during the supply of weapons on the road between Albania and Kosovo, while the other brother was in the same area, breaching the same border protected at checkpoints by Serbian soldiers. As a sign of gratitude to the family of the martyrs, they decided to employ Fitim in an inter-ministerial sector immediately after the war, even though he had no qualifications or schooling. The decision had been political and had to support families, those who had given the most to the country. But Fitim had turned out to be versatile, so that he had progressed well over time and with the support of several other commanders had been positioned as a ministerial leader, had become the holder of a government department. He had also evolved in financial terms. He had arranged his life, he had also employed his wife, whom he had married before the war, as is customary. His distant cousins had found a daughter near their home. It seemed that they had become comfortable.

His wife, Zade, had now started lecturing at one of the private universities after finishing her studies at a fast pace, not as is usually done. Now Zade was lecturing two social science subjects and seemed to be doing well, since she had the support of the system and her husband. They had built a new house in one of the most popular neighborhoods of the city. At the request of their children, two daughters and their only son, they had also built a pool in the yard. The house was quite luxurious and it seemed like a beautiful princely tale. They had managed to buy two apartments right in the city center. They rented them out and three shops that his sisters and one of his remaining brothers ran. Fitim had evolved. From that poor schoolboy, to a very important person at this time. In the party, he was one of the leaders or a regular member of the leadership. For every political decision that was made, he was there, informed or involved in the decision-making. They also began to label Fitim for the benefits, the wealth he had made during this short period of several years. They had accused him of bribery, corruption, but it had not impressed him at all. There had been no evidence or proof for all those accusations they were making. Perhaps now they have discovered it or have provided additional evidence - Driton thought to himself. He began to compare himself with Fitim.

He remembered that he had been working in journalism since the war, often with foreign media agencies since he also knew English, he also had a small family business, a grocery store below his apartment, and he remembered that after all these vicissitudes of tireless work, he had barely managed to buy a two-room apartment for which he still had a loan that had to be paid off for another three years to become his property. He had suffered a lot to make a property of his own, despite the common property that they inherited from their parents.

And this Fitim, - he thought to himself, look at what wealth he had created in a short time, wealth that was an empire for our circumstances. Fitim was not alone, all his workmates, or party members, had quickly become rich. Perhaps, he too had entered into dirty work or stepped on a rotten plank - he talked to himself. How much? - he asked himself, - how much could Fitimi's salary be? One thousand, ok two thousand euros, the wife five hundred euros, ok one thousand.

Approximately, two thousand or two thousand five hundred euros they bring into the house. Do they have to eat, educate the children in those private schools, at those dizzying prices? There were two luxury cars at home, do they spend them on fuel, servicing, home maintenance, cameras, guards at the entrance, expensive clothes from the most famous brands? They often took weekend trips to London or Paris just to go shopping with his wife and children.

Without counting the summer, winter or those in between holidays. No, there is no way that all of it can be covered by salaries, or maybe I'm wrong. We are satisfied with the government's achievements for the average salary that is close to three hundred euros, or for pensioners about one hundred and fifty euros, contributors also enter there. Big difference between income, spending and material goods in society. It seems to have become a state, a place for only for a group of people. I'm sorry to say this, but I can also mention Fitim, our childhood friend. Whether they have found evidence or not, remains to be seen. Amidst this flurry of speculation, he decided to call Fitim and to see how he was doing. He took out his smart phone, which often seems to make us feel stupid by bombarding us with a lot of information, most of it irrelevant and useful for ourselves, but anyway, we'll get to this issue another time. Dritoni wanted to push away thoughts that had nothing to do with the existing circumstances or those in which his friend had gotten himself. He tried to call him several times, but he couldn't get through, so he couldn't communicate with him and see how his situation really was.

The statement in one case by a millionaire politician, wealth created by exploiting his public position, in an interview he had done earlier in a local media outlet, in an intimate conversation away from cameras and recorders, he had said, "not a swimming pool, but he had ordered a dolphin for his large swimming pool, so his children could play and get to know the friendly water creatures." Well, it seems that a group of people are competing to see who is creating the greatest luxury in the country.

Bullshit... Don't get involved in these matters, they are not in your hands. The prosecution or the judiciary should act, if they are serious. With such thoughts, it seems that he was not taking its peace, he decided to go out and sober up from this negative influence. He thought once about Besim. It was pray time, he could be here in the nearby mosque, performing the ritual. Let's see if I can meet him, - he thought to himself. He called him, but he didn't answer. It seems he had stopped the phone from ringing so that no one would disturb him.

X

Besim notified Driton as soon as he saw the missed call on his mobile phone. They agreed to meet, but as usual, the meeting had to be held in a place where alcohol was not served.

- What's wrong, why are you standing there so helpless, distracted, you almost saw a funeral with your own eyes, - the religious man turned to his friend, who seemed to be tormented by something. The journalist was not in the mood as usual.

- Did you hear, Fitim was arrested on charges of abuse of office. I tried to contact him, but I couldn't, he had no access. Of course he turned off his phone because most people bother him, try to get an answer from him - the sad and worried friend said.

- Yes?! Aiiii, i swear to God I knew something was wrong with him. All those good things, he didn't know the end of them. From where did they come, my brother? From the salary, ...uffa, brother, the prophet has left it very well: haram, greed, it will come out at any time. To tell you the truth, I never liked that guy, - Besim spoke, as if he were one of the prophets who had a premonition that this day would come.

- Don't rush Besim, take it easy. First of all, he is our friend. The accusation and the sentence are two different things, but we hope that he will not be sentenced, although I understand very well what you are trying to say. We all have our doubts about his lifestyle, but we are waiting for the process and the epilogue of how this matter will end, - the journalist tried to make room for reason, trying to avoid euphoria, to leave some time, space for the matter and the developments that would be revealed. - Hey, I think my phone is ringing. The journalist grabbed his phone and started talking. It was Fitim himself who, after seeing the missed calls, immediately called his friend. He begged them not to worry, that everything would be fine. It was not the first time he had been accused of various corrupt things, but he had always managed to get away with it. He had engaged the most renowned lawyers in the country and abroad.

He also said that he is frendly with the prosecutors. He hoped that nothing would come of this. They have no evidence that he had done anything wrong, he repeated what the suspect said on the other end of the phone. The journalist was worried about the process that would be led by internationals. Fitim had started laughing on the phone. -Do you think they are meticulous, don't they make mistakes? - he followed his words with irony, laughing. Most of the deformations and irregularities that were made were learned or smuggled in from abroad. We didn't even know what bidding, tendering, bureaucracy, or political influence were. In a word, some of them taught us how things are done. He assured his friends that everything would be done well, that it was just a media frenzy. -Journalist, you know this best, don't you? With this tone he had ended the conversation, conveying greetings to the entire society.

The journalist immediately remembered some of the lectures of media professors and the experiences that had led him to believe that most writings and publications in our country were being done on demand, but persecution could also occur. The more you were present in the public eye, the better it was for the person. It didn't matter for better or for worse, mainly you had to be active, for each circumstance. There were set-ups of trials based on conspiracy theories that would first accuse and shame you, then apologize in the absence of evidence, and the person in question would gain a reputation from the hurt feelings or the victimization they experienced. People would rise up and then become present at every media event or their opinions would make a name for themselves, always in the service of politics. He forgot for a moment that he was not alone and turned to the religious man.

- It seems that he was good, he greeted us, saying that there is nothing to this thing. Just an accusation, he will be cleared, - the journalist spoke with such hesitation that he didn't even believe what he was saying. He made even the fortune teller doubt the way and the sound of the words he was saying.

-Clean? I doubt it! In the "Hyra bath" as the people say. Bullshit. He is our friend, but here, Subhan allah, - he stood up - Oh, we are sinners, born that way, we must seek salvation, prayers to we must convey prayers to the Almighty to enlighten our minds as to where this people is heading, what a disaster for us! - the religious man complained about the circumstances and developments in society that were not promising enough for advancement or comfortable well-being.

-Look, my friend, we have great differences in concepts. You believe and do not seek reasons. With faith you try to fix all things, you take them as such, devouring, non-negotiable. Fear of punishment and submission to God thinks that it will atone for all the sins that people commit. With a prayer, all the bad things we have done will be erased. I don't think so, my friend. Humanity must raise its capacities of awareness and self-awareness and know its limits, how far it can go without hurting others or depriving freedoms in the sense of equality. We don't need to be afraid of something fabulous or mythical that will kill us all, because ultimately fear is thought to be our salvation for the better.

Why should emotion prevail instead of reason, clear reasoning, without burdens. I have no desire to impose my position as you constantly do, who with religious narratives try to influence society. You continue to believe in what you think is best for you and yourself, but don't become dominant or tendentious in influencing others, because neither you nor I know which one is right. Maybe we are both right. I think we should believe in this way, so that both camps can develop and live as they want. Your lifestyle and the faith you preach are not a guarantee that you are absolutely right in the chosen path, but neither do I with my independent thoughts.

- I am not saying anything more, just so that we can be more aware of our actions, thoughts and aspirations. They should never be the cause of anyone else being hurt or affected in any way. I apologize, maybe I overdid it, -said the journalist or philosopher as he was known in society. He finally didn't spare himself but gave his opinion towards the religious man who was constantly preaching religious discourse.

-Wow, my friend, are you an atheist by any chance? If you are, which I suspect you are, I don't want to waste any time here with you. I don't want to waste my time with unbelievers at all. It is a sin to think like that. You are committing sins, oh sinner!

It seems that the devil is beginning to influence you, you are not aware. - said the religious man indignantly and in a reproachful tone, raising his eyebrows and hands up.

-Not at all, you are wrong, maybe I am more religious than you, my friend, because there is no measure to prove it. A person when born believes, believes in his parents, believes in his siblings, friends, work colleagues, in his spouse, in his child who will achieve something in life, in the good work he does every day for the future, and in many other ways, a person is inclined to believe.

No one denies that. Without faith, humanity could not exist, but the independence of faith in each person must be respected so that no one has the right to capitalize on the most intimate thing of the individual, not even in the name of the sacred if they try. A person believes that in this world as complicated as it is magnificent, the two opposites together create a perfect harmony that amazes everyone. All this interconnection, this omnipotent force that is holding things together and that amazes us all, we can call it whatever, however, and it is the intimate, private way in which I, you, each of us communicate with the Almighty, the force that harmonizes this divine creation on earth. I think that no one needs to tell anyone how to believe or practice faith. Rules make people do as they wish. Those rules for some may be appropriate, but for some the same clothes don't match everyone's body, they cannot all be uniform, since even the fingers of a body differ from each other, - the philosopher spoke, immersed in the debate.

-Belief and religious rules are like the flesh and bone of the human body. How do they do one without the other, without codes, rules? The great prophet left everything for his descendants. Everything is written and confirmed by the religious codex. As you say, it does not exist and it is not possible for everyone to act as they wish, according to their own whims. Where is that? You are wrong, you sinner! Look at what you are saying, I do not agree with you at all, I am even starting to get nervous from this conversation, - said the religious man, indignant, almost taking the step to get up from the table, but his interlocutor lowered him with his hand. He remained calm and wanted to keep the situation under control, not to hurt his friend who took things so cordially.

-It was not intended that the most intimate personal things of human, in some cases even more intimate than sex itself, be discussed or a model of how to act should be taken. In mating between two partners, two people are needed, and here the connection between the person and the supernatural power is even more private. Its channeling should be made separate, not public, but more personal than the love between two people itself, as I emphasized. If everyone takes lessons about their most private or sacred things, then it can be trivialized, alienated, idealized or even extremely politicized. But the truth is that meat without bones does not do, but is everyone's flesh and bone the same in this world? No! Similarly, the approach to this phenomenon should not be expected to be the same.

The key to this whole mystery lies in love, the good will to move things forward, not fear. I apologize, I will not argue further. I apologize if I overdid it, but I just want to clarify and give my opinion. Maybe it's different than usual, but as long as we have discussions without getting heated, it's fine. I'm not saying that my opinion is absolute. You should think the same way, because we're not doing great sacred things, it applies to my thinkers as well. Here, no one knows who is right and who is wrong. Once again, I emphasize, we must look at it from this prism that both sides must be right, neither should dominate the other or defeat, bias. The only question is the selection, the perception of the individual as to which path he will follow and which one helps him to ease the burden of life. Truth is said to be perception. It does not exist as an absolute, like society, life, the evolving human being, as well as the fact, the evidence, depending on which parameter it is taken or interpreted, can be seen as truth or refutation, but we'll talk about this topic another time, let's not exaggerate.

After all, we don't know whether we are alive or dead. We are used to saying that we are alive, but we have never seen death so that we can judge both sides as a fact. Is it by chance that we are living death and what is the truth if it still exists somewhere in all this mysterious mess? – Driton spoke, deeply immersed in the infinite world of philosophy. He was lost for a moment and slowed down. He stopped, didn't speak anymore, he realized that perhaps he had exaggerated even though he was always hesitant to talk about these things in public because few people understood his philosophy. He could be taken for a fool. He gave a friendly look to his friend who seemed to have also wandered in the philosophical discourse or narrative that the agnostic thinker had prepared at the moment.

- Let's leave this topic, because it seems to me that we've gone too far, Besim, - said the philosopher, wanting to end the conversation lest his friend be hurt.

- Okay! I'm asking you something now, Driton. Lately, I see that you've increased your contacts with Shpresa. Has something new arisen between you? - Besim addressed him with a devilish look, as if the heated debate of a few moments ago had dissolved into the ether and they continued in their old tone. - I understood from Arbër, I should meet with him from time to time. He is interested in religious matters, he is reading a lot and we are discussing various issues about the things that interest him. It seems that he is very smart. Speak, tell me, he began to narrow down the thinker.

- Yes, we have increased our datings, but there is nothing concrete. We are just spending more time together. After that day when I suddenly found her in the city, I think I told you, it's not getting out of my mind. I have a feeling that a mystery is creeping into her head. She suffered a lot during the war, it could be the consequences of that condition that are now appearing. She's not talking, she's not opening up, but there's something that I can't see, confirm. That girl has a burden on her. Her gait, her posture, her eyes, her body, speak for this, - the philosopher spoke distractedly about the event a few days ago when he had been a witness himself.

- Arbër doesn't talk much either, especially about the traumas of the war. He was little, maybe he doesn't remember it well. I don't even want to ask him. I also notice that Shpresa has something that is bothering her, - confirmed the words of his religious friend.

- Let's hope that our friend will have a good time and will not be accused, and we'll see about the other things. It will be fine, - they spoke in unison. They had been drinking their coffees for a long time and hadn't noticed. The conversation had distracted them for a moment. They competed like two good friends over who would pay the bill. The thinker paid because he was the most persistent, apparently feeling that he was the one who should take on the burden of the debt, the amount, as a result of the passionate conversation from time to time, that he was perhaps its initiator. The waiter made the payment, thanked the guests as he left the bar, which was very close to the city center and it was easy to reach all the desired destinations.

Driton returned to the office, while Besimi, surprisingly, could not get the beautiful Vesna who had once been in his embrace out of his mind. Her eyes didn't leave his mind for a long time. The woman from the bar reminded him of those eyes that he had once forgotten.

XI

Besa recovered very quickly. Her condition improved significantly and fortunately, from the medical checks and recordings, there was nothing to worry about. Fortunately, there were no fractures except for some sprains in her neck and somewhere in the upper part of her body that she had suffered from being hit by a car from behind. She had been released home and had slowly returned to her daily life and normal things. Of course, she was on medical leave, but she was expected to start working within a few days. She was gathering strength by resting at her home.

Shpresa once again had one of those nights that would not leave her alone, disturbing her by reminding her of the horrors and images she had experienced that would not leave her head, her mind. Several times after she woke up, she would look at her body, to see if it was still bleeding. The blood in her body was as much a horror as it was a salvation, lest by chance all that hell she had experienced was growing inside her, in a life that, with the devil's blessing, could give her breath and body. She didn't want to give up such a life at all. This thing had become a burden to her, usually in the mornings when she woke up from sleep, if we can call it that, that night, or nights. Even though years had passed, the anxiety was still inside her. No, no, it will not happen, I will not allow, I will not accept that a terrible thing i had experienced, will grow in me. I don't want to give life because of violence, pain, and an unyielding body.

But who will listen to me? Who will ask me? I will decide about this, but if it happens, I can only.... . give death. The severe depressive state often tormented her and it seemed that there was no way out. Often she saw the way out of her troubles and mental problems in her brain in permanent departure, but, but... suddenly she saw her brother sleeping like a lamb next to her. Only then would she stop, tears would flow, burning inside and making her not act, stopping. She would lower her suicidal hand, which would heal her wounds forever, as if by magic. There were serious cases when she got tired, she gathered courage, silently apologized to her brother, it seemed that she was setting off on that path, but again, again a hope would hit her hard and leave her together with her Arbër, whom he immediately went and hugged so much, almost suffocating him, He often wondered why his sister kissed him so longingly all over his face, making him feel as if she had returned from a long journey and now they were seeing each other after a long time.

Sometimes it seemed as if his sister was somewhere far away. He often felt this emotion when they were in the room. With her calmness, her long silence, his brother felt that she had left, even though he was beside her, he noticed that she was not present with soul, being, mind. Her body had long since disintegrated, it was not in sync with her existence. She was in the middle of a Dantean purgatory, where the force of the underworld pulled her more down than up. Instead of enjoying the fresh air, she was moldy and stinking from the filth of thoughts that came from the bottom of hell. She had been living dead, for a long time.

Blood for her was everything… in awakening from nightmares, liberation but also melting. Oh, how she could have all the blood in the world and keep it for herself so that every time she woke up it would be there, not that blood of violence of a beaten, torn body, but blood that could give, life, breath, body, name, fate…. like the fruit of a caress of braids or a scorched chest accompanied by the butterflies of the stomach that make the knees tremble and the earth that she treads when the eyes see the eternal.

Liria stood on her dining table with her hands on her head while she ate several types of fiber with yogurt, controlling her diet, to constantly be in good physical condition with her weight. She always took care of what she ate and wanted all those clothes, especially dresses or short skirts, to fit her best. She didn't want to gain a single kilo, she always liked to look beautiful and attractive, first for herself so that she would feel safe and confident. She remembered the day of her visit to Besa in the hospital, Besim's behavior that ruined her mood. Why do people like Besim, who change perceptions and change attitudes from one extreme to the other, always use force, "argument," to dominate women? Why did he only look at me? I have become an eyesore. For my actions and behavior, I give responsibility, first to myself, then to others.

After all, it is my life, my property, I do with it what I want, as long as I don't deny others their freedom. I have always wanted to be free like a butterfly, to have no obstacles to anything. I have chosen my desires, lusts, sufferings, pains by myself, I haven't let anyone dictate to me, why now Besimi,... the one who used to be completely different, especially towards me. No, I don't accept this idea, with the change in worldviews or judgment, to change approaches towards others, to change behaviors, no, I don't understand, but I don't want to know either. While she was lifting her spoon for another bite, various thoughts were running through her head and she couldn't find the thread of meaning.

Why are only women made to feel important about what they're wearing and never men. Why are sanctions only imposed on the fragile, gentle gender, only because they have greater strength to exert on the weaker. No, I don't want to think this way. Why is a dress code never assigned to men. Women have feelings too, not just the male world.

Women can be disturbed by beauty or a naked male body. I know full well that I'm a woman myself. When I see an athletic face or body, I want to see, or or… a devilish look and laughter seemed to take over her face. Religious sermons don't say this, man seems to be deforming it and interpreting it as it suits him. Usually the male world leads these kinds of games. There is no other rule than how it manifests itself, articulated with a tendency or background for the man to dominate the female world. I'm not exaggerating…not at all. According to some interpretations, men are allowed to have more than one wife, polygamy, with various silly pretexts. Come on, tell me now, - irritated with herself and the thoughts that were appearing in her head, come on, tell me, - she was talking to herself. She seemed to be screaming; from her inner, piercing voice, a roaring voice that broke doors, windows, all the relics of the religious world. Tell me, is it permissible for a woman to have more than one husband with codes, rules, laws, canons or whatever you want to call it. Why, if she has the ability, affinity, since a man does not meet her requirements, Why not? Don't you like it now... or, it seems that she had entered into a heated debate with all the codes, social laws that social structures prepared. This is called nothing else but discrimination, nothing else. I don't accept you.

You are not fair, you have double standards. I can't do it for myself, I think about some... - she started laughing to herself. They just come and go, none of them stay with me. They take the nectar from the pollen and run away to their hives where they make shit that someone else eats. She wanted to laugh, cry or whatever. But you men, without you we can't do it at all, but even with you we have a hard time. She thought for a moment about the Creator, am I blaspheming? - appeared to Him in the form, the image of a man with a long beard, opened the eyes and think...

 you've poked your nose into my head here too, you masculinist world..

Besim, there's something about him that sometimes behaves so hatefully. I wonder why he feels freer to talk about anything with me, or, or...he had a girlfriend once in Bosnia. I remember that some problems emerged between two families of different ethnicities that seem to have been the cause of their separation. I never asked him. It seems that the impact of the war and the two antagonistic camps also affected their love. It is said that they got along very well. Maybe this could be one of the reasons he has taken the path he has today.

After the breakup that happened in his life, it seems that in all women he sees his girlfriend and makes him talk because he couldn't protect her, have her by his side. He loved her and can't seem to forget her. Failure to have one thing can very easily turn into hatred for the same thing. When you can no longer have it, then you resort to all kinds of derogatory labels to make it easier for yourself not to have it or lose it. It's not worth dealing with these troubles, - She threw the spoon and plate in the dishwasher and went outside. It was sunny weather and it seemed to him that even his mind cleared up for a moment.

They assured Fitim that everything would be done for the best. They had released him to defend in the bail so that most of his family and friends had gone to meet him and see how he was, but he had stayed away from the media after they had criticized and scolded him for the acts they had accused him of. His friends from the party seemed to have taken all the measures to make him appear innocent, except for the defense which was well selected and very expensive. They had managed to establish contacts with potential judges who could have led the trial process. Fitim felt comfortable, there was no concern or burden even though there was a lot of hype on his behalf recently.

There was fear of the internationals that they were leading the influence and the process and sending it in a direction that would penalize the defendant. But it seems that the party and its militants had thought about this case too. If he were to be sentenced or found guilty, it would be a burden for his friends or the party interest group who did almost everything in synchronization and together, and it could also be a problem for others, if Fitim were accused.

They had managed to make an agreement even with the international justice present in Kosovo. They would try to help in the process in question, but at the same time they had to guarantee some international obligations for the country that could be sensitive or even painful for the public to carry forward, since they were the group or people who had influence on decision-making in the country. Fitim had hesitated for a moment. - Wait, is the cost of my release going beyond the limits? On one occasion they had told him: - It's not just you that's the issue, but we're all involved, the whole group is in this game. No, it won't be a big cost. Why, what more could they ask of us that would be difficult or paralyzing. Even so, they have nothing more to ask, we've fulfilled everything, they reassured him that it would be done well and all preparations had been made so that their friend would come out the best in the upcoming process, without any sanctions.

Fitim had reassured his friends of his generation about the developments around him. One day, friends had come to visit him at home and he had assured them all that, God willing, he would be with them on the expected prom night. When he left the house of his accused friend who was under house arrest, Driton was amazed by the construction, design and amenities that the house had. The same impression had been left on others by the large courtyard of the house, beautifully surrounded by a veranda in the middle of the garden, mosaicked with various flowers, and which was refreshed by a swimming pool that shone with fluorescent tiles and lanterns that it had around it for using even at night if desired.

Nearby was the modern marble counter and equipped with drinks from the most popular or most expensive and that seemed to move and could be approached if desired and enter the pool inside to facilitate the service during swiming. Expressing strange exclamations and ringing voices, they had left the fairy-tale house, not counting what they had seen within the walls, which had been more than beautiful and wonderful.

XII

Driton's head was heavy from the recent events that had happened around him. In the office, he usually created news, while he followed what was happening to his friend. He often thought about his situation and many times he had hope for it, and sometimes he doubted the entire epilogue as to how it could develop. He had doubts about the entire process and the progress that would be made. He had increased his datings with Shpresa. Besim and Arbër had recently found a kind of symbiotic relationship.

They met almost every day, Besim had taught him about the codes and rules of religious obligations. He had explained to him about the five main pillars of Islam. Arbër, always enthusiastic and very eager for the lectures of his family friend, often lost track of time and where he was. Fortunately, his sister knew that apart from school and occasional meetings with his peers, he ended up in conversations and confessions of the Besim, so she didn't worry about him.

The young man's interest and dedication to religious teachings had made him also enter into the obligations that religion preaches and he had started practicing prayer. At first, he had found it difficult to learn all the supplications, fard, sunnah and rak'ahs that he needed for regular daily practice. Besim also spoke to him about other obligations, the influence that had to be made so that everyone followed the obligatory path, to know more about the blessed land, Sham, the afterlife, the prevention of evil, the evil and about seventy-two dedicated virgins if one manages to gain paradise, paradise, with devotion, dedication and kindness to relatives, especially submission to God according to religious preaching and brotherly ties with those of the same faith.

He would delve so deeply and listen to the teacher that the student would get lost in the words and stories related to the religious world that he usually listened to. The lecturer preached to him without hesitation, spoke to him with full emotion. He seemed to be a good orator and the job of conveying the message was accepted very easily by his student or new friend.

Whenever he was late or not at home, she knew he was in the company of Besim, especially after school or at the appointed time for evening prayers. Shpresa worked regularly at Danaj's with Aunt Myrvet. During the break, they usually had their afternoon coffee break and after work she would run to get home. She missed her brother, they would have lunch together. She usually cooked the food the night before since she was away from home for almost the entire day. The sister began to notice changes in her brother. Arbër began to use Arabic more than usual at home, he had increased his prayers and began to change some of his behaviors. He would often criticize or advise his sister on certain things about how she should behave. During meals, he would ask her to pray before they started eating and asked her to also start praying and to change her appearance and style of dress.

- It seems that Besim is having a big influence on you, Arbër. I will talk to him, - the sister directed her attention to the guardian of the guilt, about all the changes that were happening to her brother recently and the changes she had noticed in his behavior.

- Sister, he is very kind and loving, he is helping me and advising me, it is for my good, don't accuse him at all. I am the one who is interested in the things he is conveying to me, - he spoke in defense of his teacher.

- I am not saying anything, but I am noticing some changes in you, it seems to me that the real Arbër is dissolving day by day, is turning into another person that I barely recognize.

You seem like a different person to me and distant, cold. Don't get me wrong, I am just afraid that you are preoccupied more than necessary, the sister spoke in concern about the only vision of life that was left to her from her former family.

- Don't worry, sister, on the contrary, I assure you that I am feeling and thinking better now, - he threw himself into his sister's embrace, who barely held him with both hands after the little man had grown taller and was showing signs of turning into a handsome young man.

Regarding Arbër, Shpresa had also discussed it with Driton about the frequent meetings he had with Besim and the changes he had noticed in his brother. Driton had only heard about all those nuances and developments in her brother that worried his friend. He had not interfered at all in meetings with Shpresa, he didn't know what to say. Besim was a friend, he knew his approach, on the other hand she was in question a young man who could misunderstand and find all that narrative baggage too heavy for him to swallow. He could inadvertently stumble into a vortex from which it would be very difficult to get out of it later. By leaving it all there, if consumed excessively, they feared that he would become alienated and instead of religious influence going to the service of the individual, the opposite could happen or vice versa in which the individual could be put at the service of religion. Driton understood, he knew her fear, but what could he say to her, how could he comfort her? Suddenly something occurred to her…

-I hope you understand completely, I don't know what to say, except that I can talk to Besim and advise him not to burden him too much with things that are probably not for his age and he won't understand them properly, and the worst that could happen is that Arbër misunderstands this whole thing and gets too preoccupied and then it will be difficult for him to listen to you. He will think that you are opposing the company and conversations with Besim, and he may get irritated to the extent that it will be difficult for us to communicate calmly with him, - said the philosopher who knew his friend's concern, which was a sensitive matter. He was caught between two fires, between two friends, so he thought that talking to Besim was the best and most reasonable method for the moment.

Shpresa agreed and thanked him for the commitment he would make on behalf of her and her brother, who seemed to have undergone major changes recently. She wanted to prevent him from exaggerating even more.

Besa returned to her normal life with her dynamic rhythm between work, children, husband and parents. She took care of everything on time, the strength and tirelessness she had before returned. She had heard about the process of accusing Fitim. She remembered the case of her accident, the visit of friends to the hospital as well as his approach, the care he had offered her, in case she needed anything. This made her worry even more about him and his family. I hope everything will turn out well with Fitim, - she thought to herself.

Driton scheduled a meeting with Besim. The friend didn't hesitate at all to respond to his request. He was intrigued by meeting him and the contradictory conversations they had, each with their own approach, their own opinion, which was usually antagonistic, but this didn't impress anyone about the differences they had, and what is best is that they didn't get angry at all. If they opposed each other, it was all taken up within the framework of the conversation and the development of the debate. Sometimes the atmosphere became heated, but they didn't part indignant or angry.

Everything remained within the framework of friendly conversation. Each had expressed his opinion and respected the other even though they often disagreed in their opinions. Driton had left work to meet, while the religious man had been in town with some friends and it had not been difficult for them to get together soon. They had started talking about many different things, they had discussed Besa and her recovery, they had mentioned the accusation against Fitim. Sometimes they had given each other hope and sometimes they had despaired of the positive epilogue that could follow by prejudice.

Shpresa was also a topic. The bohemian and free spirit of Liria herself and her lifestyle were not missing. It seemed that Fitim and Liria were very similar in their way of thinking and living. Would they have been a good couple? - the friends thought in conversation. Arbër's conversation also opened, his frequent meetings with Besim, his devotion to his friend's brother.

-That boy has entered into my heart, he is a special one. He is so kind and understanding that there is no one like him, it seems, at that age so mature. Many times he surprises me for the better. What impresses me the most about this boy is his thinking. He swallows things very easily, he is so reasonable that he amazes me, he praised his little friend and the meetings they had from time to time.

-Aren't you overdoing it with such frequent meetings? He is still very young, - he somehow began the way of opening the topic of discussion that he knew would not be easy to swallow.

-How? I don't understand... do you think I'm overreacting and I shouldn't meet Arbër? Are you saying that or are you just teasing me? - the teacher said in surprise, who noticed from Driton's face that something was wrong with him.

-Look my friend, it seems that Arbër has recently started to change his behavior and approach towards his sister, he has become strange, at least that's what his sister thinks.

As if he is not her brother. Shpresa is afraid for him. He has become very attached to religious sermons. She is afraid that he is abandoning his studies and is influencing him in some way. Don't get me wrong, but you may have inadvertently overdone it with your lectures so that he changes his behavior. He has also started to interfere in his sister's life, he advises her on how to behave and how to approach others, - the philosopher tried to gently explain the concern of his friend, who had recently noticed the change.

- Wow, Shpresa sent you to see me! How bad that you think that I am influencing Arbër for the worse, are you accusing me of influencing him or not? - he spoke sadly and sorrowfully, wondering what kind of thinking his friends had put him in.

-Slowly, don't worry, don't misunderstand, but Shpresa is afraid that the impact of your lectures has taken its toll, that these changes began when you increased the frequency of your meetings. She doesn't think they were done on purpose, but these things seem to be weighing on his brain, - he tried to calm his friend, who seemed to be affected by the accusations the thinker was making.

-It could be puberty, why could I be the cause of the change in behavior, am I doing something wrong? - said Besim, trying to justify and defend his position, without any premeditation and which affected his student.

-No, no… I understand completely, but take it a little more gently, don't charge the boy too much with those topics, he may not be able to handle them, he is young. Maybe he is not the right age for these things. - Driton spoke, trying not to hurt his feelings and create additional concern or accusations against the religious man.

They agreed not to charge Arbër and to ease the heavy charge on his friend Shpresa, who was so likely to his heart.

After leaving the thinker, Besim began to turn the conversation around in his head. How is it possible that I am being accused of influencing him? He was walking and feeling exhausted. I was just trying to support him by giving him support and advice in the absence of his parents and to ease the burden on the sister by trying to help her avoid bad paths... To see me in that light? As an enemy and not as a friend? No, no, this is too much! It seems that I am exaggerating... or they only advised me because the boy has changed, and it may be that I am to blame for this, but it could also be some other reason.

But Driton mentioned my lectures and his behavior in relation to the sister recently. Could the boy have changed so much in such a short time? They are the same ones who are also looking at me with different eyes, accusing me of having changed in relation to them. It seems that my behavior does not correspond to what they are used to, they are looking for Besim of the past, and now Arbër of a few weeks ago. Could it be that...

The philosopher, in the same way in the direction of his office, was reflecting and trying to find the thread of the conversation. Did I hurt him, was I harsh, or did I overdo it? We now know Besim's worldviews and his changes in thinking about the world and social relations interpreted through a religious eye. We have accepted him as such, but sometimes it seems to me that he does not want us to accept him as we are, he wants to change us in some way, to make us more desirable for himself and closer to his attitudes. He can go too far with the interpretation, to the extent of indoctrinating or radically changing the individual with worldviews that could be a topic for sociological studies.

How can they so quickly and so strongly embrace the new things that are imposed or presented to the public? Perhaps the feeling of belonging to a certain group may be decisive, the identity role may have a strong hand here. The individual feels that he belongs to someone and it makes him feel good, strong and secure. His brain in such cases seeks fusion, evaporation into something more inclusive, where each one tends to give something of himself in the service of the common goal, a kind of ego-altruism that turns into self-satisfaction.

All is done in search of the salvation of the soul. Sacrifices, dedication are made for personal matters in the service of individuality, even though solidarity is thought of, they are done only in the service of personal ego. A gift is required for all the goods of this world that makes one a devoted participant in religious obedience. I think that nothing is done without purpose or only as a gesture, a voluntary desire without profit in the service of releasing positive energy, necessary and felt as spiritual food, but all the goods are expected from the servants to return and be rewarded, where the individual benefits from the cost of the investments he makes over time

One must make a profit in this world if possible or, in the other option of the afterlife, it is intended and predicted that it will happen anyway. All this is known to be something mysterious, undefined and can come into play as a rule of the afterlife since in this life the epilogue can be known, little room for maneuvering while the eternal world remains an undiscovered enigma, and can very easily be swallowed as truth, as faith with the reward of the afterlife. A stream of thoughts constantly overtook him until he saw himself entering the office. He had not remembered the path he had taken because he had been deep in thought. Suddenly he stopped all thoughts and dealt with the objective, with the things that now surrounded him, with his work colleagues, the office and the tasks that awaited him.

XIII

Besim continued to ponder in his head for days what he had talked about with Driton. He felt bad and the conversation of the previous days made him feel guilty and a little touched by the things that were said to his face. He decided to minimize his meetings with Arbër in order to change his student's behavior and perhaps remove the blame that had been placed on him before. Arbër, as usual, expected to meet him, but his teacher always found excuses and avoided the regular meetings they held. This began to last for days, then for weeks. Arbër, in the absence of his teacher, found other like-minded people with whom he spent his free time, and who seemed to replace his teacher, but he felt his absence more and more, until one day he began to suspect. - Sister, I don't know how much you know, but it's been a few weeks since I've seen Besim. If he avoids me, if…. - he was left speechless and with a piercing gaze he shot at his sister in case she had a hand in this.

- What do you mean by that? - his sister replied firmly.

- No, nothing, but I said that you haven't talked to him about anything, I'm just curious, - the brother addressed his sister, speaking through his teeth.

- It's been a while since I've met our friend, I'm sorry, I don't know, - the sister spoke as if she wanted to interrupt the conversation to move on to another topic, to leave behind her brother's mistaken suspicion.

Arbër, thoughtful at times as if talking to himself, pulled away from his sister and went through the main door into the courtyard, always trying to find the reason, why? The sister remained silent. She sat down on one of the old, cracked chairs at the table that made a sound if you leaned on it, so much so that it seemed like she was crying, suffering from the tones of a music that called for elegy or classical melodrama.

Little Arbër appeared to her and the tubes of soap bubbles that he often played with as a child. She didn't want to enter into the memories, the anxieties that often became one with reality. She concentrated on the bubbles, but now she no longer saw soap bubbles, they were some fragments or rather fragments of a life that dissolved in the air. You didn't need to stir them, they disappeared as soon as they came out of the tube of life, without seeing the sunlight they managed to sink into the darkness. The bubbles spoke a lot about Shpresa. They were bubbles that could grow on their own and create a shape that would evoke a flash, a glimmer of a future or would become heavier, shaped by the rushing winds and turbulence of memories until they exploded on the ground, unable to reach the desired heights and fly free, but as if a force of gravity or heaviness was pulling them to the ground. Sometimes it seemed that they had been split in two. Those of the heights avoided gravity and challenged the laws of physics of their sisters against those who constantly fell down and splashed through memories that created stains in the brain, in personality, name or identity in what perhaps they are trying to call themselves. There were more of those who crashed to the ground than those who flew free. It was Arbër who channeled all those bubbles of life for Shpresa, everything revolved around him.

Driton met his friend and they talked at length about everything he had talked about with Besim. Shpresa was informed about the questions had asked her about Arbër's teacher. They were left a little doubtful that they had gone too far with the way they had approached their religious friend, the consequences of which now seemed to be felt most by her brother himself, due to the lack of his company.

After a night of partying with work friends, Liria woke up tired and exhausted. She didn't remember much from last night, but she remembered the way Besim had begun to treat her once affectionate friend. She wondered if he still held that contemptuous opinion. Liria had begun to suspect that something had changed in her friend, not only in his new lifestyle, but also in his behavior with women, especially with her. He had remembered a lost, wasted love for her. She decided to meet him and try to clarify some things that were bothering her. She was looking for explanations, she wanted to know that his way of communicating with her was only temporary, of the moment.

Besim, after talking to Liria on the phone, agreed to meet her. They agreed on a meeting place, which helped ease the tension between them a little, created by prejudices in relation to each other. The religious man had just begun to reveal it, while the extravagant woman only felt the burden of pride getting heavier when his friend constantly scolded him with words. During a simple conversation, when two people meet like that, the conversation between them also began. They were ordinary questions, "how are you, how are you doing, what's new" as a preparation or pregame, to get to the essence, to the main topic.

-        -Besim, lately I've been noticing a tendency, or an intention to offend me. Maybe I'm wrong, but my impressions are leading me in that direction and you're not giving me any room to think differently- Liria interrupted him without a second, right where she wanted to send the conversation. Surprised and lost in thought, her religious friend just listened and didn't react, didn't answer. When they had met, he hadn't extended his hand to his friend. This had made her even more nervous because she wasn't used to him addressing her in this way. There were arguments, facts for all this.

-I don't understand anything, but I have a feeling that something dark is developing in your head. Maybe I'm wrong, but I have this impression. Explain, tell me what's happening, especially in relation to me. I've noticed that you also look at other women with the edge of your eye and with a dose of contempt that comes out of your eyes. Have you started to hate the female gender? Am I the reason, or, or.... You had a lover once, I heard... by chance... - Liria faltered during the conversation, as if she was walking delicately and very tactfully along the edge of a strait. She knew very well that an abyss was waiting for her at any moment below. One's steps had to be very careful, such were Liria's instructions so as not to irritate her friend, she walked with those stiff heels, from one topic to another. Her words made Besim smoke.

- Do you smoke? I haven't seen you with a cigarette lately. What's going on? - Liria would verbally hit him like a matador when he shoots his prey for the first time right in the head with his sharp knife, and he gets so hurt that he only waits for the final blow to conclude the last part. It seemed that she would shoot him right there. From those blows the prey would not rise again in a duel. The matador with his prey between his legs would receive ovations for the masterful fight he made.

In our case, Besim, the prey, had not yet become capable of the curtain falling. His feet were still tapping on the melodrama boards. He didn't need a prompter because he knew the text in his dreams, while he had already learned the role from his life as a director.

- I had a lover once, - he began to speak. It seemed that he would swallow the entire cigarette in one puff. The smoke that came out of his mouth and nose resembled a dragon when the scorching fire through words melts the furious soul. - We were very close, for a while. We met by chance when I was in Bosnia with my uncles. She was very beautiful. Her name was Vesna. She had black eyes in the shape of a fish tail, a face that perhaps Picasso could make more shaped and beautiful, as only God knows how to do it.

The body had the shape of a fish's eyes that seemed to be about to burst at the waist. Her body was long and thin. Just looking at her made me lose everything, myself, time, memories, identity, and for the first time I understood why I existed. I was made to complete her half in a deep, meaningful sense.

Liria was stunned by the words she heard. Even though they walked together, her legs felt heavy on the road and wouldn't move. She had become all ears, she sympathized, she had a premonition that something bad would be the epilogue.

- We encountered difficulties between our two families. Both were against it. Vesna's uncle was known in the public, and I had not heard before that he was an Orthodox priest, he had been one of those who had blessed most of the Serbian fighters on their holy path to the war front. He was a politicized priest, burdened with nationalism. He had led several caravans before towards the Serbian enlightenment in Gazimestan. Where hundreds of thousands gathered and indoctrinated had awaited the heretic who attempted to become a saint towards declaring war on Kosovo once again after six hundred years. It was the same priest who was always at the forefront of leading church liturgies and supporting warmongering policies towards non-Serbs. As soon as my uncles heard, who had gone through the olive groves during that time, and had barely escaped all those sacrifices and persecutions, mass murders by people of that kind, soon came to us. The priest had made the same opinion and influence about his niece after hearing who she was related to.

They took me away from Bosnia. But even when I no longer saw Vesna, we tried to keep in touch. It seemed that the devil had mixed his hands there too, we had it impossible. I lost the love I once felt and became a prey to politics. My uncles immediately offered me advice, identity, religious, and religious that made me somehow separate myself and gain strength to overcome the pain I had been carrying for a long time. I entered different religious circles and began to look at the female gender differently, which helped me forget Vesna. It seems that from time to time I think about it. That day often becomes turbulent for me. A few days ago I saw a woman with eyes that looked a lot like hers - the religious man was talking while mechanically, without knowing it, even though he had a cigarette in his hand, he took out another one and lit it. He noticed that he had two in his hand. He threw the one that was at the bottom to the ground, stepping on the remaining cigarette, while he operated on the other. She was still holding her foot firmly, stomping the cigarette on the ground, so that for a moment she saw that she had made a hole from the force of gravity, and in the meantime he had also smeared dust on his shoes. She stopped.

- You had a love drama, my friend. I am very sorry, but it does not mean that you have the right now to hate the entire female world after your love failed. You can find her again, you just have to have patience and faith in this matter, - her friend spoke with emotion, wanting to calm down a little the pain that seemed to have revived in her during the conversation. Besm felt as if he had been struck by lightning while she spoke. His anger didn't go away, but it increased even more. He made a sign with his hand as if asking for forgiveness, stepped back and left. Liria began to call out to her. She thought about following him, but she was in two minds. She decided to let him calm down. It will be fine - she thought to herself.

On the way she thought about everything he had told her. It was hard for him. He was between two fires: in one he was burning from lost love and the other from identity traps that, as Malouf described, are very difficult to control when they rage. From that bohemian life between love affairs, social outings, drinking, various teenage experiments, to cross over to another line, that of religious holiness...?!

Did this event direct him, create a turn in his mind towards the garment of a religious man and perhaps it happens that he hides his suffering towards her in the constant prayers he makes in the service of his soul. It is clear that he is hurt. The potential prevention of accidentally being possessed by the devil requires more control than he can do for himself. Religion seems to be able to give him what he is looking for, but I have my doubts. It seems that he has not forgotten yet. He suffers... But why should he see the woman with a different eye now? It seems that the failure to do something for himself, more easily removes the failure through hatred if one manages to convince oneself by giving it a completely different, uglier meaning, - thought Liria, confused as she walked along the road. She managed to understand what she wanted, but this made her even more agitated.

XIV

Arbër and the teacher clearly had changed their relationship. He could not meet him at all. Besim always avoided meetings with him and left no room for reproach. Driton and Shpresa usually discussed their meetings and often thought that perhaps they had exaggerated the relationship between them, while Arbër was even more different with his attitudes and behaviors that he extremely surprised his sister.

-Maybe he does it on purpose the way he behaves... maybe he wants to get revenge on me about this, since he suspects that I have a hand in Besim avoiding Arbër. He has started meeting some other friends who seem to be having an even worse influence. He is more closed off, does not discuss, looks at me with a certain disgust. He often instructs me on how to act and asks to put a hijab, saying that I have an obligation. His worldviews are clashing with mine day by day. He also demands that I commit myself to the five obligations of the Islamic religion, and when he sees how I think, he gets upset, angry, and tells me that I will pay in the afterlife for everything I have done and for what I am not doing. He thinks that the situation we are in is due to the lack of commitment to religious obligations. God is punishing us and is not rewarding us in any way for the path we have chosen, so according to him we must change course - the sister spoke worriedly about her brother who, at a young age, seemed to have taken things too far. Emotion had overwhelmed her and reason seemed to have been replaced by the dogmatic, unsubstantiated way of believing. Driton could understand from a socio-psychological perspective the child who, with a conditionally limited world and a simple life between the edge of existence and poverty, in the absence of parents and family authority, at that age the adolescent had trouble embracing his circle which was not very kind and often vindictive, he seemed to find rest under the claws of the eternal world without yet enjoying the world he found himself in.

Since it didn't promise him much, he had hopes that in that world, according to religious sermons, he would achieve eternity and gain paradise. From a kind of social isolation where the real demands for a better and more dignified life are dissolved by limited monetary power, the individual has no choice but to dream and hope that beyond the limit called life, there could be salvation not only for him, but for the vast majority who found themselves in such a position due to the lack of the so-called existence or dignified life. Now this word had a different meaning, it was not only to fill the stomach with food, drink or shelter, by existence you also understood the material goods that you had to possess if you wanted to have status, a name, a sense of being, presence, not of articulation, but of possession that showed that you truly are, have or dispose of.

Fitim was getting ready to participate in the court process that would be held today. The media had also found out. Some of his friends gathered, including Driton, Besa and Shpresa. They were sitting in the back benches of the court and waiting to see what would happen. It seemed that the defense of their strong friend had taken all the measures to release their client or had done everything so that their fellow party member could continue his life at liberty. The prosecution, with all the papers and documentation, had engaged the lawyer who would lead the charges against the defendant, while the defense seemed to have engaged an entire team. Two of the defense lawyers seemed well synchronized. The session began with the judge's order. The part that sought punishment began with all kinds of charges from low-level to the highest. Fitim otherwise felt comfortable. We watched with curiosity how the process would continue. Shpresa had started to bite her nails nervously about what would happen next. The defense objected to everything he was accused of, there were some facts, arguments that he was faced with, on the other hand there were other opposing facts that the party that was suing Fitim had. It offered writings, letters, documents with which it was attempted to argue the mismanagement or misuse of public money.

- Look! It was signed by his hand. Here is the facsimile, where it is clearly seen that for this contract money document, we don't have the support of legislation and procurement procedures, it is seen that with only one signature the contract work came into force, which you see is worth several million. The subsequent signatures are said to be made with pressure and blackmail to make this document seem legal.

Look at the dates, the bidding, registration, opening of the boxes and further proceedings don't match. There is no way all these processes can be done within one day - the lawyer addressed the jury and the honorable judge who listened attentively to the emotions displayed and the argumentative language of the accuser, who sometimes gestured with his hand and sometimes with the papers he was holding so much that it seemed like he was going to fly with all those pieces together.

The defense side had a counter-argument saying that everything was done with legal proceedings.

- Since the bidding has probably exceeded the procedures and had to be repeated two or three times, in the case you mention, the circumstances have been created such that due to lack of time we have entered with a quick procedure but all the relevant authorities have been involved in the process and as the other side is saying, everyone's signatures are there. Only time was in question, we didn't have the luxury like in the past. Nothing is illegal, there is a regulation there, here... - the defense approached the jury with a look at the judge and began to read the article of the law which seemed to be in accordance with everything he said.

The plaintiff objected, trying to prepare the judge who was avoiding the main point. He was diverting the fact and the way of arguing. The judge intervened and it seemed that things began to escalate to such an extent of arguments that you didn't know which was the most correct. Both sides were right as much as they were both wrong.

At one point, the accuser decided to call the witness who he thought would be of great help to the accusation's argument, but something happened in the meantime, two or three times the witness didn't appear. The judge called both parties together and asked them to be well prepared next time with witnesses and procedures already announced. It seems that the witness didn't appear at the hearing. This caused the judge to end the hearing for today and until the next one in two weeks, the defendant could defend himself at liberty.

Fitim, with a glance from the front rows, continued to be calm. He saw us, nodded and with a light smile assured us. We thought that things would turn out well for our friend. Of course he is innocent, he was our friend, we wanted it to be so, we didn't want him to end up accused, regardless of the fact that all the good things he possessed seemed to be... maybe.... no no no it is not possible, - Besa and Shpresa were saying. Fitim does not do that, it is not possible...

After the session ended, we all left together. Fitim realized that he had to go with the group that followed him and kept him close. Like a pack of wolves they removed him from contact with other people and from the media pressure that was being put on him. We barely got out after that crowd that had formed in the meantime. We didn't have the chance to meet our friend up close. Driton had many doubts about the process, about what was happening and about the epilogue, it was not as it should be, usually things are guided and delegated by reason as they should be, it seemed that many things that happened in this case had no reason. If you calculated the life and income of his friend, they didn't correspond to the achievements, but if you listened to the arguments of the parties in the dispute, both had provided basic arguments. Likewise, for his friend there was an interpretation of things, it was said that there was an irrationality of the rational, again even the evils were justified in this whole mess. But it was also done in this way, in this form of action, judgment and reasoning, but this seemed only to a part of the close society, like some secret clans that after appearing on the scene with a kind of antagonistic articulation take on dimensions. Most didn't know and didn't have the power to understand this kind of incomprehensibility in all this rationality that was presented.

Besa had been familiar with these kinds of processes for some time, as she was part of a ministerial sector, she had heard about them several times, and in some cases she had been closely acquainted with such cases. Her colleagues with whom she shared offices had been part of such processes, or were part of some other public sector that had contact with her. Shpresa, meanwhile, kept her mind on her brother. He couldn't get out of her mind. For a moment, she wondered why her mind was constantly on him. Was it some sign, a premonition... But Driton's presence, his company, seemed to give her security and make her feel good.

XV

Arbër had increased the number of meetings with his group of like-minded friends. He was often late for home and his sister would get worried every time he did this. He began to withdraw into himself and rarely discussed things with his sister. Shpresa often asked him questions, tried to start a conversation, but his brother would answer very briefly, usually with "yes" or "no", "I don't know" or "maybe", these were words that showed that he was not up for conversation and wanted to be alone. He seemed to have the whole burden of the world and didn't know how to cope. You could get this impression from his gestures and facial expressions.

His sister noticed this but pretended not to see it and they continued in their old ways, hoping that he would open up and tell her what was bothering him. It was known that the lack of meetings with Besim was one of the reasons. He still believed that his sister had cooked this up so that they wouldn't communicate, trying to change the behavior he had been displaying lately. She thought that Besim was influencing him. Now he seemed even more frantic with his mental and psychological state. He was harsher in behavior, often raising his voice, but now it wasn't religion that was clouding his mind. Who was influencing him now? His friends, his classmates? It seemed that the influence on him was inevitable, he wasn't immune to some viruses if I may say that they would destroy the immune system. It seemed that his body had no defenses, it would submit and surrender as soon as they attacked it, transforming it into something else, only not in Arbër.

Driton often tried to talk to him, to calm him down with the help of his sister, but very little seemed to work. He often offered him company, to walk, to go out somewhere alone or with his sister, but it seemed that the situation remained the same, unchanged. He didn't open up to conversation and, out of respect, kept a neutral course and at the first opportunity, the offered chance, he withdrew into his own world away from those present. This made his relatives worry.

-Today, sister, it seems that I will be a little late, don't worry. After school, we will go to study with our classmate Agim, then we will meet after lunch with the group that attends religious lessons. We will stay at the mosque until after Asr. I will try to come before five in the afternoon, - he spoke and tried to justify today's day that he had planned, preventing him from creating panic in his sister.

-Okay, since that's what you want. I know Agim from school, but these other friends, who are the ones you've been meeting lately, I don't know them, I don't think I've ever seen them, - she spoke carefully and with a sense of humility he approached his brother, trying not to hurt him.

-Are you going to take these away from me as you took Besim away from me? He was a bad influence on me, of course these brothers of mine will hurt me too. If I let you know, I'm afraid you will take them away from me, you will find a reason not to see me. You want me to stay alone all my life, without company, to spend time only with you, - Arbër spoke furiously. A flash caught him and seemed to ignite and explode like a gunpowder shell.

-I'm just asking you, I think i have the right, you're my brother.

Before she could finish his sentence, Arbër left the room and then the house, raising his hand as a sign of protest that I was leaving. The whole house spun around for Shpresa, the ceiling seemed to fall to the ground and part of the floor rose up the other way. This happened to her several times until she managed to sit down in a daze to calm down on one of the chairs at the table. She held her head with both hands and covered her eyes. She didn't want to open them for a moment, she tried to believe that she was dreaming. It seemed easier to believe closed. It seems that she squeezed her eyes a lot, rubbing them with her hands, and after she opened them, after a moment, some flashes began to shine, balls of sparks, an aura that reminded her of those ball bubbles, but now they were shiny. It seemed that they always followed her, there were no days, weeks without appearing in her eyes. The soap bubbles with contents as cold as death had turned into bubbles of fire that seemed to constitute everything before her eyes. They didn't disappear for a moment. She opened and closed her eyes, but they were still present, as if they were mocking her. "We are here as long as you are, we can change roles, shapes, colors, but the bubbles will always follow you." It seemed that Arbër too had completely turned into a bubble. Wrapped like a balloon flying. She was afraid of exploding, of falling and getting hurt. She went to the bathroom, washed her eyes in order to clear her head and all those images that disturbed her went away. She escaped.

Fitim seemed to be slowly returning to everyday life. He began to go to work, after the court allowed him to defend himself at liberty and until he was charged or not charged, he could exercise his duties in his ministerial work. He began to meet friends, the media pressure faded day by day, those were the first moments when, with euphoria and in an attempt to create news, they would not leave him alone, but within two or three days everything becomes real and people are said to get used to it. It was a clever tactic in which it was said that if you want to do something that could cause a stir or mass dissatisfaction, whether in society, people, the collective by making a decision, do it on Fridays, since the hot blood of Fridays will be extinguished, subsided until the next meeting after the weekend on Mondays.

By avoiding constant contact, you are far from dissatisfaction and it is said that over time, even that momentum or harsh reaction will, after a while, make the new reality acceptable, without being punished or escalating the situation more than it was at the beginning. The reaction and dissatisfaction will fall to a level that will be acceptable for any act that initially made them furious. It is very surprising how time, not only heals but also influences the acceptance of things about which there is a lot of hesitation at first. Realities are internalized by the various decision-making circles even though they often conflict with our rational views. They are swallowed as well structured and we seem to tell ourselves that it was written to happen. From that rebellion against the institution that channels decision-making, we move to another stage of acceptance as easily as possible, once with ourselves then we articulate it in such a way that it becomes credible for others, why all that turn in approach. Interpretation is the sister of perception and both together can very easily create realities either imposed or injected with tendency, where the masses as indoctrinated can very easily start to believe in what they like. It is known, it is related to the ego, character and cognitive system of the individual, or the suggestion of the mass in the psychology of the crowd.

The sessions, as usual, based on processes of this type, lasted endlessly. The scheduled schedules often failed because one party or he was not ready for the hearing, requested a postponement, or there were no witnesses who had previously appeared. This seemed to be because there was influence on the witnesses, who were unable to testify in the case to make the verdict easier to understand and reflect on. They were hesitant to come even though they had accepted at the beginning. There were doubts about their failure to appear in court. So the process was only postponed. Once upon a time, even the media got tired and no longer aroused interest in following them, they predicted what would happen. The defendant continued his normal life, while the plaintiff found itself in an unenviable position, failing to document the situation he had observed. It often happened that in such cases, the defense was very well organized. The influence of the defense and interest groups had taken its toll, they had poked their noses into every pore of social and institutional life so that they had people, connections and ran things the way they wanted. This was also enabled by the monetary power and power in which they were. Sometimes the whole process seemed like a kind of theater, as if we were trying to fight crime and corruption, but in the meantime, due to the lack of evidence, their release was the result. They emerged even stronger before the law and social structures, being seen in the eyes of the public as victims and insulted in their pride, demanding retribution in the de jure aspect, while in the real aspect there were many reasons for suspicion and unfair processes. This made Fitimi and other Fitimas feel comfortable, since the entire range of services for preventing accusations was available and there was no room for worries.

XVI

During these working days, Liria had connected its procurement department with a workshop together with several relevant departments inside and outside the mission. There were three working days that were organized in one of the most popular restaurants in the city. There they ate and drank more than they worked. They had an agenda filled with various breaks for cigarettes, coffee, lunch that fell every hour or an hour and a half. There was a five to fifteen minute break, until around twelve o'clock it was lunch time when they paused for an hour and a half, usually moving from one part of the restaurant to the other, where the food was served. It could be in the form of a buffet or with waiter service.

This way of organizing the workshop lasted three days in a row, the participants complained especially the women who had gained weight from the abundance of food on the various menus. There were also other ways of organizing the workshops. They also took trips that were usually organized in the warm months of the year and selected one of the most beautiful coasts of the Adriatic or Ionian Sea. These days were more like tourist vacations than seminars, but what was best was that the workers earned honorariums for participating in this type of event. But due to budget cuts in recent years, they had decided to hold them in city restaurants. They had to come to terms with the new circumstances that had arisen, since in such cases there was no honorarium since they were within the city and it was not considered an official trip. Local institutions, various ministries, and departments had also begun to learn from these types of missions, but as in the worst case scenario, they had acted by imitating them.

Some had taken a family member with them, all at the expense of public money, not to mention the official cars that had described private agendas and various destinations, all in the name of the state. It was an unwritten rule that during the evening hours they would have a party night, after the planned work was finished or rather tired from the food and frequent coffees that came, all to create a better working environment. Due to the heavy glucose, especially after lunch, there were times when their eyes would close from the cool atmosphere created by the many air conditioners, made some fall asleep while sitting down from the quiet speech of the internationals on the podium. Usually such meetings were organized just after five in the afternoon when the working hours and group work ended. Standing and helping yourself to what you wanted to drink, you were available to meet many faces moving around the counter that was often in an open garden environment. The drinks were lined up one by one, the conversation seemed to have started to heat up and the alcohol did its job by creating a good social atmosphere.

The drinks were limited in how much you could consume and usually if you calculated it, there were three to four drinks that you could consume within two hours. The service closed and usually the time didn't reach eight in the evening and this only ignited the catalyst within the guests and made them move to another bar to continue drinking. There, the companies began to split into groups and each independent group headed towards its own destination, to continue on. That night, Liria noticed that the drink had begun to affect her after three glasses of wine, she didn't leave her work colleagues and together with them they ended up in one of the most popular bars in the city center. She continued drinking and found herself among various flirtatious conversations of the colleagues who were there. Fortunately for her, she had changed her drinking habits since she had not had the same wine producer and this seemed a little bitter compared to what she had drunk before, it seemed that she had become accustomed to the previous taste. Tired of the high heels that she had worn especially for this day, she made her stance even heavier, so from time to time she leaned on Andi or Drita. John stood next to her and often glanced at her as if he wanted to remind her of one of the nights when he had ended up in bed with her. Danica, part of their company, also contemplated what was happening, although it seemed that she had also started to drink. They slowly began to separate into pairs, after all that drinking, it seemed like the end of the party. There was little chance of continuing further, if we can say so with the state that most had entered from excessive alcohol consumption. John offered to accompany Liria, but she refused, saying that everything was fine with her, she still wanted to stay there. After not finding support, he took Danica with him and they went out together, leaving the rest

still inside the bar. John, as usual generous, paid for all the drinks. Liria and her friends were left at the end after most of them had dispersed.

-I'll drive you home - Andi said. -I can drive since I haven't drunk much, I'm in good shape, I've had one or two drinks - he turned to Drita and Liria. They accepted. They had no choice, either to call a taxi or accept their colleague's invitation.

The three of them got in the car and Andi began to create his driving line, calculating which house was in front. It seemed that they reached Drita first and she got out after showing him the address where she lived. She greeted her two friends and it seemed that she had trouble keeping her balance because she almost fell. Andi wanted to walk her to the apartment door, but she refused, it seemed that she could do it alone. Andi, after seeing Drita enter the gate of her building, continued driving towards her second destination, that of Liria. She was standing behind in the car. It seemed that upon her exit into the fresh air, if we could call it that from the exit of the interior of the bar, the air had cut her off, as they say in alcoholic slang, and she had barely gotten into the car. Andi tried to somehow spark a conversation, but it seemed that Liria's tongue was stuck. She spoke slowly and was barely decipherable. She would leave words half-spoken and continue after a few seconds, the conversation with her was not uniform, it sounded like a broken gramophone when you leave the needle speed at the slowest.

- Liria, you live alone in the apartment, don't you have a family there? - Andi spoke, wanting to get some information about her in these early hours of the morning. It was past two in the morning.

-Yeeees, I aaaaam aloooooooone, - Liria was sobbing and could not maintain her upright posture.

He didn't like it at all if her family members or parents saw her in this state, so he was relieved about the situation she had become.

-I think we're close now, after two blocks of apartments we'll arrive, - Andi said. He was looking for reassurance about the road he was driving, while he was wondering from whom he was now asking for an explanation and reason.

- We arrived at your place. - Andi said. He immediately got out of the car and offered her help.

- Okayyyyy, I'm fiiiine, leaaaave me aloooone, good niggght. - said Liria. Her legs couldn't hold her and it looked like she was going to fall. Andi ran to hold her, when she started vomiting like a prow with a high pressure. Trying to save her from falling, Andi got involved in his friend's vomit and the entire top of her clothes got dirty from it.

- I'm sooorry beeecause I've beeeeen feeling like voooooomiting for a loooong time, you weeeere driiiiving baaaadly, - said Liria and tried with her hands to find some air to walk further.

Andi, seeing the state his friend was in, decided to help her, to take her to her apartment. He grabbed her by the arm and helped her, while she tried to say that she was able to take care of herself, to leave her there. Andi thought that if he left her there, she wouldn't move and would sleep right on the street, stairs wherever she could find a place to rest her head. - Tell me which door is yours and give me the keys to open the door. She waved her hand at that door and that door again, she had no idea where she was or where she was going, like an unconscious plant, she somehow took the keys out of her bag. At first she confused them with the work ones, which Andi recognized well. Finally, she managed to give him the ones he needed to open the door. Instinctively he decided which door he should try to open, since his friend was already opening all the doors by hand. Andi didn't have enough keys to open them all, and where could he find the one he needed?

He took the keys from Liria, who reluctantly offered them to him, tried them, and luckily opened the door on the first try. It seemed that he had found exactly what he was looking for, with his other hand he was holding his friend by the arm so that she wouldn't fall and hurt herself on the ground. There was no other option, he just threw the things his friend had with her into the hallway after opening the door, and with both hands he grabbed his friend in the air and lifted her up and carried her to the first bed he found.

-Hey, you bastard, where are you sending me like this? Are you thinking of ending the night with succes sex? She wasn't lying down, she was trying to get up, but she didn't have the strength, she looked like a zebra after a fight with a lion that tries to get up but the many vomits don't allow her, when the predator in front of her waits and knows the tempo of the time when she will fall to the ground and not get up again, so Andi was standing in front and every reckless movement he tried to correct so that she wouldn't fall out of bed.

-What the hell is going on, oh owl,- Liria started screaming. She let out a ringing sound and fell on the bed without moving at all. It seemed like the zebra had reached its timing to surrender. She didn't move for a while. It was the right moment for him to deal with himself. He entered the bathroom, looking very nicely arranged, just like the other rooms. Liria reflected extravagance everywhere, at home, outside, at work and elsewhere. He found some clothes solvent and started rubbing the shirt and the bag he had been wearing while his friend was vomiting with a cloth. He rubbed it a few times and for a moment he heard a sound, ran to her room and saw that she wanted to vomit again. He hurried back to the bathroom, found a plastic basin and took it and ran back to her, brought it close to her head and like a rag he vomited again. Luckily he had managed to get there in time so as not to dirty the room with the solutions that were coming out of her stomach from the mixtures of excessive food and drinks that she had consumed during the last two or three days. He thought about going after Liria had sleep, but the awakenings with vomiting made him wonder if he should leave her in this state alone or go.

He waited a while longer to see if she was waking up or if she needed anything. The clock had weighed down the tiring night, it was past three in the morning, so he decided to stretch his legs on a sofa near her room for a moment and go if he didn't need it anymore. The night had taken its toll. Andy had fallen asleep sitting down until he thought about going home.

A sigh woke him up. He opened his eyes and realized that he had fallen asleep in the chair that seemed to have made every part of his body ache. He looked at the clock in front of him in the shape of cubes on the wall and somehow managed to decipher how they were arranged in the most irrational way and that the shape of the hands moving around it seemed very beautiful. It seemed to be fifteen minutes past eight according to his calculation, the position of the hands that had kissed the cubes without number. He hurriedly straightened up from the back pain and went to his friend's room.

-Oh my head, my head hurts, I don't remember anything from last night, you Andi, - he held his head half-stretched with one hand and tried to remember something from last night, but he had difficulty. His friend stood there without making a sound, just looking at him, not thinking about anything.

-Something happen to me and you..., - she glanced at him in order to find out something from what she couldn't remember.

-Nothing happened between us last night, don't worry, I stayed close to you in your vomiting, until you calmed down, with the thought of returning home I had fallen asleep on your couch in the waiting room. Now I'll go, - Andi said, touching himself and trying to smooth out his clothes, which were wrinkled from his uncomfortable sleep. She gave a sign to withdraw, not feeling well in this unenviable position she was in.

-Wait, don't go. Let's have a coffee because it's good for both of us, to sober up, - said Liria, trying to stand up and almost fell from the dizziness she was in. She somehow escaped and remained standing in the direction of the kitchen, holding her heavy head with one hand. She managed to make the coffee. She seemed uncoordinated with the clumsy movements she was making.

-Here's the medium coffee you asked for. I made sugger free for myself, maybe it'll wake me up from this drunken state, - she offered the coffee to her friend who stood next to her like a guard to take care of the state she was in. As soon as she took a sip, Andi pursed his mouth. It seemed that she had mixed up the coffees. Opening her hands, she apologized to let him know that she knew what she had gotten herself into and who she had next to her.

-Those stains on your clothes, wait until I see them, - she said, feeling bad and trying to remember what had happened, while as if hypnotized she looked at a point right at the buttons of his shirt, but she barely managed to understand.

-I didn't put you in this state, oh… now I remember. I'm sorry for everything I seem to have caused you, I'm starting to understand what happened last night, - she glanced gratefully at her friend with an intoxicating smile given in the form of special sympathy, which Andi noticed and returned with an approving and kind look.

- Maybe you and I could have been together as a couple, - Liria said, casting a penetrating and exciting look on his face, so much so that Andi felt ashamed and at one point spoke through his teeth.

-Maybe, but in other circumstances, not in this way, - he gave reason to assure her friend that in no way he thought of taking advantage of the opportunity or the situation she was in.

She clung to Andi's body, who was drinking the last sips of coffee, entering his intimate space, giving him reason for an attractive flirtatious act. Her heavy smell had not yet passed, it was mixed with vomit, alcohol and the smell of tobacco. Andi didn't move from his seat so as not to offend his friend, but he was cold towards all of Liria's actions. He thought that maybe she hadn't yet recovered from last night's actions. It wasn't that she wasn't attracted to him, but it seemed that she wasn't in a good state of reasoning, and the hasty steps could make both of them later regret their reckless actions under the circumstances. Liria kissed him on the forehead as a sign of courtesy and stood up.

-I have to go, I'm late, - he said, trying to leave everything behind, not focusing on what was happening between them, he asked permission to leave. Liria grabbed his hand and said:

-Maybe I overdid it, I understand you completely. I'm sorry for rushing in like this! I appreciate the respect you have shown me and the trouble you faced last night with me. She held his hand and didn't let go until she spoke. This made Andi turn and remain facing her, looking into her eyes.

-You are very beautiful, Liria, but I have to go - he said, pulling her hand slightly from her and with a caressing and admiring look he left the room. Then he felt the door open as he left the apartment. He didn't feel comfortable in her presence at that moment. Liria stood there stunned. She remembered that she hadn't had his coffee yet. She approached, but in the meantime she searched the medicine cabinets for a painkiller. Her head was still throbbing and there was no sign that it would pass, not even after a suggar free, heavy coffee. She wondered for a moment at herself when she thought about her desire to have a husband. She began to laugh at herself. Such a thing had never occurred to her before.

XVII

Shpresa was increasingly worried about her brother. Arbër was rarely at home and when he was present, he was just in body. He was constantly closed in on himself, in his thoughts. He often behaved harshly with his sister, he had an authoritative problem or perhaps he had entered the turbulent months of adolescence. According to the years, he should have been at the end of such a phase, since he had now turned eighteen and at least according to the psychological aspect, Arbër should have already in some form created his personal identity that could change up to a certain age, but he was in the stage of maturity, he resembled a man, a mustache and beard had appeared on his face, he let his hair grow in the form they wanted without interfering to give them direction or path. Driton didn't leave Shpresa alone to face all these problems, so he often met her, talked to her and tried in one way or another to help her, to support her in the formation of her brother in the personality disorders that appeared from time to time. In addition to her own life anxiety, she now had another burden, she had to find a way for Arbër to return to the way he used to be, to become more fair to his sister and to be more polite. She often thought that now all those horrors that he had experienced were appearing to him. She had never talked about this matter with him. He was little then, but of course he remembers the murder of his parents, since he never mentions them, as if he tries to forget it or it seems that nothing happened to him, but to someone else. Maybe he does not remember, he was little, how do we know in what form all that experience has affected a six, seven year old child. If he remembered his sister's experience, what happened to me, it might be a big bite to swallow, especially now that he's starting to understand things more. Could it be that all of this has to do with his recent behavior? That old wound may have hurt him so much that the symptoms or the old incubation have now begun. Maybe through religious belief and religious practice, ...who knows, he's trying to make amends and wash away all that he found, which in his mind could be considered a sin, an help to his parents and sister. Or, what he found was a merit in the absence of submission to God, the cost of the bill was what happened to us.

There is no way to think like that, today no one knows which path is right, everything has changed, time, people, circumstances, mentality, approach and perceptions towards life and the things that surround us. We see many people who have become rich in various immoral ways, have built palaces. Forgive me my friend Fitim, for me they are "crossing the fence" nothing is happening to them only as it is best. God seems to be pleased with them or has forgotten them. It seems that he always rewards them after the sins they commit, while the vast majority who try to respect rules, sophisticated principles, courtesy and solidarity ... with others, yes, yes. . precisely these in most cases are suffering or the existing burden they have is becoming even heavier. The challenge that must be overcome, leave those nonsense. Tell me where justice lies in this world?! I have often been fighting for years, yes, even with God, if He hears me. I would address Him in all languages just to say a couple of words, from Hebrew, Arabic, Latin, or Greek, Slavic or even Mandarin, if one of these languages has the primacy or is closer in words to God. I would never have had a hard time addressing Him, but not in the way they are trying to impose on me, since in Albanian He is not answering. She was aroused by the many thoughts that exploded in her head, she was in an internal war with herself, and her ego. Her being seemed to be divided into three parts and each one was pulling her in the opposite direction in an attempt to dominate one side over the other parts. She didn't know which one to listen to or follow, sometimes one and sometimes the other became stronger and led with her ego.

For Fitim, it seems that the process would end as it is best. After several postponements and lack of adequate evidence, the judge in one of the next sessions released him. The verdict was in his favor. His entire political and party group were perhaps more happy than the accuser himself because they avoided the path towards them in case their friend was accused. The hugs didn't stop, the accurate predictions about whether I told you that it would end like this, as it is best to tell each other. Fitim remained calm as on the first day, didn't move from his place, sat down, while his lawyer received congratulations and praise for the defense he had organized. He was happy, because now he had one more reason to be paid for the services he had provided to his client. It was a lot of money, but the group paid a large part of that money, which eased the burden on their friend.

- Get up, man, come on, I'll congratulate you on your release, we've fought hard to get here, get out of here, Fitim aga, - the lawyer happily addressed his client, trying to encourage him to experience the positive energy influences that surrounded him, but he seemed to be immune to them.

-Now we have a chance to go for a drink, one, two or as many as you want, - said one of Fitim's fellow party members who was organizing the attendees, the relatives to gather somewhere and celebrate. Congratulations came to Fitim from all over the hall, while the other losing party stood indignantly watching their joy and the victory of the process. He gathered all the documentation he had in front of him, congratulated the winner, shaking his hand, and ran out of the hall.

He sent word to his friends of the generation that he knew this whole process would end this way, now he would be freer and he couldn't wait to meet them at a party and think about the dates for the prom night and the usual organizations that are made for that occasion.

For several days, Andi couldn't get the incident with his friend out of his mind. He had her in the office and they often found each other looking at each other. The look was a little different now. Before, they would see each other, but their eyes didn't say anything, while now they looked at each other intentionally and remembered the incident of the previous days, the look made them both remember the same thing, maybe one of them would avert his gaze, not wanting to reveal his thoughts, he had the feeling that everything that was in his head was read by Liria, who by nature was not at all shy, was always open, communicative and natural. If at one point you thought that she was very beautiful playing the role of extravagance, you were wrong, just a few moments with her, you would notice that she was extravagance itself, modern, she was born that way, so that everything seemed to suit her, life had given her a lot in her name, she was original. She glared at Andi more, he seemed more reserved, more shy.

-Let's go have a drink outside because I'm tired of working on a project for a while, my eyes are tired, I need air and a change of environment. Andi, will you accompany me? - she addressed him as if smiling with that sharp look that said: here you have me.

-Okay, I'm in the middle of something for just five minutes, I'll be done soon, okay? - he replied, as if he was eagerly awaiting such news from his work colleague. She gestured with her hands open as if to say "as you wish.”

After entering one of the closest work cafes, they sat on the terrace after finding a spot exposed to the sun with a good view of the city and the street where passersby could be seen frequenting. They both took an espresso coffee while Liria gestured that these would be on her account, as a sign of gratitude for the suffering she had caused him the night before.

-I know that you could have used the opportunity in the most masculine way possible that night, but you didn't. I know for a fact, you respected me, but it seems that with this gesture you have now made me like you, you have entered my heart, - she spoke and looked him straight in the eye, trying to strip him of all the things he had on his body. Andi noticed this, he knew where this approach of his friend was taking him.

-Liria, don't you know that I have a girlfriend? We have been close for a while and our relationship is going well. You are very beautiful, attractive, every man dreams of spending a night with you, but…. now I am in a relationship, I really like her.

-I'm not telling you to break up, never, I just offered myself as a sign of admiration and liking for you, but it seems to me that what I'm doing for you is very complimentary, if I'm not mistaken,

- she spoke, trying to excuse herself for flirting with her friend, transforming her views into a gift of courtesy and in no way into his appropriation. She tried to remove the misunderstandings.

Andi was attracted by his friend's generous offer, but now his mind was divided in two, he was tormented by the temptation towards Liria, but on the other hand he also loved the girl with whom he often went out together recently. If he went with Liria, he would betray the relationship that had just begun. The male hormone pushed him towards Liria, his conscience told him not to, that he should have consideration and feeling for the relationship that had begun. This feeling is nothing other than betrayal. Many things were running through his head. Part of it led to

him towards his work colleague, the other part was trying to stop him, to reason, to respect his newly started love, while the greediest part of human lust was telling him to keep both, as much as possible. He rubbed his head as if in distress. He looked at his friend in front of him who was waiting for a sign, an answer as to what he was going to decide, what he was thinking.

-We'd better go back to the office because we have work to do. I'm halfway there.

He needed time to think further, he didn't know how to answer. He decided to change the subject. Liria understood that he wasn't ready to make a decision yet, she didn't push him or pressure him. He stands up, asked for the waiter, paid the bill and followed Andi, who cleared the way for him by walking behind him.

-I almost forgot, I have to stop at a store nearby, so you go ahead, I'll be back in a bit, - she directed her friend as she immediately entered an alley that connected her to the main road. Liria remembered that she needed to buy underwear for herself. Even though she had dozens of pairs, she followed the most popular and provocative brands that were on sale. She had seen on one of the websites that a new model had arrived, very innovative and extravagant that she had really liked. Wearing them, she thought she would look very attractive and irresistible. Unfolding and looking at the top and bottom in the store, her mind flew to Andi for a moment. She made a devilish laugh to herself and decided: she bought the transparent underwear made of thin silk. After a little while, within half an hour, she returned to the office and submitted to the work that had been waiting for her continuously for several days.

Andi immediately noticed when Liria approached the office. In the meantime, an e-mail had arrived that concerned most of the local workers. He asked his colleague if she had read it and how she had understood the message conveyed by the decision-making circles of the mission.

-No, I didn't manage to read it because I immediately got down to the rest of the work. Is there anything I should know? She could see from his face that something didn't sound right.

-It seems to be related to some process, some kind of reshaping, or restructuring among the workers, if I'm not mistaken, a kind of reduction but with a slightly softer term. Maybe I didn't understand it very well, but that's how it sounded to me. Liria immediately opened her electronic account and noticed that she hadn't read it even though she had received the notification. She started reading it, holding her forehead with one hand. Andi stood near her head while she tried to understand what was written in the message.

-As far as I understand, it seems to me that's how it works. We will undergo tests and interviews, a kind of competition between us and whoever comes out the best stays at work, those who don't achieve good results will lose their jobs.

Both remain surprised, but also worried.

XVIII

Shpresa woke up startled from sleep from the nights that brought her through the anxieties and horrors experienced over time, she woke up between her blood and Arbër's bubbles. She had become porridge in sweat, dripping with water. She looked at the body as usual when she sees such dreams, wondering if it had been torn apart again by the teeth of wolves tearing the flesh or if it was just a dream where they failed to plant a devil's plant that the light never wants to see, a plant without a name, without an identity, but one planted in the meadows, in the nights between dancing bats, torn clothes on a Luciferian altar, where Shpresa always saw herself being dragged through the doors of hell. Her body was nothing but a sacrifice in the name of sin, where I drank from her virgin blood that would sober the power of evil against good, in the underground hell where the cries from the depths were heard on the surface, pulling chained hands, a stream in the whirlpool of evil spirits, where heresy in their name raised the tower of eternity.

Somehow she found the strength and desire to get out of bed. It was still early, just past six in the morning. She went back to bed. She tossed and turned from side to side. She went to see his brother, but he had woken up from his sleep and was performing ablution to proceed with the morning prayer. He didn't disturb him, she let him continue in peace; she didn't even wish him good morning since he was immersed in the work he was doing.

She decided to start with the usual morning chores, thinking that she would do them slowly, without rushing. She had all the time in the world to get ready. She laid out breakfast with what they have at home, which was not so abundant, but it seemed delicious, especially for Arbër who seemed to have woken up in a more cheerful mood than usual. They got ready for their duties: the high school graduate had prepared his books and uniform to continue his studies, while Shpresa got ready with the few cosmetic items she had at hand. After they saw that they were almost ready, and it was already early, they also drank some tea together, brother and sister, chatting about routine things. That morning seemed so pleasant brother so much so that at one point she wondered if it was possible that the previous Arbër had returned. Let it be at least for one morning. Her sister was overjoyed. On the way out, they both greeted each other in the direction they were going, but Shpresa was stunned by her brother's embrace, something he hadn't done recently. She was very happy, but at the same time she had a strange feeling that she couldn't decipher. Inside, a cold chill ran through her body, regardless of the warmth that Arbër gave her. The whole way she thought about him, she couldn't get rid of her brother's loving and warm behavior, but something kept coming to her mind, a bad premonition. A fight with herself drove all those thoughts away, saying to herself, "What's the matter now, you asked your brother for a love once, you took it, he gave it, and now what do you want? Speak up! "You still have resentment in your mind, why, why are you ruining the moment" - she spoke to her mind. Her inner voice made her fight hard with the outer one. In the conversation, she saw that she had reached the Danaj family where she worked. Her working day was not so tiring, or so it seemed to her because she had received strength from her brother with his pleasant brotherly behavior. They had drunk their usual coffee with Aunt Myrvet during the afternoon in the tastefully arranged yard, full of colorful trees and flowers, adorned with various stones that separated the green part from the soil cultivated for flowers of a wide spectrum of colors. Uncle Bedri had also joined them for lunch. Throughout the meal, he had told stories of hunters and chess conversations that were similar among his friends. When she left the house after working hours, she had also prepared food for Arbër.

-Take these pancakes with you because Arber really likes them. Say him to come have lunch with us some day, I know he has teaching commitments, but we would love to. It's been a while, - the charitable lady gently escorted Shpresa out of the house, while Uncle Bedri waved to the girl who took care of them almost all day long.

- I will tell him, but you know how peers are these days. Thank you very much, Aunt Myrvet, you are very good to us! - said Shpresa with gratitude, leaving quietly.

The road flew by, she couldn't wait to meet her brother at home. He usually arrived shortly after her sister arrived home. She hurried so that the food she had with her wouldn't get cold, she wanted to experience the feeling of being supported and loved by her brother for once more. The road seemed shorter than usual.

She soon reached the yard. She got comfortable, got some housework done and immediately set the table for her brother because she knew that his time to appear was approaching. The moments when Arbër was supposed to be home passed. Another hour passed, two, three, eight o'clock approached. Shpresa began to worry, something had happened to him. She panicked, she moved, sat down, stood up, in her thoughts she didn't know what she was doing, she ate her fingers, looked at one point, her brain was blocked for a moment by all the things that were going through her head. She decided to call one of his friends. The answer was that he hadn't seen him at all today. She called Driton, told him that she was in trouble. The friend assured him that he would come to her as soon as possible. He didn't delay, he arrived. He found Shpresa in a very bad state, confused, lost, looking at the clock on the wall, without taking her eyes off it.

-He'll be fine, calm down, we'll find him. - the friend tried his best to give her hope for her brother that he would be found and that nothing would happen.

-My whole life is him, I have no one else in this world but him, as long as he is healthy and well, I don't want anything, even if he is rude, just to see him at home, - she cried, moaned to herself with her head down and her hands on her face. Driton took out a napkin and offered to wipe the tears that were flowing down her face.

-Has he gone to a friend we don't know, - Driton tried to resolve the situation.

-I spoke to one of the friends he usually hangs out with and occasionally spends time with, he wasn't there.

-He'll come, he'll come, he has nowhere to go. He'll show up now, you'll see him, -the friend consoled his friend in distress.

-I hope, but I don't know... that morning feeling... I knew something was trying to tell me. He was so kind, so gentle and sensitive, when we woke up. He hugged me so tightly, it seemed like a goodbye hug, said Shpresa and burst into tears again.

They both looked at the clock that didn't stop, it walked on its own itinerary. The hands moved, showing more than time, pain, uncertainty, the lost path.

-It's too late for you, Driton, - said Shpresa with the feeling of not burdening her friend more, holding him hostage and in anxiety too.

-No, we will be together in this work, I won't leave you for a moment. I have Arbër as a friend too, I worry about him too, so... (in thought) I will go and ask all the friends he frequents. Give me the names, the classmates, and I'll go to the city mosque to see if he's lost his way while talking to them. Driton headed for the door to leave, leaving her friend unaware of what was happening to her brother.

-If we hear about every new thing, we contact each other on the phone, if he comes home or if I see him. Meanwhile, Shpresa stopped him, informing him of the names and places he often frequented.

-It's not time to call the police yet, let's not make a big deal out of it without exhausting all the possibilities we have, I think, - Shpresa agreed, hinting that if the police get involved, she thinks something bad will happen to her brother. She wanted him to return without making a fuss or causing trouble.

Driton spent more than two hours walking around all the corners of the city, the bars, his friends, he even went into the mosque and talked to some people there who knew him, no one had seen him that day. He also started to worry about him. Something didn't feel right here, in the meantime he contacted Shpresa, she didn't have good news either, he hadn't returned home. It was almost eleven o'clock, no sign of her brother. Dritoni stayed with her in those moments.

- I'll stay here with you tonight, I won't leave you alone, maybe he'll come back in the meantime. Tomorrow, in the morning, we'll go to school and talk to the guardian to see if any of his friends have seen him. I'll lie down in Arber's bed tonight. Don't you have any family members you could call?

- his friend advised or reminded her. She approved of his attitude, nodding in gratitude for the care and support he was giving, but she didn't give any sign that she had any relatives she could call. They hoped that he would appear at the door in the meantime. They remained silent, remembering where he could have gone that didn't occur to them. Shpresa didn't close her eyes all night. Every time she sat down, some voice that she heard on his feet would get up and go out into the yard, walk around the fences, but there was no sign of her brother. Usually such noises were made by stray dogs or a cat rolling over things that came across the street. "Something has happened to him, he has never been this late", - she said to herself. Dritoni did not sleep well either, only some idleness from time to time and he heard every movement that Shpresa made, especially when she wandered around the room, the corridor, or went out into the yard.

- Rest a little, Shpresa, we need strength for tomorrow, come and sleep, - his friend spoke from the other corner, knowing that only she made those movements in the steppe and in anticipation that the person she was waiting for so eagerly and longingly would appear. She imagined his image, which never disappeared from her imagination for a moment.

- I am fine, I am not sleepy, I cannot sleep, he is not coming back in the meantime. He will come, I know he will come. Her voice, which had been calm, began to rage, trying to calm herself and give her courage, in those moments of anxiety.

Morning approached. From fatigue, Shpresa had fallen asleep, she was sitting as if waiting for her turn to continue. She had dreamed of her brother who seemed to be riding a white horse, dressed in the clothes of a knight, with a shield in one hand and a sword in the other. He looked exactly like a man. He had long hair, a mustache with a beard tied together, while the horse's white hair shone and contrasted with the black eye that he had, just like a spot that resembled some kind of cute panda.

He raised his sword, shouted in a ringing voice, but the sword itself was dripping blood. He looked around and saw his sister piercing him so much that it seemed that the blood on the sharp blade of the sword came from the stab in her eye… She was scared, she woke up making a sound. She saw that she had fallen asleep and the dream had not left her alone, which made Driton hear her and come closer to see what was happening to her.

-Nothing, just a dream with Arbër. We better get ready and go to school, so that no one knows anything. You see, the morning had just dawned. Her friend nodded, approving of what she was saying. The two of them got down to work and were soon ready to leave.

-Let's go to school first; Let's talk, and if they don't tell us anything... maybe it's better to report the case to the police, - she spoke in a low voice and not in joy, she let out the last word.

- We'll do as you say, Shpresa. - said Dritoni. The words got stuck in his throat from the burning and grateful look of his friend, who apparently had never seen that look before, and it made him tease his heart and brain for a moment.

Fortunately, they didn't suffer much and found Arbër's guardian. He was in class, but he didn't hesitate, for a short time, to meet them. He assured them that he hadn't seen him in class yesterday, he had been absent. At one point he had wanted to contact Shpresa to see if he was sick or if something had happened to Arbër. Not even his friends knew anything about him. Desperate and surprised, she left the schoolyard, wondering where he might have gone. Has she found something bad, has someone hurt him, has he been beaten and left unconscious somewhere, street dogs…

there's no way, he's not afraid of them, he knows how to defend himself, has he had an accident or has someone drowned him, yes, someone, someone… she was screaming to herself and tears were streaming down her cheeks. Dritoni was talking about the actions they had to take now, what they had learned from their teachers and friends, but he wasn't there, she wasn't listening to him at all. Dritoni saw that she was lost, she wasn't present. He stopped the pace of his speech, seeing that she didn't react at all. He stopped, looked into her eyes while holding her by the arm, and saw that she was in tears.

-Are you crying? Don't despair, we will find Arbër. You can't give up, - he looked at his friend in the eyes and tried to instill security and support in her. It didn't take long before Shpresa hugged her friend tightly and burst into tears.

- Cry, cry, if it makes you feel better, vent, throw the pain away, be relieved... - Dritoni spoke.

For a moment she stopped, raised her head from her friend's chest and looked into his eyes, the tears slowed down.

- Thank you! Now I think I feel better - said Shpresa. That hug, that warmth of her friend with all those streams of tears seemed to ease her emotional state.

They left for the police station that was closest to their residence. After they entered the corners of the building, a police officer on guard stopped them, asked them where they were going. After they indicated that they were going to file a case, the police officer directed them to the entrance corridor on the left to office number four where the investigating police officer on duty would be waiting for them.

- You are ordering, - said the policeman sitting by the desk, after seeing Driton and Shpresa entering his workspace.

- We are here to report the missing brother. He did not come home at all last night, since yesterday morning for school, I do not know anything about him, - Shpresa spoke with difficulty, her voice trembling.

- Are you her husband? Are you talking about your friend? - the investigator addressed Driton.

- No, I am her friend, I am just helping her, - Driton justified himself while looking Shpresa in the eye.

- Have you contacted friends, professors, have you talked to neighbors to see if anyone has seen him, or has there been any confusion, conflict with anyone, threat, or anything that can come to your mind recently - the investigating policeman spoke thoughtfully.

Shpresa said that they had been at school, their friends had also contacted them, she confessed that he had not had any trouble recently or any trouble with anyone. As far as his sister knew, she was talking and one thing was constantly on her mind: should i say it or not?.

-Mr. Policeman, lately I can say that he has been more nervous and not very well-mannered with me, like an adolescent protest, in fights with authorities and putting meanings to some things that sometimes seem to not need so much meaning. He tried to challenge some rules, codes to replace them with new ones, if we can call them that, to the one that seemed more appropriate to him. He often seemed confused to me, because there was no question of conflict. By nature he has always been withdrawn and calm - she tried to describe the situation in some way that could perhaps come into play and help them find Arbër.

-We will wait today because there are cases when children of this age go to a family member or friend and after a day or two they return home, there is a fuss unnecessarily, only in the context of miscommunication. Do you have any photos of him for evidence? Shpresa took out his photo from her wallet that she always carried with her and offered it to him.

- Do you have parents? Does Arbëri have a mother, a father? - asked the policeman.

- They were killed in the war. Apart from me, he has no relatives, neither he nor I. - said Shpresa.

- Listen, we will wait just today to see if he comes back. Here is my business card, with my phone number on it. This one is always on duty and open. If he comes home, let me know, if there is no sign of him the next day, we will then declare him missing, - said the policeman as he offered the card with his large, conspicuous hands. We pray that he is not coming to your house so that your friend can stay close to you and we hope that it was just a reckless gesture by your brother, not announcing his whereabouts. We will stay in touch. I got all the notes I need for the report in question, but I won't open the case until tomorrow. Then by the time we declare him missing, God willing he'll be back today, - he said, approaching the door to escort them to the corridor and motioning to the exit. The chubby policeman returned to the office, while Shpresa and Dritoni left the police station. As soon as they came out, they noticed that it had started to rain. Dritoni asked to go into one of the nearby places that served pastries. Hunger had begun to bother him. Dritoni took some pancakes and a curd pie,

while Shpresa only drank tea. She was hungry, but hungry for Arbër, she didn't want bread at all.

Dritoni returned to his journalistic work, while Shpresa decided to somehow pass the time at Danaj's, often trying to contact him at home, just in case Arbër picked up the receiver. She tried, but no one answered the phone. She didn't stay with there long, decided to go back home, to wait for any news from his brother. Dritoni worked as hard as he could, he didn't even care about work. Shpresa felt sorry for her brother and was afraid that something bad had happened to him. She once thought of making a media announcement about his disappearance, but it occurred to her that she might hinder the case after the police suggested waiting until the next day. She got up from her chair at the exit door of the office and called her friend. She said that returned home. The voice didn't sound good to her, so she decided to go and stay with him.

Neither the afternoon, nor the evening, nor midnight, nor the morning brought anything new about Arbër. He was declared missing through police reports. Dritoni helped here by making it public in several print and television media. They hoped that any one had seen him or knew where he was. Shpresa seemed no worse today, but at that moment when his case became public, it seemed to her that he had been stolen and would never be found again, ever. She remembered her meeting with him, the last one before she left the house, that generous behavior of his, that look that seemed to reveal a hidden sadness behind the scenes, the warm hug he gave his sister. All of this made her experience pain once again and burst into tears again, but now she was as if were crying, speechless, she had no strength to make a sound, her voice did not come out, it seemed that she was exhausted, from the broken spirit that burned the crushed flesh and that he felt in her stomach. Those twists were like a turret drilling where all the air that the body has inside is exposed and released through a combustion that rises up and comes out of the mouth, and the diaphragm never manages to fill up with oxygen again to release tones, just like a punctured balloon that not even the wind carries, but remains torn and the only one to be stepped on.

Dritoni standing at the table and talking if we can call what they were doing with his friend a normal conversation, after many calculations, reflections, assumptions or prejudices, all about their brother seemed to escape from simple rationality, swaying or shaking and entering an irrational world just because it suited the expectations or the epilogue they prepared for themselves. With words, it seemed that they gave solutions to everything. They often said that he did this on purpose, that he was tired of his sister and had found some rest somewhere else and what not.... they talked so much that sometimes they contradicted each other what they were saying and the debate heated up; for a moment they looked at each other and said to themselves that it seems we are going crazy.

A moment after they saw that they had no reason to spoil the atmosphere, they had to have a clear mind, they began to get closer, to take each other in good terms. At one point, intimacy took its toll, but in this specific case, tinged with anxiety, so much so that Dritoni pulled Shpresa closer to him and brought her into the halo of personal space, caressing her face, when suddenly something furiously contradictory flashed in her that confused and worried Dritoni. Her eyes widened, she saw once again what she had not wanted to see... the sparkling bubbles appeared that turned into those bubbles of war. She imagined the drooling policemen, stinking of alcohol accompanied by the stench of boots and sweat... in her eyes, Dritoni's hand appeared to her as the policeman's. She had never touched any hand before except that cursed, rotten hand dressed in black that tore the veil of virginity right in front of her parents, where the blade of their knives was a sacrificial act of the wedding that was being prepared for her. It was a funeral wedding, both of them were tied in knots and they wouldn't leave her alone like the vines of trees that tie around the trunk and hold you tightly and don't let you get up or feel free. Her soul was imprisoned, the man's hand disturbed her so much, it couldn't be deciphered otherwise, even though she sympathized with Driton immensely, in her imagination it seemed like the hand of the enemy.

-You don't need to stay anymore, you have your own things to do, I'll manage. Thank you and you're free to go, - she spoke as if she wasn't very determined to her former friend and sympathy, but who still had feelings for her.

-But how, why, was I wrong to approach you? I saw a fury in your eyes. I apologize, but why, I don't understand!- Driton spoke confused. She stood firm, waiting for him to leave, but inside, what she felt was not revealed, she hid it very well. Dritoni said that he didn't want to leave her alone at all, but he was persuaded by her insistence. He went out, but he was completely confused. What happened, what did I do to make her so upset? Did I become so stupid? - he said to himself. Why did I have to approach her? It seems that I have fallen far short of her expectations, but it seems to me that I have tried to approach her and take advantage of the opportunity in this difficult situation she is in. It seems that this is what she has in mind, there is nothing else, - he thought as he walked. He was so confused that suddenly noticed that he was going in a completely wrong direction. He had gone through several crooked and narrow streets that for a moment he stopped and said: "Will I know how to get out of this labyrinth?" After her friend came out, Shpresa knelt down and cried. She didn't know for whom more: for her brother who was lost and it was not known whether he was alive or dead, or for her eternal love that for her it seems will be a forbidden apple. What if we get closer. We both love, especially me, but what if he realizes that her sympathy is not pure, has mixed blood, polluted by the secrets and fluids of the murderous hegemonic authorities." The entire unbridled arsenal of Kalashnikovs, the rapists, have shot my body. None of the men want to have the remaining shells in their hands, until the gunpowder has been fired in the name of someone else.

No one will ever take the dregs, the waste like me, when you have the opportunity to choose from the best possible modern assortment today. Why get involved in something that centuries-old foundations will place you in the cradle of tradition where the soil called mother will turn into mud with the caress of a life stepmother who will never be ashamed to spit on your walls of social code. Dejected, she threw herself on the sofa and lay as if dead without moving for hours. Her sleep was fleeting. In the dream, Arbëri and Dritoni had come together and were fiercely shooting her until she tried to escape the shots. They both laughing to each other, the blanket, their tongues sticking out to see who would be more accurate in shooting her right in the head, they played, they had fun with her as with a toy that is about to break and you help them more to achieve invalidity and non-functionality, thrown beyond. It seemed that a stone was headed straight for her, and before she reached her destination, she woke up in sweat and cold. She was uncovered. The cold of the night had entered through the outer door, while the sweat from inside was not leaving her in peace.

Dritoni was not at all comfortable, he could not find a pace. He called Shpresa several times, but she did not answer, apparently she was asleep. He thought that she was cooking such things on purpose, that she had some whim that he could not discover. He could not bear it and decided to return to his friend.

As soon as he reached the door, a cold shiver gripped his body. He opened the door to the courtyard, turned the latch back on the railings that connected to the entrance to the garden. No one was heard, silence from the courtyard, sadness for a single woman in this entire house, he thought to himself. Here fear seized the man and not the most fragile…

He knocked on the door, waited a moment and after a while the door opened. A surprise hit Shpresa's face, while Dritoni thought that she had expected her brother to open the door at this moment and not him.

-Maybe you thought it was…. Is there any news from Arbër? – he spoke politely and without emotion asked his friend who opened the door.

-No, there is no news, there is nothing new – said Shpresa. She turned back, but left the door open as a sign that he could come in. He said that he had tried to call her several times, but had not succeeded. He had been worried about her and had decided to return to where he had left her before. Until Dritoni entered, he looked up at his friend again. She seemed even more beautiful than when he had left her before, perhaps the time he had spent without her in his thoughts had made him see her a little differently, more beautiful, more attractive and more loved. Her curly hair, which was slightly disheveled on her forehead, looked quite beautiful even though it was not combed or arranged in a straight line. Her tearful and suffering eyes were the most beautiful he had ever seen, while her slender body, with a cotton dress that occasionally hugged her body, created the shape of her thighs and buttocks in a way that often tickled Driton's mind. They were not extravagant and contemporary clothes, but they were clean and had the scent of roses, not from perfume but from the aroma that his friend emitted, an aroma that it seemed that only he could smell and was specially prepared for his taste. He looked at her in a certain way, but he did not dare to reveal himself or take any initiative to transform these moments

in terms of intimacy. He tried to have self-control so as not to upset Shpresa in any way because then the epilogue knew for sure what it would bring.

-I don't know what we're going to do, I'm starting to lose hope, it's been almost two nights without a word from him. It's just that something happened, he was the only one who kept me alive. How am I going to do it now? She held her head in her hands and leaned back in her chair.

-You can't give up. Whatever happens, you have friends close to you. I talked to Liria and Besim earlier. They had heard about Arbër from the media. Everyone is there to help and I share the same opinion. No matter what comes, you can count on me, - Dritoni said and tried in some way to pave the way for her faith and future that regardless of the end, she had to continue on.

She looked his friend in the eye and took his hand. This surprised Dritoni. He was stunned and waited for what would happen. She begged him to go at night and rest because he was tired all day from dealing with her; to return to his life and not worry about her problems, since he would also find support with the help of the police in searching for the missing person, so that things would go more calmly without euphoria. While she was talking to him, it seemed that he thought that now their roles had changed, instead of him giving her the go-ahead, the opposite was happening. Where did that strength come from, that rise in all that vortex of perceptions and premonitions prefigured with a mosaic of anxieties that you face as soon as you open your eyes, injected as if it were real. Even though you try to avoid it, your conscience tells you that it is unreal, don't believe it, you still can't resist it, it becomes like a part of you or something planted that grows from you and it itself slowly becomes the murderer of what was born from you, so the hand that once fed you turns into a hand that takes life. How could you leave it in that hand that could now kill you, regardless of its narrative that supposedly had things under control? Is it left in this state numbed by paradoxical curiosity where everything now seemed to be in order? It plays its assigned role in this whole significant act, as the main character tries from time to time to overthrow the secondary just to have the authority and dominance that the director grants him, but the script

i'm afraid someone else has it, so that even from the dark corners if a wise word is spoken, the whole scene will still turn around where the boards in the name of glamour from the patronage of the main character will be overturned like a flood of question marks, where did this suddenly come from.

XIX

Dritoni spent another night at his friend's house waiting for Arbër, but still no sign of him. This undefined state began to torment him. The wait seemed long, tiring, often bordering on boredom and neurosis, feelings that disturbed his peace of mind and made him suffer more for his brother, or rather his little friend. Other friends came to Shpresa as a sign of support and help. Fitim with his monetary strength put himself at his service. Besim with his prayers did not stop, asking the Almighty for mercy to open the way that would lead his friend home. He felt a little irritated that he had influenced in one way or another in all this mess. Besa approached Shpresa to spend a few days with her, not counting Driton's help, so that she would not be alone, she was able to spend this period together by keeping her company. Liria was also willing to try to organize some contacts with higher authorities through some connections with internationals to help clarify the fate of the missing person in question. In this way, with his influence, Fitimi was also willing to contribute. Shpresa felt very good after everyone joined together, showed solidarity and sympathized with her. It seemed to her now that the world was no longer as small as it had seemed two days ago.

Condolences came from friends, but with this she could not console herself at all. She often felt guilty for this whole incident. She was closer to Driton now, her first sympathy, but as close as they were, it never seemed to her that they had been further apart. She was afraid that this relationship could be broken if he let her get closer, and even more so, that the gates that had been locked since time immemorial would be opened and all the news, the events, the things would become known. The doors could be closed again so that they would never be opened again. Something bad could come out of those doors, so it was better not to disturb things, to let them flow in their own way, without interfering or blocking the way, without any impact, it could then cause an explosion between the two and they would be separated forever. It is better to have him close in this form of a friend than to have him come closer to me like a loved one and then lose him forever - she always thought to herself. Sometimes to have things closer they don't have to be in the way and shape we want. The closeness or distance between people will never have a meter or instrument that can determine what the limit of one or the other is.

Suddenly someone can appear out of nowhere and open all the doors that you could never have imagined would happen, but here it is, while the one you have closest, his presence can seem like the most distant person in the world you have, never seems to be close to you. In his or her presence you always feel lonely. To leave things as they are, or to intervene, was the question for which she had only half an answer at the moment. Besim did not feel good about the loss of his student. He decided to meet Liria. He went to her. When she saw him, she let him in. He looked bad on his face. Liria noticed this immediately after her friend appeared at the door. There was some guilt inside him that he thought of sharing with someone, and Liria seemed the best address for this. She often knew how to bring out in him what many people did not know how to do. She was good at all this. Her social relationships were well-sophisticated, her manners and way of approaching people were in accordance with the needs and demands that the opposite side usually expected, so she was very close to people and knew how to make them her own. She always listened carefully when they had something to say, and her modern appearance only helped her more in this regard by creating sympathy and a desire to be as close to her as possible.

-It seems to me that this escape of Arbër may have happened because of me because it also ruined his relationship with her sister. This is bothering me, I haven't been feeling well for a while, I spend my nights between Arbër and Vesna, who always appears to me in my dreams, almost trying to tell me something through them, confess something, or ask me for something. It seems that I miss her a lot, - he said and threw himself on the sofa as if he had been struck by lightning. It seemed as if all his ships had sunk.

-You're no longer interested in her? It seems that you're afraid or don't want to, let alone dare. Now, in these modern times, you can make any person, anywhere, close to you through the kind of social network.

that enable virtual communication. You don't use them, but they can help you a little to see her photo if you want - said Liria. This teasing from his friend intrigued his mind even more. It seemed that he was suffering from just looking at her face that he had projected deep into his mind for just one more time.

Liria took her name and through her private social network account found Vesna's profile, enlarged the photo using her smartphone and brought it closer to Besim.

- Is this the Vesna you're talking about? - she said, bringing the device closer to Besim, who remained frozen. He didn't speak but it seemed as if a thousand visions passed through his mind and made him look very tired, as if he had aged in a minute.

- Yes, this is it. Thank you for making me see her once again! Isn't she beautiful? - he sought support and approval from everyone he passed by to justify the situation he was in, whether he was right.

-Yes, she is very beautiful, if you want, you can even contact her, this type of communication allows it, - she pushed his feelings that were now showing in him even further. The magnetism of his emotions seemed to touch Liria as well. Besimi's complexion changed. He slowly left the phone on the table, with a gentleness as if he didn't want to hurt the photo or ruin her beautiful profile, he turned to Liria, looked at her sharply and headed for the exit with a sigh with which it seemed he wanted to relieve his soul or the fire that was burning inside him. He stopped at the door, once looked in the direction of his friend with his head lowered and the respect he offered her through the bodily movements he made, in humility he said "thank you" and went out.

Liria remained in thought, she didn't understand why his mood suddenly changed, she saw how he reacted, like his eyes sparkled when he saw her photo, but why is he hesitant to go any further? Just to talk. Maybe he's afraid of the worldview he has now, maybe of his family, or of himself. How can he know what she's like, or who she'll be with. He doesn't want to understand or doesn't have the strength to contact her, lest the old fires be rekindled and then nothing can stop them,

nor the worldviews on identity, religion or social codes that families erect as fortifications, the prestige they want to leave in the name of nobility by breaking the most elementary rules of being generous.

She remembered to call Shpresa and see how she was, if there was any news from his brother. Before she could finish the conversation with her, a call that did not offer hope or anything good for Arbër, she suddenly heard the door. Thinking that Besim had again forgotten to tell her something or had just remembered, with the phone in his hand, while finishing the conversation with Shpresa, she opened the door. She was surprised when saw Andi. She immediately stopped the phone conversation and decided to go to him. Andi did not speak, he just looked and stood stunned in front of the door. The two of them met each other's eyes for a short time. He had come to take what was served to him earlier. Now he was more determined than ever. He pushed the door open with force, grabbed Liria with one hand behind her head, pulled her closer to him, and kissed her hard. Wracked with lust, after pulling the kiss away from her lips, he bit her bottom, making Liria feel all those bursts of passion. Her bitten lips remained swollen from his greedy teeth. She kept her eyes closed for a while until he caught her, carried her with both hands in his arms, while kicking the door that he left behind to close and entered straight into the bedroom where she slept. He looked like a hunter holding his prey in his hand, which he seemed to enjoy being given to him. She was now his. She surrendered completely to the dominator, so that he could do whatever he wanted with the trophy won on the divine altar, donated especially for him. Their bodies merged, they melted into one. The whispers, the lustful sounds they emitted, permeated the room with a tendency to exceed the limits of the walls that had become the nucleus of an unwanted seed that had within itself the nickname of deserting martyrs driven to betrayal. The desire to immerse oneself in her pool made the moment even more magnificent, made both of them feel free, especially Andi, to whom the aroma of shame and guilt that carried in this entire act, gave the strength of immortality where with the nectar she inhaled, she reached the limits of being present, existing, permanent and sweetly obligatory sinner.

He moved away from her body, took the pillow and threw it behind his back. Half-sitting, he took the pack of cigarettes and lit one, focusing in a point. She pulled back lying down, took the sheet and covered her exposed thighs that felt like they had run a marathon. She didn't manage to point out the underwear she had just bought. She started to get dressed slowly while he didn't move from his place, only inhaled the cigarette smoke. It seemed as if he would swallow the entire room with the force of attraction, continuing to stare at the same point as if hypnotized. She threw away the sponge and the cigarette that he had so quickly finished, got up, put on the pants and shirt that she had barely found because he didn't even know where he had left them, and turned to Liria with a reproachful look.

-That was a big mistake. It was the first word he had spoken since he appeared at the door. He took his things and went out. Liria didn't speak, nor did she move at all. Sitting on the bed, she just watched what Andi was doing, who seemed to feel guilty. The door slammed shut, footsteps were heard fleeing. He went.

XX

Besa had just been invited to an official meeting regarding education in the country. There were many different defects in the education process and system, so much so that one of the representatives of this ministry and competent person was invited to a public discussion to elaborate on topics that affected the public's interest.

Many irregularities had been revealed in this system, so much so that there was a fuss and mutual accusations about who was to blame, the system as a whole or the incompetent participants themselves who were exercising their duties right there in such a sensitive segment of social life. Some employees in the public sectors were caught with forged diplomas. There were cases when they had not even seen what the school's halls looked like, let alone the academic units, but they were equipped with certificates that gave them the strength to get employed.

If we add the connections with various interest groups or party militants who sought to consolidate their ranks and accommodate the network injected into the representative system wherever they could, with the aim that those diplomas issued, if converted into today's denigrating social circumstances, would be equivalent to nothing more than a strong political vote. In high schools, due to overcrowding with students, the lesson had become more between reprimands for silence and the breath held by forty or more clergymen, in classes where two by three sat, in some cases there were not even chairs to sit on, quality was required in that whole mess where the breathing of those present was heard more than the teacher's voice or any new thing taught. There were cases when this irregularity or disorder in the system had created indifference towards the teaching process which had very often heated the students' blood in the absence of focusing their attention where it was needed, and they had turned into hunters of conflicts among their friends or in relation to the teacher whom the system did not protect at all, had left to the mercy of fate.

Such an apparatus had sanctioned him to such an extent that he could not control his own lesson at all due to the unfavorable circumstances created by the parades and the uncontrolled noises of those who had no place there at all or the attention and dedication in the entire regulatory and channeling apparatus of the teaching process. In the absence of concentration where it was needed, energy was spent on delinquency, so violence began to break out in schools between different groups over who was more dominant in creating authority that, in the absence of the institutional one, had slipped into the hands of those who least deserved to lead the school, the vandals.

Many curricula, methods and teaching units were shaped, complicated with the intention of supposedly increasing the quality and teaching methodology, but it was the opposite. Many things were politicized, from history, trying to shape even the most modern past of the country through the interpretation of the discourse of power, to geographical subjects where each distinctive map in itself had something that sowed evil. Those who were still in power took credit for installing the knowledge system through it, similar to Faucalt who takes the example of the intervention of power in knowledge and the production of knowledge by itself in the service of doctrine and the realization of propaganda aspirations with a tendency to return the desired interpretations to a reality accepted by the broad masses of society.

Improvisations as much as you want, from various supposedly necessary titles, profiteer authors influenced on behalf of politicized publishing houses that tried to make the written word as controlled as possible, more "populist" and not at all in line with the real prism or critical panopticon.

Education remained in recent times between the screams of the degraded teacher or dressed in the suit of the lethargic pedagogue, the slaughter of students where instead of a pen they held the sharp knife that coincided with their future and that reflected the current state. All these attempted reform phenomena, organized or paid for by the over-honored who tore through the treasury of public funds like hungry dogs running after a piece of meat, all in the name of decadent enlightenment and the search for an enlightenment refined by ignorance and the executioner's hand that awaits the future of a country without causing pain and blood, but a euthanasia injection.

Headless bodies lined up in the fabrication of the processing of knowledge that benefited those who exploited society in the most bastard way reminding them that here the knowledge and bright preparation of generations is being cultivated in succession. It was Besa, who had accidentally shot at the wrong place and time. They had been put on the front line or the firing squad, while the planners stood somewhere behind the curtains and watched how it was going, whether the work should be undertaken or the plan changed in action. Besa was criticized, insulted, and nailed without knowing much about what was being talked about. Later, she realized that the cooked cake was nothing more than a project that needed to be tested or a pilot plan made, how it was going, whether there were any obstacles and what needed to be undertaken in the future. If you managed to withstand the labels, the denigrations even though you were not part of it, you would be rewarded with your steadfastness and the defense of the defenseless that you had done and you would get as close as possible to the planners of the social master plans.

If you couldn't argue irrationality or unreasonableness, then in their eyes you would be seen as an extended part of the opposite side or a collaborator. Unable to argue irrationality, demagogy, you would find yourself thrown somewhere in the trash, so far away from attention that it seemed identical to public elimination. Nervous and very worried, she left the spaces of public discussion. She seemed to be in a daze. She stopped for a moment where she could find peace, in a corner where there was no movement, she held herself with both hands on her hips and said to herself: "I've eaten what I didn't eat, they've cooked all this dough for me, there's nothing else." She began to touch her face, she felt the heat that had gripped her everywhere, especially her cheeks were burning. She was going to leave. She looked for Bekim, her husband. She needed to open up to someone, to talk about how until now she had only heard accusations in the lowest forms of human expression against her, directed at her on behalf of the institution. Now, she needed to express herself to someone else, someone who would listen to her. Bekimi agreed to meet her. He left work for a moment and they soon met in their often-frequented place.

Liria seemed to be ready to undergo tests. It seemed that she had passed the test with Andi, and in the most beautiful way possible, but now professional challenges lay ahead. Andi seemed haunted. Ever since the lightning-fast meeting a few days ago with Liria, he had not found peace. He could not get his work colleague out of his mind. This had also affected his relationship with the love he had.

He was very cold towards her, either from the guilt he felt in his conscience that constantly gnawed at him or from the burning desire to see Liria again in the form he had met earlier. Andi was not very focused on work, while Liria was not affected at all. She seemed to be experienced and did not shake or move her focus from the events that surrounded her. She was always attentive and focused. It seems that she had successfully completed the written test and was now waiting for the interview to come out. She did exercises and lessons from the literature that had been provided to her. Andi had prepared very little. He did not read and had not taken this job seriously, but he knew that it could cost him his job if he was not successful. They submitted to all obligations and now they were only waiting for the results of the oral interviews.

XXI

Shpresa was always waiting for some news from her brother. She was between Driton, the media and the police investigator. Any spark regarding Arbër would make her day or even evening, which in most cases she spent in tears, easier. Friends visited her from time to time and offered her support or anything she needed. Driton was constantly by her side, although she hesitated at his insistence. Besa spent some of the difficult nights with her, and the first week quickly passed and the tenth day approached and there was no sign of the missing man.

Shpresa went to work from time to time, but knowing her condition, they often let her go and calm down. It seemed that she was always in thought and wanted to lighten her burden. Uncle Bedri tried to support her and said that he had connections through the hunters' association to some decisive circles in search of the missing and would try to find some connection to be more agile in the search for Arbër. Aunt Myrvet prayed almost every day for him and hoped that one of the prayers she made would perhaps find him and bring him home to his sister.

Fitim through the Ministry of Internal Affairs had done his best to get the special search units involved and through the media and other circles of information and publicizing the case they had left no stone unturned to get any news about him. They had also offered rewards if anyone saw him or reported where the much-wanted man was now. Besa through the school system and teachers, had created an information network so that no one saw him or knew him because in every corner of the places, institutions where he attended they had left his photo available in case he appeared. But nothing had worked so far.

One morning she decided to go to work at Danaj's. She thought that perhaps she would refresh herself in the company of the pleasant couple, that she would get away a little from that atmosphere of endless waiting that suffocated and irritated her at home in the constant absence of her brother. Trying to recover from the night from which she mostly woke up tired how relaxing. When she was leaving the house, after getting ready, the phone rang, making her turn. She thought it might be Dritoni since he often contacted her. She approached the receiver and picked it up. Nothing could be heard except the rustling of the weak connection and a breath that could not make a sound. Shpresa answered "hello, hello, alo, alo" but the other side could not utter a word. Thinking that it might be a mistake or that someone was joking, she thought of putting down the receiver and ending the connection, but something stopped her from doing so.

-Sister, sister, - suddenly a voice was heard. It seemed to come from a very far away and could be heard faintly.

-It's me Arbër - was heard from the other side. He was the words half-spoken, it seemed that he was emotional. Shpresa, as if in a dream, was completely stunned and did not speak, but she had become completely deaf. She couldn't even begin to talk. Unable to speak, tears began to flow.

-Brother, are you okay, where are you?- she spoke in a voice that sounded more like a wail than a normal conversation. She could barely get the sounds out of her mouth, which seemed to be tied up and unable to move.

- I'm okay, don't worry about me, everything will be fine, I'm here for both of us. We need to fix the mistakes we've made, we need to clean up our past and our lives, you just have to trust me, I hope we'll see each other soon. I miss you, for everything… - Arbëri spoke as if in tears.

- I left a letter for you, sister, in my closet where I leave my clothes. I have to go – he continued in a trembling voice that the receiver transmitted to her sister's ear.

-Stop, brother, where are you, what's happening, are you okay, brother…. – she started crying, covering her face with her hands and holding the receiver in her hand, but the connection had been cut off. She tried to call him several times but there was no way, he had left. Everything was boiling in her head. Why, what's happening, where is he, is he in some kind of trouble with someone and many questions that were seeking answers in her head.

 She was confused by the many thoughts. After she calmed down, she called Driton and told him about the phone call. It didn't take long for the friend to arrive home. She told her everything that had happened and what she had managed to talk to him about. In that shocking state he was in, it seemed to him that he had not managed to do what he was supposed to do. He criticized himself for not being able to come to his senses and figure out something that would be helpful in finding and locating him. Dritoni was trying to understand and resolve the many confusions that were in her head.

-Now we will contact the investigating police officer and tell him about the phone call. Maybe he can help find the location where he is. This apparently gave will and hope to the sister who seemed desperate. It didn't take long for the police officer to appear at the door. Dritoni met him and he entered, finding Shpresa sitting with her hands tied behind her head. He removed his hands to meet the newly arrived guest and began to tell what he had experienced a few moments ago. Going through the same experience, he could not finish his words due to anxiety.

-Okay, don't rush, calm down - were the frequent words of the policeman, who in a small note managed to write down many of Shpresa's words that seemed to be choking as they sometimes got stuck in her throat. They had not managed to learn where he was and why he had chosen to disappear in that way.

-We will try to somehow locate this call made. As soon as we find out something, we will contact you. For any new information, please inform us as it may be important for identifying the place where her brother is. Do not spare us at any time. Thanking him for his commitment to solving the case, Dritoni and Shpresa accompanied the guest.

On the way to the station, the policeman kept turning Shpresa's words over and over in his head, trying to find a thread of connection, or some sign that would lead him even slightly towards a solution or Arbër's location. It was difficult, nothing made it easy to create an idea or decipher a problem that required how to proceed. For the moment, everything seemed enigmatic Dritoni asked her to go out together in the fresh air, perhaps it would do her friend some good. She accepted and they ended up in a place that looked more like a promenade than a place to drink something. They spoke very little. Both were absorbed in something that could easily be detected as to where their thoughts were going.

Each one of them was creating events in their heads that had a positive ending, they did not want to think about any other possible scenario, nor did those kinds of thoughts cross their consciousness, they did not correspond to the wanderings and expectations that conflicted with their entire being, especially with that of Shpresa, they were unacceptable things so much so that the brain did not absorb them, but threw them away as something like antibodies and unnatural for their consciousness projected into the much-sought and possible reality.

Shpresa decided to report to Danaj, while Dritoni continued with his daily duties, leaving it to be understood that they would see each other again soon. As she was leaving, his friend seemed different, it seemed that she had aged in a short time. Her beauty still stood out, but her posture and the way she walked made her look like she was almost a hundred years old. Her body had also shrunk, while her morale and motivation had wavered more than ever. But her eyes, her eyes still held hope. It's good that she's alive, I heard her voice saying several times to herself and in public. Sometimes she was so agitated that it seemed to her that it could be someone else and it wasn't her brother's voice on the phone, she had as many doubts as she had hope in all this unexpectedness that had just hit her.

Another wound had opened: the old one seemed to be lying there open, often dripping blood, but there were other wounds this kind of hope had in itself, when it often cursed its own name, thinking that its name was not fitting for the life it led. "I am hopeless," it often addressed to the omnipotent. "This is what you wanted… to trample on me, to humiliate me, to denigrate me. Has little been done to my name and family? I seem to be an unfinished cost, I still have an open account in all this? What else must happen to me for it all to be closed to me? Tell me, tell me, take me and everything, but why are you touching the red borders of my mind and soul? Why are you touching that untouchable? Why are you playing with my fire and my limits, you want to see how far the pain of a living person can go, that is what you are looking for? Arbëri is not only my pain, he is time, love, death, everything that can be felt, tasted, but also touched. He is the purpose for which I wake up in the morning or fall asleep at night, for his laughter, a brotherly embrace and a growth of stature from a young sprout into a trunk that will expand branches, buds and with its crown will shade me from the breeze when I have a hot head. It will make me see the world, life, differently, and hate death, which I once loved so much."

Friends gave her a lot of courage when they heard that her brother had been called home.

-He is alive, healthy, that is the most important thing, it could have been worse, - they told her, trying to evoke positivity in this whole drama.

-Yes, it is all right, thank you, but where, why, for what reason…- sometimes she spoke incoherently, it seemed that this situation had hit her hard and tired her immensely. Now she didn't move from the house for almost the whole day, waiting for the phone to ring again and for Arbëri to call. She was so attached to that phone that it seemed that she often dreamed of the phone ringing itself. She thought back to the conversation with her brother several times, but she couldn't remember something, it seemed to her that something was missing, but she couldn't decipher what it was about due to the surprise and sudden manner of his phone call. Lying down and contemplating a point of view, she suddenly stood up and it seemed that something came to her mind. How could I forget, how, how…. she was talking to herself. She thought of the letter that Arbëri had mentioned, that he had left especially for his sister in his wardrobe. She couldn't remember if she had mentioned it to anyone and she ran to the letter. The phone rang, she stopped, stunned, unable to move, she didn't even go to the phone. The bell rang several times until she left and started moving around. He arrived before she could stop. It was the investigating police officer.

He told Shpresa that they had detected Arber's call, it had been made between the Turkish border and Syria. She listened and did not react; she had become completely deaf. The location from where he had contacted his sister was a military camp where usually the beginners had received their first instructions to join the Syrian front. He had told Shpresa with regret, assuming that his destiny would not be the war there, but that he would find a way to return home anyway. Very young people had attended there, but most of them had never returned alive to their families. Shpresa could not be supported by her legs. She sat on the floor while she spoke and when the conversation ended, she threw the telephone on the ground in anger.

-Why, why…she shouted and with a murderous look she entered his room. She searched through his closet, dropped clothes on the floor, saw a pair of pants that Arbëri was wearing, picked them up and hugged them. Suddenly she changed her mind and threw them away. She turned her eyes to the drawer and saw a green envelope that was there. She took it with both hands, did not even close the closet, she ran to her room and sat down to read it. A shiver gripped her body. Sometimes she felt cold and sometimes she felt hot. She ruffled her hair, rubbed her eyes and opened the envelope.

XXII

She couldn't bring herself to read what he was writing. She put it aside, brought it closer and smelled the scent of the letter that reminded her of his brother's presence. She didn't know what to expect from that letter, her mind went back to the phone conversation when Arbëri, with his voice trembling, mentioned this letter. The entire mystery of his disappearance must have been explained in this envelope. But what would he have written? As much as she was curious and eager to read it, she was also a little afraid about what would find in all that story from Arbëri, it seemed that something scared her in this whole drama. She threw the letter away and left the room. I don't want to read it, I don't know why, but I have a concern - she thought to herself. Something seemed to hit as she was leaving the door. She thought about going out into the yard for a bit to get some fresh air, because she was suffocating, the room, the house seemed to be pressing down, it had become claustrophobic.

She returned to the letter. She changed her mind, took it in her hands and decided to start reading the letter at any price that would be presented to her. She gathered herself, braced herself, regulated her breathing that had been rapid. She closed her eyes for a moment and opened the envelope. At first glance she immediately recognized his brother's handwriting, it seemed that she was now calm and began to read the first letters while standing.

My sister,

I wish that this letter finds you healthy and well, that you are always happy as I would like to see you and the way I met you for the first time, the memory of you in childhood is always in your laughter. In recent years, I have hardly seen that facial expression that I once adored, but I know what our family has faced and what pain we have come out of that situation with. I was little, perhaps it is understandable that I could not perceive things the way I do today. Sometimes I think, I was better when I did not go through them at all in my mind, to understand you and the illnesses you experienced, we have never discussed them, but in your eyes I have often seen the sadness and fear that tormented me so much.

I did not have the strength and did not know how to face all those horrors that exhausted your mind and made you close yourself in the corners of the fortress where often I could not find the key to enter you. Shpresa could not stand, she felt a tightness in her stomach, her legs weakened. She suddenly sat down on the sofa and continued reading. Tears began to form, she suddenly removed the paper from her eyes, wiped the pages and returned to read it again where it remained.

I have often fought with myself, asking questions about how I could have at least slightly eased that burden, but I could not find a way. I connected with Besim with the only reason, perhaps God's mercy and the prayers I made for you, would hear me and we would find rest and salvation. I thought that the horrors we experienced were perhaps punishment from the Almighty and we deserved to lose our parents, perhaps the sins we committed without realizing it brought the deserved punishment. I wanted, with the help of Besim, to pay off everything and the debt we have in front of God, through my friends I headed for the holy path where we will be washed away from all evil, mostly for you, sister, we will be cleansed, both body and soul from the scars and burdens we have carried for years in our souls. It seemed to me the only way to reach spiritual peace, first mine, because I could not bear to see you that way, but also for you. I think we will succeed in this journey and God willing we will see each other again. It is said that there is a blessed land where we want and all good things will come to us after we fulfill our obligation, in the name of the holy, being rewarded in this world or the hereafter, and that they will await us with all the good things that we do not have today in this life

After reading these lines, she burst into tears and the flow of tears would not even let her read. She put the letter away for a moment. She began to feel sorry for Arbër and the way he thought and foreseen things. She never managed to talk to him. Now I understand that he knew more than I thought, suffered just like me. After her eyes cleared and was able to continue reading, returned to the letter.

Whatever the epilogue, you never give up, keep going, I have chosen my path now, I am sorry that I was not able to at least say goodbye to you, but maybe it is better this way for both of us. It was easier for me in those moments, I apologize if I made the situation difficult in any way. I see Driton who is a very kind and quite generous guy.

-I notice how he looks at you. It seems that he will always stay close to you, you can rely on him, he has great sympathy, it is something that is visible at first glance. With your brother, everything you decide for yourself is permissible, it seems that I am leaving you in a kind of betrayal, but don't look at things that way, you understand me too. I had a very difficult time too, I was helpless from all this, until the decision I made, now I think I am calmer, I hope you are too.

I love you always, Arbër

Shpresa collapsed on the bed and started crying so much that she lost consciousness and suddenly she was caught in a bracket between sleep and subconsciousness, sometimes in a dream and sometimes she seemed sober. This state lasted several hours until Driton appeared at the door. He was surprised when he saw her collapsed in that state. Distraught, until she sobered up, he began to tell her what had happened. First, he explained the phone call from the investigating police, that they had detected the location from which Arbëri had contacted her and the letter he had left for her. His call was very much in line with the direction in that letter. His mind was made up in such a way that he had foreseen that he would go and fight for the good, the sacred and the reward that he would receive both in this world and in the one that follows after the one we leave behind, from the devotion that he had given himself as an obligation.

Dritoni was cut off after hearing all this from Shpresa.

- Besim is not in any way influential in all this, - he said, thinking silently that he wanted his desire, obligation and conviction gained to go and fight in the land of Sham not to be known.

- No, no, in the letter he tries to completely excuse Besim. He mentions some friends, they may also be influential.

Maybe it would have been better if we had left him with our friend, but who knows, phiiii, - she sighed, trying to get out all that duc that was tied right to his chest.

-Maybe it's better to notify the police officer who is dealing with Arbër's case about the letter, the message he left. Dritoni agreed and with a phone call from the business card he had left with Shpresa, he contacted him and explained in short points what the letter contained, which was very consistent with the detection of the location of his phone call by security circles. The policeman wished them luck, hoping that Arbëri would return home safely as soon as possible and that they should be strong enough to face this challenge. He assured them that he would always be available for any news or anything new that could help in the return of her brother and asked them not to hesitate to contact him at any time.

Dritoni asked her to go outside together, perhaps a change of environment would do her good. Shpresa did not hesitate at all. It seemed that the house was different now, bigger and stranger without her brother's presence. There was something meaningless in his absence that made her sister feel unwell, almost to the point of hating the house, it seemed like it was eating her whole body, so that she was just waiting for an excuse to avoid it.

They walked for a long time, his friend didn't know how to comfort her. He knew what state she was in now. Sitting on a bench, they watched the passersby. Some walked briskly with dogs, they seemed to be quite large and were pulling their owners so hard that they seemed unable to control them, others had come out with their children, holding the children while they rode their bicycles, they didn't have good balance so one of the parents had to keep the child's balance so that wouldn't fall to the ground. Birds were flying around in large numbers, people who had taken corn kernels with them were feeding the wild pigeons of the city. The pleasant sound of the flashing wings that came from their large flock, every time they landed and sometimes when they rose up, making various beautiful figures in the air for the eyes, in the presence of many walkers who looked there, made most of them almost hold their heads up from their heavy life that was often with their eyes on the ground. Here and there there was a tree that provided shade and tried to save them from the strong rays of the passing sun with its shield. The number of trunks was limited so that there was a lot of concrete space that, with the reflection of the sun's rays, made the heat unbearable. It was mid-May. This month is often known to be rainy on most days, but these days were not exactly hot and if it weren't for the presence of some fountains there, as well as some cafes and some of the well-maintained promenade, it was hard to stay in that hot spot without the support of the trees and the coolness of the flowing waters that made the vacationer merge with nature to some extent. This made Driton adapt to all that surrounded him in the background. He looked at Shpresa in the eye. It seemed like it was a call from nature as he put his hand on her shoulder and looked at her. He looked at her so deeply that it seemed like he discovered everything about her since her birth, but no, he didn't see anything he expected to see, they were hidden very much suppressed by her past.

-I like being with you, I feel somehow fulfilled when I have you by my side,- said Driton who tried to kiss Shpresa on the lips, ignoring all that mass that was passing by, but that everyone was looking at their own work.

-I like you a lot too, but you don't know me at all, my friend. It's better if we don't get too close - Shpresa said nervously. She lowered her eyes, almost ashamed to look at him, as if it were the first time they had seen each other and not that they had known each other for so long. She began to feel uncomfortable in this whole conversation.

-I know you, as much as I need, I don't care about more. I love you and all that is important to me, I want to stay close to you as much as possible, - he said, sure of what she was saying. She addressed him with full conviction and enthusiasm and did not hesitate to express it, but this made his girlfriend start to feel very bad, especially when she saw the children playing in passing, making soap bubbles, she went back in time to exactly where she had not wanted to be. She was sweating so much that she was stunned by the memories, she was afraid that she might return to the state she could soon enter, like that rainy day when she met Driton on the street. With a supportive look, she begged her friend for help. The change in her face made Driton think that it was not his words that had an effect.

-We better get out of here, I was upset. Driton, we can't be together, you have to understand me. There is something stronger than you and me, please don't insist, don't make me suffer more, - she mercifully asked her friend to change the subject and together they got lost in the crowd of the city that looked like a flooded river that has no bed but is spread out like a mouth that swallows everything, covering the entire surface of the earth with people walking.

XXIII

Besimi, through the crowd, tried to avoid taking a different direction and not seem to be present. There were parades, events in the city center. Now it seemed more like he was running than walking, it seemed that he needed to be somewhere else. Something was bothering him. From the facial expressions and gesticulatory expressions, you got the impression that he was talking to himself.

-Where are you going, my friend, so quickly, - Dritoni came forward. Besimi looked at him with surprise and it seemed that he had gained momentum and would not stop, something he could not control.

- Let's get out of here, don't let any camera eyes catch us because there was a protest below. I was leaving the crowd, I came across it, passing by, I was not aware of it…. - he spoke and did not stop walking. His friend started following him and suddenly they ended up in a place where they were calmer and away from the protests or parades that never left him alone for a moment.

-What are you running away like that, who is following you, man? - Dritoni tried to understand what was happening to him.

-Don't you see what is happening, it is a parade, support, maybe even a voice of protest in the service of homophilia and the LGBT community. I don't like this way of marketing, - he spoke angrily and it seemed that some tremors had taken over his sacred body.

-Hey, what's wrong here, everyone has the need and opportunity to express themselves as they feel, there must be space for everyone if we want to be a society with values, - he tried to somehow emphasize the thought and give support without making the things that were being expressed by his philosopher friend tragic.

-Driton, I don't agree with you. I can kind of understand the community and I have absolutely nothing in this regard, but the children, the children of elementary school, what are they doing here? Don't you see? - he waved his hand towards the crowd, which was far from them and from that place the schoolchildren with rainbow flags could be seen marching through the city streets.

-Why, children, tell me! These people don't even know what this phenomenon or community is. They use these young people for tendentious sensitization. This age is fragile, juvenile, if this type of marketing is done in the name of homophobia, it will first push these young people in these sensitive years to experiment and try to explore these ways of sexual desires or changing their identity and gender preferences from those they have. They will be guessed at, doubts will be created in their attitudes with all this pomp and show of them in public. I am very disappointed with this state of society. These kinds of impositions are making me more of a believer and relying on the great, seeking salvation from the evil that man is bringing closer and closer, intentionally or unintentionally. It seems like something cooked up. This kind of lifestyle stops natural reproduction, creates diseases, epidemics. Look at these kinds of diseases that can very easily turn into pandemics. Cancer, Malaria, Zika, formerly Sars, and many others are bringing human victimization, all of which is creating a way of thinking, acting, and living different from what we were once used to, new things do not mean that they are always good without ever being tested. No, no, I will never accept this progress of humanity, this kind of unbridled debauchery that is turning like a boomerang against it. I am afraid that these kinds of conspiracies are being cooked in various corridors, against man as a result of global overpopulation. Who has the right to show or determine who dares to live and who does not?! Tell me, am I wrong? – he spoke and trembled like a birch tree while he spoke. He was more than worried. Dritoni felt his worry in his entire being that seemed to be haunted like a liquid fluid trying to stop itself from melting or alienating itself into something it did not know. The things that a person does not know, does not recognize make him afraid of them. It seemed that he was trying to prevent his social and moral disintegration by relying on relics and religious narrative as a preventive measure against all the evils that have befallen societies today.

- Look my friend, each individual in this world has their own direction. We must enable and understand each one in their own way, how they want to be shaped, develop or communicate with others, we must not stand out. If they are different from us, we do not have to be afraid, we will get used to everything. The freedoms and rights of each one must be respected. If our worldviews differ, we may not agree, but we must not denigrate, isolate or not give them the opportunity to express themselves. I completely understand your concern, I agree with you in the way of raising awareness of some things, phenomena that we are giving more attention to than perhaps was necessary, but we will also get used to these new and different ways of articulating preferences and lifestyles. We cannot see the whole world with just one pair of eyes. Everyone has the right to see it in their own way, how they feel, want and aim to be comfortable in this entire sphere. If you or I are different, it does not mean that we cannot communicate or coexist where each can follow their own path without hindering or getting in the way of the other and blocking their progress. As long as we act calmly and in accordance with the law, then we are fine, while with the social code we must constantly negotiate and get used to the differences between us. But if we honestly look at each other, we will essentially find more things that bring us closer than that which separate us. From that aspect, my friend, we must learn to live.

These children come out today, maybe even more will be made tomorrow, but things that are not made for you or for me will never fit, the measure and proportion of the stature of each person is different. Likewise, these kinds of phenomena, if they are not tailored to our bodies, will only be a momentary flash, as they will kill us from the inadequate sizes that have been offered to us, then we will no longer wear those clothes, or they will be too wide, which will make us slide around our bodies, or too tight and we will not feel comfortable in them and will get lost along the way over time if we use them. So do not be annoyed by these things, they can only be realized if they adapt to the genesis, demand and cult of our thinking. How many novelties will come and go... so we should not become irritable and react to each thing that comes. We will let things flow by themselves. If there is a bed, the flow will find rest, if not, the momentum will be exhausted or dissolved by the branches and the flat shape of the surface that will not leave space for the flow to come to life

and the accumulation of perceptual mass. Don't worry my friend and take things a little easier. The day before yesterday, it was different, admit it, but even yesterday was not like what it was, but it is by no means the same as today. The days we spent can never promise even for tomorrow that it will be like today. Things change, move as we move in relation to the environment, nature and thinking influenced by the creation of new circumstances in social life. Only you my friend, look at how you have changed in worldviews; we know how you used to be and now you are diametrically different, right? Human nature is like that.

The context determines human actions so that the external world in most cases determines what we have inside. Oh, if only we were able to be unaffected by these circumstances and control all the good things that the spiritual world brings, but temptation is strong, strength, power, dominance, greed, excitement, desires, the pleasures of life, pains, feelings, demands, always challenge our inner self by surrendering our weapons in the face of traits such as those in the service of ethics, empathy, sympathy, altruism, love, support, sincerity, justice, respect and tolerance towards others. But it is better to leave these things and go sit somewhere and refresh our minds because these things do not stop, - he spoke and looked at Besim who seemed to be a little calmer now. That sudden momentum that ignited his fire seemed to have already subsided a little.

-Okay, we will go somewhere, but still I can't understand at all why all these things. We weren't like this before, why all these new values? Why now? They couldn't have come earlier? We were here, the same. While I, yes, it's true, I have changed, but I have adapted to the new circumstances created. We have been living in confusion, now it seems to me that we have come to our senses. Our soul has not had the opportunity for faith, we have been deprived in our past. The former ideology left little room for religion and it seems to me that those who preached it, I say from my point of view, did not do it in the right way. But anyway, let's leave these for another occasion. I know what you think my friend, you have often told me that religion is the opium of humanity. If it were true, we need from time to time for that kind of feeling, when many problems come before us, we find support and rest there. I have talked a lot, it seems to me, and I have begun to tire you, I see from the way

how do you see me, the religious said, somewhat relieved. Okay, shall we go there? He waved at the road, which now seemed quieter than before. Besimi had the same thought. With the crowd leaving, he was also freed from a pressure that tormented him and had made him worry. Dritoni and his presence did little to lighten the burden that he had taken so seriously. His hand led them both away from the center, into an alley that led straight to a neighborhood that was full of cafes and taverns that were lined up like the platforms of a bus station. It seemed to him that with the physical departure from that area, his mind would also leave the turmoil he experienced until he saw children singing and dancing as they walked with banners and various slogans in support of the phenomenon that seemed to him to have also been overcome by that state. It seemed as if something had stuck to him so strongly that he could not or would not ever be able to remove it from himself. They sat in one of the nearby taverns, together with his friend. It seems that they had talked so much that now each of them was silent in their own thoughts, drinking their own coffee. Each sip contained a message. It was a swallowing of the world, of things that very slowly moved down the throat, but it was also a breath of relief after that sip that escaped down the larynx towards its known destiny. Besimi was preoccupied with thoughts of Vesna. He remembered the photo of her that Liria had shown him. He wondered to himself, how he managed to remember her under these circumstances. This thought made him almost laugh to himself. It seemed that Dritoni was in the same state. His mind was on Shpresa. Tell me, what was he doing? Why isn't he letting me get closer? What's on her mind? She seems disconnected and inconsistent in all this mess. She remembered Arbër and the path he had taken.

- Did you hear that Arbër had ended up in one of the military camps in Turkey on the border with Syria? - he said, trying to dispel the thoughts that were bothering him. They started talking again. He turned to his friend who seemed to be in the same state as he was. The traps of love had tied them together through the chains of love and they wouldn't let go at all.

- Yes, Shpresa told me. I apologized if I had influenced him by chance, but she tell me not… - she spoke somewhat absentmindedly. He was shaken by the expression of guilt that seemed to have been more on his than he actually had.

Dritoni noticed that it was a sensitive topic for his friend, so he decided not to prolong it any longer. They continued like that, each in their own thoughts. Without disturbing each other, they had found their oases of peace and seemed relaxed for a moment.

XXIV

Shpresa was sitting in her tavern in front of the house's doors on one of the chairs that made a sound as if they were wailing while she tried to wake up from the heavy sleep that had tormented her all night with her morning coffee. She was faced with her own blisters, with the red liquid that was never being removed from her body.

Often, it seemed to her like blood, shame rather than sacred, the dismemberment that the dogs of war did, sucking everything from her body, leaving her without soul, honor, or anything. She had seen little Arbër in her dream with those same eyes, along with that same tube of soapy water that he never let go of, but at the same time she had also seen him as an adult with long hair, a mustache, and a military uniform, holding aloft a sharp sword. At that moment, she woke up when the sharp weapon had cut her dream in two like a guillotine, and she woke up alone in the house. It had taken her some time to understand the reality between waking up and the nightmares she experienced. They had seemed so real to her, she had barely deciphered that it was just one of the sad dreams that were frequent. While she smelled the coffee, the images of the nightmares crossed her mind. The shivers would not leave her alone. She thought about going to work at Danaj, but Dritoni and the expression of love he made never left her mind. How could she face him? How could I tell him that my body was killed by the teeth of wolves that had long since turned my blood into murky water, and that I was neither a girl nor a woman in these circumstances, but something in between, something undefined, or nothing. Virginity or the most precious thing of a social and traditional codex among girls, these zombies tore off, desecrated and muddied it right in front of my parents. Now I can't even call myself a woman after my girl was stolen and taken away.

I couldn't sanctify, give blessing to the relationship, with the one I would love. I had lost the key to coexistence, understanding, love and honor between a couple. How can I get through to him, how can I show that I'm not me, I'm someone else now. I love him too, but how can I tell him, how can I act. It's better to keep him away from my heart and maybe he'll be closer to me. But I'm having a hard time, she's giving up, but her body isn't in line with her heart now, she had been wasted before, or stolen without asking me, and made the other half being suffer. Several times I wanted to end this work, but I didn't succeed, it was Arbëri who removed the noose from my neck several times, while now he is preparing the grave for me, - she thought constantly and whatever was going through her head. He tried to change his approach, to break those thoughts and focus on a moment of joy, happiness, but it was very difficult to find such moments. She needed an optimism, a strength that would push her through today to make it easier to continue beyond. She stood up, put her hands behind her head, tried to stretch, her muscles maybe these movements would awaken the good feeling in him. She did some physical exercises, filled herself with air and talked to herself. He gave her courage not to despair, but her subconscious with its pessimism stayed on her other side and wouldn't leavealone. Suddenly, from a bright ray of light, her mind was clouded, so that from that sunny morning it turned into a night twilight and the expression on her face revealed everything outside. It seemed that two souls in the body were fighting among themselves, angels and devils had been internalized in her. The only question was who would prevail in that body with so many wounds in its soul.

Besa and Bekim were drinking their afternoon coffee in one of their favorite places and in the meantime they had seen Liria and Besim. They had stopped, they had greeted each other. They had not wanted to disturb their peace since they had seen them deep in conversation. They had continued on without accepting the invitation to accompany them.

-What are you thinking about, should I write to Vesna, let her know, how do i feel? I am always thinking about her, - Besimi turned to his friend in distress.

-I don't know what to say, but you can write to her if you want and see how she is and how she is responding to you first. To see how she feels about you after a long period of several years. You can expect anything from that communication. It can be kind, rejecting, so you have to take this matter seriously, and be ready for good or bad, - she tried to guide the religious man. Who knows how his former girlfriend would react to his current evolution. In her mind, she was afraid that his friend would be hurt.

Dritoni had met Fitim and had the task of taking a statement regarding the process he had previously had, the accusations, and his release after the court verdict. It was more of a friendly conversation than an official meeting. Dritoni asked questions in his capacity as a journalist and the latter answered as he knew how. He had to write an article about such events and corrupt affairs in society. His friend's trial was a typical case.

-Do you think that business and politics are interconnected in our society? -was one of the questions of the journalist on duty.

-Look, in the public opinion it is said that there are public figures who have achieved great material benefits through politics, but there are also those who have invested capital to become politicians. It seems that I was saved from both. With the last court decision, I was declared innocent.

- He laughed to himself, now addressing his friend more than the journalistic report in its form.

The debate between them did not last long and over coffee and two glasses of cold alcohol, the meeting ended, more friendly than official. They also discussed the events surrounding them, mentioned Shpresa and her problems with Arbër. Besim's behavior in relation to the events in the country and relations with the extravagant world of women. They did not forget Besa's troubles in the education process and the attacks that had recently been made to her as a representative of the lower and middle school teaching department within the said department. How they are facing various problems and proposed that one day they get together and set the date of the graduation party, a night that will perhaps heal all these days full of events and challenges that surrounded them. Wrinkling their faces from the deliciously cold alcohol, pushed with a sip of plain water or dry as Dritoni drank it, they ended the conversation and meeting they had. They separated and each took his own path that was diametrically opposite to the other. From the large number of people on the streets, they disappeared like shadows among the crowd. Dritoni immediately came across Liria and Besimi.

-Hey, you two who are arguing so much, you can't stay away from each other. They say that those who argue love each other. Misunderstanding is just a step towards rapprochement between couples if they continue to communicate, - he laughed, teasing the two, who were surprised when they saw their friend coming out of nowhere. Why have you made such faces, hey, especially you Besim! What's wrong? You look like all your ships have sunk. By nature, you believers don't give up, you have strong beliefs and you face all challenges. Are you talking about something and I'm stopping you? Should I back down? - Dritoni spoke, sometimes mockingly and sometimes seriously, which created confusion among his friends who had difficulty distinguishing which was his true face and thought. They had such a face that it didn't change without taking into account Driton's spiritualism in relation to them.

Liria began to tell him about the topic they were discussing. They talked about Vesna, the feeling that had reappeared in Besim, the doubts, the desire and the confusions that were in his head. He needed someone who would perhaps solve all those complications that had gathered in him. Should he be informed after a period of time, how will she react when sees his way, his approach different from what he had had, his faith and religious dedication, which usually did not leave room for a connection between a couple who had differences in identity, especially a believer or one troubled by recent events in this part of the world. But in his case, it was something different, stronger that sent him down that path. He wondered how his head could not control his heart, such a strong feeling reigned that sent him towards it.

Dritoni had heard about Besim's love case and did not know how to approach it. His worldview was known and he was in a paradoxical state where his heart and mind were in opposite directions.

-Will you listen to your heart or your head, my friend. In these moments, loving with your head is sublime because in addition to your heart, your mind is also synchronized, but in your case it seems that only your heart is in line, your religious head seems to leave you no room to act if you look at things from an identity perspective, when you add to these the family genesis and its relationship with politics, to understand that many things are clouded and doubts are created, - the journalist tried to understand and reflect the situation. But - he continued - love knows no limits, identity, preferences, desires... it is a feeling and not an emotion that can be ignited as well as extinguished. So you decide for what you have in…

-But you have all the words on the tip of your tongue.

A philosopher rather than a rafter. It is easy for you to talk about the opposite, I tried to forget it, I know I shouldn't have, I'm alerted, but a feeling that I can't describe pushes me to her and lately I can't get it out of my head, why... I don't even know why I'm feeling this, - he spoke and confessed to his friend with head down, facing his entire external and internal world.

-I would have told you to raise it from a glass, but this doesn't suit you,- she turned to the believer, who looked at her through the eyes, making her remember what she was talking about. Liria burst out laughing, taking all these conversations with humor.

-It seems that Besim was losing his head when he was in love. He has such a nature, we didn't know this, it really seems that he still loves her. Do you still love her, or not? - she also joined in the humor, making their friend in trouble feel bad.

-I'm sorry but I fell into the trap of Driton's words, I was caught in that state he created and I joined in the mockery. I apologize, don't misunderstand me, - with half a smile on his lips he looked at the believer who began to feel better. Driton gestured that he would keep his mouth shut and not speak. All this created an act of melodrama, where it was not known when to laugh and when to remain serious in this whole conversation. Driton made a gesture that he was withdrawing to leave his friend alone and it seemed that his agitation would end. On the way he laughed to himself that if anyone saw him, they would think that he was communicating with "them", "those" who are not seen when they are present. Suspicions would arise in the circle that he had crossed the line if anyone saw him, he felt it and with self-control he returned his state to other circumstances, if they could be called normal from what he had a few moments ago. Which is normal is a separate issue. It does not mean that if the majority has such a disposition that it is standard towards the minority that behaves differently. Can we call it imposing the will of the majority, if the minority does not accept such a thing, - he thought to himself after it seemed that he had returned for a moment from the madness that perhaps this could be normal. I normalized the madness, I accepted it as the standard for all of us… - he hummed to himself. His mind went to Shpresa from his friend's words about Vesna and his girlfriend, but the memory of his former girlfriend was not absent either. He tried to compare the feeling, but

it didn't turn him on at all, while as he imagined Shpresa, he felt a fire, an indescribable feeling for her. It seems that my Vesna is Shpresa, - he said to himself and hurried to meet her.

XXV

-Dritoni found Shpresa leaving the house. It seemed that she wanted her leave to get away from the events of the last few days; she thought that with this departure all the problems that were tormenting her would also go away.

-- Shpresa, where are you going? - her friend asked her. She seemed to be distracted.

- Driton, it's better that you and I don't meet again. You still don't understand anything about what's happening, - she said, moving her hair from her forehead that was weighing down her eyes. Standing together in front of the main gate at the exit, Dritoni gently grabbed Shpresa by the arm and led her inside the fences of the house.

- I'm sorry, Shpresa, I don't understand you, you need someone, for help…. - he spoke in a low voice, barely able to get the words out.

-- I'm telling you again, my friend, that you're just wasting your time with me. Better leave me alone, - she spoke as if hesitantly and not full of strong conviction. - Driton, you still don't know me, so you better continue on your way. We've become very close lately, it's a mistake…. - his friend spoke intermittently.

- Listen, Shpresa, you know how I feel about you. Since the first time we met, I have always sympathized with and adored you. This feeling is still with me to this day. Let me be close to you in these moments, to share our worries together. Why do you want to send me away? - he spoke with his hands and feet covered in gestures and sometimes looked around so that some passerby would think they were fighting and it would seem that Shpresa was in trouble because of him. He lowered his voice from time to time, as soon as someone passed by.

- I'm not for you, Driton, I don't deserve you at all. I have always loved you too and I still love you, but there is something you don't know... - while she spoke, her tears flowed in streams. They seemed to be arranged as if by a needle and the volume of the flow increased as it came and went, while her voice and words they also flowed without changing the time interval and sound frequencies. It seemed that she was still restraining herself. Dritoni opened his eyes so that he would not understand anything more from the sight than from the words she spoke. He wanted to take in everything she was trying to tell him.

- If you have been looking for a lover, you cannot find her in me. If for a moment you have dreamed that fiery kisses or a warm body for a moment would immortalize eternity, if so… you are very mistaken with me, I am not her. If you thought that you would swallow the scent of flowers or the fragrance of laughter in the nights with the scent of pine trees, I think you will regret it. The eternal moment when two lovers, with the carving of tomorrow in stone, make an oath where neither the years nor the strong winds will erase that common path or whatever is during the walk together, I don't know how much I can offer you, or be only yours... because I was first the devil Driton's. I was his rest, in the game between sacrifice, blood and the worldliness of evil that with the stench of girlhood burned my soul, while from that day on, my cold body is nothing but a corpse that before the bridal altar from a bunch of devils instead of a blessing I received the eternal curse of being myself... They have taken everything from me... I am wasted and extinguished, only the shadow of being a girl is left to me. A dedication or a log house without a will left me.

Her eyes were down while she spoke. She often made some mechanical movements that were out of sync with her mental state. Driton's face was pale. It seemed that there was no blood at all; with open eyes, he swallowed everyone around him, Shpresa, the yard, the house. It seemed that his eyes were still hungry for something, they could not be deciphered, while his wrists were cracking with the force exerted on them without his knowledge, in the deepening and experiencing of his girlfriend as she spoke. - Driton, I was raped during the war... that day when my parents were killed. I am no longer the Shpresa you have in mind... I'm sorry, I am not... - she spoke like a calm, determined man. It seemed that a great force went through her body and she felt better, as soon as she spoke and released her words. It seemed that all the burden, the burden that had accumulated inside for years, dissolved for a moment and made her forget her troubles.

Dritoni was stunned. It seemed to him that his entire surroundings, which he had previously been swallowing with his eyes, suddenly turned backwards. He began to feel dizzy. He held his head in his hands and leaned against a log in the yard, while he looked into the eyes of Shpresa, who was strong, stoic and more beautiful than ever, with shining eyes and an unparalleled self-confidence that almost told him subconsciously that "I tried to tell you, but you didn't understand." Dritoni did not speak. He was still lost. Thousands of flashes through his mind, flying like images of comets, whistled in his brain. None of them gave any connection, meaning or idea. In a lightning-fast and unbalanced way, they clouded his mind.

Looking into her eyes and the state she was in, Shpresa began to walk backwards, approaching the door of the house to enter.

- Wait, wait, - shouted Dritoni, which made Shpresa stop her step and turn towards him. - This does not change the opinion I have of you at all, Shpresa…

- What do you mean? - Shpresa intervened with an irony. While his friend spoke confusedly, she continued walking towards the entrance to the house.

- Stop, stop... I think I'm confused and distracted and I'm not expressing myself well, clearly. I wanted to say that I still want to be with you. Everything you're going through, I want to share with me... it's not just words... we'll give time space. Maybe she's wiser and will know how to behave with us, but I want you to give me a chance to be with you, nothing more, so we'll leave the rest to the course... In time, we'll heal what can be healed, alongside each other.

It seemed as if a tear rolled down Driton's cheeks. His eyes were bloodshot and he couldn't even look up. He felt very small and guilty in front of Shpresa, who was now radiant like never before. A strange feeling of guilt had been running through him for a while and he felt humbled in front of her, while the tears began to flow more strongly, while he tried to secretly wipe them away without Shpresa noticing. He tilted his head left or right until he spoke in a trembling voice.

-Better, let's leave it at that, my friend, - said Shpresa and with a sharp and domineering look, entered the house and closed the door.

- Don't! - shouted Dritoni. He stretched out his hand as if he wanted to grab her and stop her from going inside. He approached the now closed door and began to cry like a child. He was careful not to hear Shpresa who was also locked in the room, crying and wiping away the tears that were dripping non-stop. Dritoni, for a moment, recovered himself. He thought that perhaps it was better to leave the woman he adored alone for a while until she calmed down and then he would find a way to meet her again. He straightened up and headed towards the exit from the yard. For a moment he turned his head towards the window of one of the rooms, but he saw nothing. He thought once again about what she had been through, what she had experienced and how she had carried the pain inside her for years, he wanted to push the thoughts out of his head because they made him emotional and unable to contain himself. He would be noticeable to passers-by with the state he was in. How many Shpresa does this country have, that we do not know about, and we cannot help what they have gone through during those years of war, but his Shpresa hurt him more than the others. For a moment he also remembered his neighborhood friend Roni, who was said to have been raped by paramilitary soldiers when they had found him at home, right in front of his parents. Roni was naturally more feminine, his way of speaking, gestures and intonation seemed more like a woman, while his physical appearance gave the impression of a rock for which many men envied his physical build. His friends in the neighborhood often made fun of him, but unintentionally. He accepted the insult very well. The paramilitaries had called him "you are our woman" and had raped him one by one like four rabid wolves hungry for hunting trophies. They had made Roni bleed and hurt a lot after they had also inserted the large rod of military equipment that was worn on his belt into his anus. After the war, he had been unable to bear the pain he felt inside his soul. One morning, his family had found him hanging. It seemed that he was imagining Roni and then Shpresa. As he walked, he tried to dispel his thoughts, but they were stronger than his own conscience and the strong emotions could not be emptied. How many of them, how many of them, are like that, he repeated to himself and it seemed that he did not know when he had set out. He walked, just walked, did not stop. He walked for hours, without any destination, he needed fresh air if the circumstances of urban traffic and the surroundings allowed it. It seemed that he had a claustrophobic feeling and his entire city made him suffocate. He sought space and movement without stopping, without an address, until he began to feel his legs starting to get tired. A few hundred meters away was the park of one of the city's neighborhoods and he decided to sit down for a while.

Shpresa seemed to have gathered strength, she seemed somewhat more liberated from the moment she had talked to Driton. A relief and a great physical weight seemed to be lifted from her. She was surprised at the feeling she had. She had not felt so good, so strong, for a long time, but her mind still seemed not to leave her at ease, her momentum went to Arbëri. She wondered what he was doing at this moment, how he was, did he have anything to eat, where to sleep, and many, many things she wanted to know about her brother in distress and longing for him. She took some things or household chores to fix in order to distract herself from the things that were weighing on her mind. She took some clothes to wash, approached Arbër's closet, found one of his shirts, took it, squeezed it, hugged it and brought it to her nose and smelled it. It seemed to her that for a moment she smelled her brother and brought back good memories of him. She gathered the clothes and put them in the washing machine and continued with some other household chores to pass the difficult time that had been preoccupying her days lately.

XXVI

-Besimi had found the courage to contact Vesna. It seems that she had responded. She had welcomed the contact with him quite well and for a few moments they had exchanged a few words via phone. They had not seen each other during the conversation, but the messages and communication had made both of them excited and welcome the initiative of one party. Besimi felt very excited while writing, while his enthusiasm grew even more as he received a response from his former girlfriend. Vesna had also revealed her private life during the conversation, as with a subtlety and sophisticated manner she had slowly begun to unravel it for Besimi. She worked for an international organization that dealt with the consolidation of relations between different ethnicities in a post-conflict situation. Meetings, talks, various trainings, and social gatherings were organized solely to improve the cold relations of the peoples who had emerged from the fratricidal war. She had had a few love affairs, but nothing serious and she was still single, which Besimi welcomed very well and which interested him so much. In conversations with Liria, who was close to her, she would occasionally advise him on how to approach the conversation without hurting her or being aggressive in the development of communication with her. When the conversation started to get heated, he offered to meet her if she was of the same opinion. Vesna accepted very well, but he had a proposal for her. Through her organization, she would visit Kosovo and stay in Prishtina for a few days in connection with a seminar organized by various regional circles in which she would also participate. This made Besimi so happy that they agreed that they would not leave it to chance, but would meet as soon as she was announced to be in Kosovo. She promised to let him know in time and the conference in question was expected to start in a few days. They ended the conversation and left room to continue the communication.

- Hey, how was I? Tell me Liria, did i overdo it, don't be impulsive in all my questions, proposals, requests, don't appear a bit banal, feel free to tell me - he was addressing his friend.

-Ha, ha, ha, - his friend let out a laugh. - A… I didn't know that you religious people love so much, I thought you were only devoted to sermons and dedicated religious figures, …love…. ha ha ha - she started making fun of her friend again.

- Look, what are you talking about, look, - the friend interrupted. It seemed that this raft of her friend did not like it at all.

- Listen, I'm telling you seriously, you were very good, you are not banal at all, it seems that she accepted you well in the conversation. What interested you to be able to understand, I don't think that she should have felt offended, not at all, so only success in future communications, Don Juan, - she finished the sentence again with a light laugh and with her lips on a smile.

-This atmosphere of laughter was interrupted by a phone call that rang on the Liria line. - Hello… Besa, I can hear you… When?… Who? Are you sure… not by chance…- as Liria answered in broken words, the color of her face changed and a weakness seemed to encompass her. She put her hand on her head and tried to grab a chair to sit down. Surprised by what was happening and following every movement of her friend while she talked on the phone, Besimi quickly brought the chair closer to her, which helped her keep her legs from slipping.

- Okay Besa, I'll come join you right away - and ended the call by throwing the phone on the table without closing it at all. The lights it was emitting indicated that it was not yet turned off.

- What happened Liria, what news did you get that made your face turn pale? Tell me, bye, God willing! - shouted the religious man, while bent over trying to quickly understand what had happened, not taking his eyes off his friend for a second.

- Arbër... poor Shpresa... it seems that her brother has been killed in Syria, during the fighting these days, ouff...! - she let out a groan, grabbed her waist with both hands and stood up.

- What are you saying?! Is this news true, is it wrong? - shouted the religious man who could not believe that his friend would meet his end there so soon.

They had just announced the case on television. We need to find Shpresa and see how she is. Besa was on her way to her, she will also pick up Dritoni on the way. Let's go too. Let's go, what do you think? - she said, gathering her clothes and things in her bag with a well-known brand. She gathered herself to leave. Besimi, who was scattered, nodded and in his thoughts he also tried to gather himself and leave together for their friend. They got ready, calmed down for a moment and without a word, without communication, they set off towards Shpresa's house.

-With his ministerial influence, Fitimi had just received the news. He had put all his close circles to confirm if the news was true and what the family should do to take his body at the first opportunity to perform the funeral ceremonies as it should be done and a dead person has the order. Everyone seemed to be mobilized and wanted to share their pain, worries, troubles, and obligations with Shpresa. Dritoni, as soon as he found out through the media, had set off for his friend, his girlfriend, and on the way they had met Besa, who had left the children with her next-door neighbor, since her husband was still at work.

Everyone, speechless, each in their own thoughts, were heading towards a single destination, Shpresa's house. It seemed to everyone that the house was so far away that they could not reach it, even though it was not far from the center and it did not take long to get there, but the situation they were in seemed like the road they were walking on had no end and they could not get close to their friend. As if something was pushing them away as soon as they got closer. This feeling accompanied them until they got very close to her yard. Besa and Dritoni arrived at the yard first, they were faster. It seemed that they had received the news first, but Liria and Besim were not far from home either. They would arrive at any moment. They walked so fast that Liria would occasionally fall behind and complain to the religious that she could not keep up with his fast steps because of the high-heeled shoes she was wearing. Dritoni opened the door to the courtyard with a rush, Besa followed, approached the gate, knocked several times. She turned her head left and right to see if she could see any sign of her friend, and then turned her head back

from Besa who anxiously awaited what would happen when she met Shpresa, for the bitter news. No sign, no sound from Shpresa.

- Is she not at home at all? What can you think of, huh?! - thinking, she spoke through her teeth to Besa. She knocked again; now even louder, maybe she didn't hear the door, but still no answer. Dritoni, turning his eyes to Besa and with greater force, somehow wanted approval to try to force his way into his friend's house. Besa read his mind and approved what he started to do.

The door barely opened and Dritoni found himself in the hallway with the gate open. Besa followed him. The voices of Liria and Besim had just come from the yard. They had both arrived, out of breath from the rush. They gathered in the hallway of the house, looking each other in the eye and without words, asking Shpresa where she could be.

- Shpresa, Shpresa, Shpreeeessssaaaa, - they called their friend incessantly, now one and now the other. They began to disperse throughout the house to try to find her in whatever condition she might be. Besa and Liria went to check the bathroom, while Dritoni and Besimi went into the rooms that were small in number. Besimi went into the bedroom, while Dritoni went into Arbër's day room, the only rooms in the house.

- There's nothing in the bathroom, she's not here, - Shpresa's two friends said in unison. - There's no one here in the bedroom either, - Besimi said. While Dritoni approached the living room, which was connected and open to the kitchen. In the furnished alcove at the end of the room, he saw a body lying down. He didn't have a good view from the door. As soon as he entered deeper, he approached the table, and recognized Shpresa's body, lying on the sofa. For a moment, he held on to the table nearby and his eyes immediately went to a medicine box that was lying on the floor. It was open and empty, where its rolled-up lid was a few centimeters away from the rest. Shpresa, asleep or unconscious, was lying as if dead. One of her hands was hanging from the sofa to the floor. Her position spoke volumes about the state she was in.

-Come here, quickly, I found Shpresa- shouted Dritoni. The room quickly filled with all her friends, who as soon as they entered were surprised and saddened by the sight they encountered.

-Someone call an ambulance, - Dritoni addressed everyone, until they began to approach. He tried to calm her down. All the lost people were moving around chaotically, while for a moment it seemed that Liria was more sober. He grabbed her phone and notified the city hospital, gave the address and described the case.

-Woe to us! It seems that she found out about Arbër and wanted to end everything, her life, - Besa spoke tearfully. Besim sat on both knees and began to pray. He uttered all the possible prayers to save his friend from the worst. Driton's attempts to revive her with water or to wake her up from her sleep were unsuccessful. The moments of waiting for the ambulance were endless, it seemed like centuries passed and they never arrived.

-Maybe it's better if we send her, but it seems to me that many are being delayed, -Driton spoke with emotion, who was between boredom and nervousness.

-Only two or three minutes have passed since my call, it's still too early to arrive, but let's try to wake her up somehow from these medications that she apparently took, -Liria tried to summarize. Besa approached the medicine box, took it in her hand and read it aloud, -Diazepam five milligrams. It seems that she took a sedative, who knows how many pieces poor Shpresa swallowed, -she snorted oil into herself. She brought the box closer to Driton so that he could see it. He did not let go of Shpresa from his hand and tried to do everything to wake her up.

With one hand he took the plastic box that his friend had brought, to see what she had drunk earlier. He glanced at it for a moment, squeezed it with one hand while holding Shpresa with the other, and threw it with force, smashing it against the wall and breaking it into pieces. Fitimi, meanwhile, called and received the news of what had happened. He assured them that he would contact the emergency center once again and have them arrive as soon as possible. He told them that he was also on his way to

Shpresa's house. The situation at home was the same, as was that of Shpresa.

-Everyone counted the seconds. There was little talk, only crying, tears flowing. The only sound that could be heard were the harmonized Arabic and Albanian words that came out of Besim's mouth during the prayers he made on behalf of his friend, while Dritoni did not let go of Shpresa's hand for a moment. He wanted to wake her up at all costs, it seemed that he would fight with the whole world, curse her. He resembled a Don Quixote who was trying to do the impossible.

-The emergency sirens announced that help was approaching. They did not delay and arrived at the house, at the same time as Fitimi arrived. The state in which he found Shpresa made him feel bad, very bad.

-Here we are, - Dritoni shouted in order to let him know about the location of the help. Nurses in special clothes arrived with all their equipment. There were three men and two women who quickly organized her transfer. One nurse checked the pulse, the other measured the blood pressure, while the men grabbed the body on a stretcher to carry it to the car to transport it to the emergency center.

-It seems that she took drugs with the intention of ending her life, - said one of the doctors who was trying to take some notes while the other two carried the body. Are you family or... - he first addressed Dritoni, then looked at everyone in turn.

-We are friends, the only family she has, replied Dritoni, who followed the body and did not leave it alone for a moment.

-It seems that there is still a pulse, weak but I can hear it, - said one of the doctors, who still did not take hands off her throat and sometimes from the wrist on her lap. She was not impressed by her carrying either. She managed not to leave her to do her job, on condition that they would buy time to send her to resuscitation. I don't know what to say about her blood pressure, the machine doesn't seem to be measuring it, her heartbeat, if there is one, is slow and light, which means we need to rush to the responsible ward, - said the nurse who was trying to take her blood pressure, if there was one. They put her in a recovery position, checked her breathing passages, opened her mouth, and looked at her nose beforehand, are they freed and they quickly put her in the ambulance. Dritoni also entered with her.

-I'm in a car, come with me, - Fitimi called on the road towards Shpresa's destination. Liria joined Driton not to leave him alone, while the other three joined Fitimi who were following the ambulance behind.

XXVII

Shpresa was placed in an intensive care gastroenterology ward in order to clear her stomach of the many pills she had taken and to wake her up from the deep sleep she had fallen into. There was no difference between her state of unconsciousness and normal sleep. Everyone gathered in the ward in question and at the insistence of the doctor who asked not to gather too much since she was now in their hands and they had to wait, hoping for her condition to improve. Dritoni was categorical about staying by her side. Fitimi was also worried about Arbër's body and wanted to deal with that issue as well, so that it would not be forgotten. Liria insisted on being with Shpresa, so Besa, with an obligation to her children and family, decided to go and stay in touch with everything about her friend. Those who had declared that they would stay stayed while the others, Besimi, along with Fitimi and Besa, got ready to leave the hospital.

- I almost forgot, if you are not satisfied with the treatment of Shpresa here, let me know and we will take her to a better, more modern hospital where the care will be better, - Fitimi addressed Driton and looked into the eyes of Liria, who was still left to be cared for. - Okay, let's see how things go. We will stay in touch, - Driton cut her off in a hurry, while Liria nodded in agreement with what the previous speaker said. On the way out, Fitimi greeted the remaining friends, once again seeing Shpresa who was still in a deep sleep like the beauty from the beloved children's fairy tales. He wondered if the prince would come to wake her from this lethargic sleep or if it was better for her to be in that state and not hold back the pain for the circumstances that have gripped her life, her loved ones, her brother...

-Driton, you look tired. Go and rest, I will take care of her, - Liria spoke to her compassionately. - No, no, I can't leave her for a moment. If you want, you can go, I'm here, rest and come back later, - Dritoni replied firmly, looking at his friend who couldn't keep up with her, wandering around the room that was only with her body, Shpresa's bed

while he held the sleeping girl's hand while sitting next to her.

- I'll stay with you a little longer, I won't leave you alone, - said Liria, biting her nails with her teeth, in a not so defining voice she gave support to her friend who seemed to be suffering the most from this incident.

- I have a worry, a torment that is going through my head and is disturbing me a lot. I can talk to you openly, it's not for discussion, but I need someone...to talk to, - he turned his eyes to Liria, exhausted.

- Speak, speak what is troubling you. We grew up together, I consider you a brother,

- Liria said, approaching him. She stretched her hands on Driton's shoulders which had become as strong as a rock. He was still sitting, but his eyes were directed at Liria, who with a warm look gave him support and reassurance that made him speak and get the torment out of his chest.

- Yesterday we talked to Shpresa. She was talking about her life, her past, the struggles she had had. I didn't know what she was going through. She wanted to push me away from her even though I could see that she felt the same way about me as I felt about her. From the way she looked at me, I was more than sure...but only yesterday I understand. She had been a victim of war, abuse, rape that day when her parents were killed. Her brother had almost escaped, it seems that she had become a victim of all of them, of the humiliations as long as she was alive, she will always be dead in the life she will live. Driton's voice was calm, almost fading, without emotion, intonation, like an echo that comes from afar and is lost in the air, but that pierces the ears even if it is in a low tone because the words are what hit.

- What!! What are you saying, my friend?! No, I didn't know that, look... what she's going through now, plus her brother... phew!! - holding her face in her hands, she sat down next to Driton. Her legs could barely support her. We won't talk about this with anyone, no no... how is it possible for our friend?!! - she rolled her eyes around the room and spoke in a low voice, not wanting to disturb the sleeping beauty, lest she hear the voices of the conversation near her.

It was her reason that pushed me away from myself. I could see that she was behaving differently, but I couldn't understand why, until I insisted on being closer to her, she confessed. Those were very difficult moments for me and for her. I didn't know how to comfort her, how to behave... I tried to stay close to her, but she needed some time, space... Ehhh! If I had known, if I had been close, maybe this wouldn't have happened to her... -- an unsolved puzzle seemed to have taken hold of her mind, with both hands she rubbed her face so mechanically that it made her feel pain in her nose. Her movements were not very well thought out.

- I need to smoke. Will you keep me company? - Liria spoke and made her way towards the exit. Dritoni nodded and, as he left, looked at his beauty, who seemed to be in a very deep and comfortable sleep, as if after a tiring day of physical work.

Liria did not smoke, but almost swallowed the cigarette with two or three raised lips, completely digesting it. Both were in thought. Only the smoker's breathing could be heard as she inhaled and exhaled the smoky breath, it seemed that all this had affected her friend.

- I need to walk, get some air. I'm leaving for a while, then I'll be back. Don't worry, let me know if you need anything. I want to calm down and see you later. We both don't dare to leave, so you'll be left alone, - Liria spoke with a feeling of regret, while Dritoni opened his hands as a sign that everything would be okay even if she was left alone.

After seeing Liria off, he returned to the room where nothing had changed from the previous moments, not even the patient had made the slightest movement. He sat down in the chair next to her bed and began to contemplate her. Such an atmosphere brought him back for a moment to his childhood when he had his grandfather in the hospital. He had contracted an infection or illness after a flu that most of the diagnostic doctors had not been able to find out what he was suffering from. His condition in the hospital had deteriorated so much that his father and close family members had requested his transportation to other more prestigious hospitals in the former Yugoslavia, those in Zagreb and Ljubljana. They had contacted the hospitals in question, prepared the patient for the local hospital, but his grandfather's condition had become complicated,

and after arriving at the hospital in the city of Ljubljana in Slovenia, he passed away a few days later. It was too late, too late for him to achieve any improvement; the illness had taken a turn. He remembered the frequent visits to his grandfather in the hospital that made him return to the past from the circumstances that had overtaken him today. Shpresa is not in the same condition as my grandfather, he thought to himself. She will get better, she will soon come to her senses, he told himself. Grandfather, just like Shpresa, had experienced war, but the Second World War. He had been born in Gjakova in 1916 into a merchant family, but progressive and patriotic. Soon after they had begun to grow up a little with his brother, through the caravans of those times and the bajraktars who had conveyed from one prince to another by means of a sensitive letter from the patriots of that time such as Bajram Curri, they had arrived in Albania from Gjakova. The brothers had attended the normal school in Elbasan and my grandfather the technical school in Shkodër. My grandfather had also been a pioneer in establishing the Albanian national football team and had played during his high school years and later in the "Vllazërinë" of Shkodër or the "Partizan" of Tirana. His ball shots are still commented on today by the precision and strength that sometimes made them break the weak nets that were sewn especially for football goals at that time. With the influence of the Albanian authorities, educated people like my grandfather, his brother and many others from Kosovo are advised to return to Kosovo and help in educating society and eradicating illiteracy. I remember when my grandfather used to say that first in our homes, we took off the headscarves of our women and sisters, then we set an example for other families to follow us. The first children, girls who attended school, were from the same families that made this trend follow, immediately after World War II. The state circles of Serbia, such people as my grandfather called undesirables, Albanian immigrants and were always persecuted by the regime for their contribution to Albanian education. Such persecutions affected her health and accelerated her illness faster than usual. Shpresa has the same fate almost a century later, but she is stronger, has a younger body, she will face this challenge. There is a glimmer of hope in all this, my Shpresa. His thoughts were interrupted by the doctor who came for the visit.

- It seems that they left you alone, or, you have a relative. From the care you give, it is clear that you are taking care of the patient. Well, her condition at the moment is not alarming. Her fate is the timely intervention, drinking too many sedatives made her sleepy for a while. We have cleared her stomach of the drugs she has taken and we hope that she will soon start to wake up. We will also consult with a psychologist about her mental state and we will do some additional tests to make sure that we do not suddenly notice any obstacles. While he was talking to Driton, wearing a white coat with the initials of his name on the edge of the pocket and with a thin athletic figure, a long face and an d'Artagnan beard, raising his glasses he would open Shpresa's eyelids to observe them and sometimes with a small hand flashlight he would look into her eyes.

- She will be fine, don't worry, -he said, extending his hand to the patient's only friend in the room and with light steps like a sprinter, he left the room.

Liria was Shpresa's most frequent visitor, while Dritoni stood by her constantly. It had been two days and Shpresa still hadn't woken up.

XXVIII

Liria was thinking about Shpresa, but she had to be at work. Dritoni was always by her side. While Liria was standing in the office, running a ballpoint pen through her hair and sitting, lost in thought, the announcement of all the tests and results from the organization's reorganizations arrived. The list of names of those who would continue working and whose contracts would be cut short created dissatisfaction and a gloomy, almost conflictual atmosphere among the workers of the different units.

Andi had lost his job. Surprisingly, at first he had received the news without any concern, he did not like it at all, but he did not show any nervousness in the workplace, but he looked at Liria, who was calm and out of any danger. She was spared from this process.

-No matter what names had come to the fore, or the results, there will always be dissatisfaction. Let's each try to select the candidates, someone will still be worried. It is a sensitive process and no one wants to lose their job in these difficult times of crisis. Everyone thinks they deserve it more than the other, - Drita spoke in order to relativize the situation at work and calm things down for the moment. She was also out of danger for her job, it seemed that for that reason she spoke freely.

The entire list of unit leaders is a fabrication, the names that came out we know how they were selected. Most have been loyal to their bosses, or rather, assholes, that's how they secured their jobs, never with honor, but with favors, or with a little bit of footwork. Excuse me, colleagues, but I have to vent, after almost ten years of honest work and two years certified as a distinguished worker, now at home. How, how… - Fadil spoke angrily, who in an electrician's work uniform had just received the bad news. His hands, black from the color of cables and physical labor, had made his short body beautifully muscular, while his sharp nose and round eyes, now squinting as he spoke, had been covered in dust marks from an intervention on one of the building's office ceilings. He wiped his face with a paper napkin.

sometimes he sighed, revealing the veins on his face and the red color that stained his throat in high emotion. Unconscious and extremely angry, he could not choose the words to express himself. All that speech was accompanied by excessively bared teeth and sometimes his saliva flew around during the strict intonation of the words that came out of his mouth full of bile. He spoke what he had, nervously slammed the door and went out.

Fitim that was dealing with the Arbër case through contacts with embassies and relevant circles for the extradition of his body, encountered an obstacle. It seems that his body was not found. It was said that he had been buried somewhere after the murder and they had no way of bringing him to his homeland. Meanwhile, his name began to circulate in the media again as a result of a process that was involved as a case of nepotism in which some of his close relatives had benefited. This made him a little distracted from his routine and absent from regular visits to Shpresa, although he was always in contact with Driton if anything was needed. Besimi had received the news that Vesna was in town. They had arranged to meet at one of the city's bars, which was near the hotel where Vesna was staying. His friend had difficulty recognizing her from a distance due to his visual transformation, until she had approached and called her by name. Besimi had no difficulty recognizing her. She had immediately noticed her image and knew without a doubt that it was her, his former lover Vesna. The first few moments had made them feel a little anxious. The distance and the long time of lack of communication had taken their toll. At first, the usual, routine conversations had ended, then they had remained silent for a few moments, not knowing where to start or begin the conversation. He not had Liria nearby, perhaps she would have advised or helped him, but now he had to solve the problem that was stuck in his teeth.

-How do you feel here in Kosovo, how are you doing? - he asked this formal question that came to mind and motioned for them to move from position zero.

-Good, very nice. The people are very hospitable, kind, I didn't think so, I was pleasantly surprised. We are socializing, we take walks when we have free time after the work we have. I am doing nice and good.

The city is well built, I like it, I didn't expect it to be in this condition. There are good places to eat, - Vesna replied with a twinkle in her eye.

- If I may, what happened to you, this drastic transformation in appearance and attitude, it's not like I knew you like that, - Vesna spoke somewhat hesitantly or as if she was walking the edge of a blade with great tact, heading towards Besimi.

- It's true. The phase I went through these years made me feel everything and perhaps leave some consequences in my behavior and worldview. It seems to me that I feel better this way, more fulfilled, since a part of my fulfillment was missing for years…- she said these last words as if ashamed and after her eyes burned, she lowered them to the ground and within a second her whole body was red.

- Ha, ha ha, - she laughed out loud. She brought her hands closer to him, shyly not reacting, but no, their hands joined and both felt a warmth pass through them for a moment. It seems that the conversation heated up and in that way they continued for hours, losing track of time and the obligations they had. They agreed to continue meeting and continuing their friendship, especially during the days while Vesna was in Kosovo. Besa called Driton and asked if she needed anything. She was planning to come visit the hospital and see Shpresa. Driton assured her that she did not need anything and welcomed her company. According to the doctors, the sleeping beauty was expected to wake up at any moment. The doctors' impressions and predictions gave that news. There had been no need for Shpresa to be re-admitted to another hospital. All the services were on point and the care she gave her made everyone optimistic, especially Dritoni, who was waiting for her to open her eyes at any moment and shoot her there, next to her. It had been three nights since he had left her room, in the same clothes, he stood next to her nonstop. He looked tired and his face had become unshaven, giving the impression that he was older.

His friends had begged him to go and rest, relax and take a warm shower, but he had refused.

-I want to be near her when she opens her eyes, I don't want to be anywhere when she wakes up from this lethargic sleep, - he had told his friends. They had understood his concern and worry and had left him as he had asked.

Looking at his girlfriend, he felt a thrill in his chest. He didn't know if it was a tightness from fatigue or a warning about something. He looked at her body covered with a sheet and the beautiful face of an innocent angel. A feeling of empathy caressed him, but inwardly he objected. I'm not doing this out of pain, but out of love. There's a difference in this job. I love her, I love her, that's why I'm here, not out of compassion, I know very well, very well, even though I'm tired, my mind hasn't yet been disturbed. Now there's no one in this world to take care of her. I will do it. No, I don't say no, out of sympathy, but out of a desire to be close to her. They remembered for a moment the previous moments when Danaj, Uncle Bedri and Aunt Myrvet were visiting immediately after they had heard. Their eyes went to a bag of food and an envelope that they had left near her. They were very upset when they had heard about the case. The whole time Aunt Myrvet had been crying and mentioning Arbër.

-He enjoyed my food. He has always been grateful and loving. Why should this wretch find him?! He would clasp his hands and with a beautiful and delightful language make the prayers that she had learned since she was a child in one of the city's highlands among friends and girlfriends. Uncle Bedri had not wanted to aggravate the situation any further. He had taken his wife and with an athletic stature like a seasoned hunter had left without being noticed, helping his wife who still had sciatic problems.

Dritoni approached the bag of food. He opened it completely and besides the food inside, mainly various fruits, he saw the closed envelope nearby. He was hesitant to open it, but he was curious to see what was inside. From the rotation in relation to the sunlight and the touch around, he felt with his fingers that there was also something that seemed solid with an oval shape and a kind of metal plate attached to a written letter. He could not bear it. He opened it and saw what was inside.

It was a note on which she wrote:

Dear Shpresa,

I am giving this necklace with all my heart. It is a memory from my mother, when I was a girl. I have kept it all my life, it is a talisman that has always brought me luck. Now that I am old, I do not need so much luck, together with Bedri, we wish that in the absence of our daughters we give it to you, so that, like me during my life, luck will also guide you after you have it in your possession.

With love, Aunt Myrvet

After reading the letter, he put hands in the envelope and took out the necklace, which was made of silver with some beautiful stones and with an old and sophisticated archaic work. How kind and generous they were. They have noticed Shpresa's beautiful soul, they have come to reward her in these bad moments for her. How good people, - he thought to himself. Look how with her behavior she has made people for herself. Everyone who has had the chance to meet her loves and respects her. He noticed that there was something else in the deep envelope. After reaching in, he also took out a five-hundred-euro note, with a note. "Let them be here for now, Uncle Bedri."

Besa entered the room and interrupted all of Driton's thoughts, who had just put things away and was sitting with his eyes closed. He was lost. When he heard the door opening, he opened his eyes and staggered out of his seat. Besa approached Driton.

-How is she? Is there anything new, - Besa asked about her friend until she was relieved of her heavy breathing from the walk she had taken. It was clear that being overweight was affecting, taking its toll on her physical form.

-You are obviously tired, my friend. Listen, that's why I came, to relieve you of your care for a while. Go rest, freshen up, gather yourself a little and come back. I'll be here, I'll let you know about any changes that happen, don't worry, - Besa tried to convince him, the tireless one who hadn't closed his eyes for days, but had just been sitting in the chair from time to time when he was too tired to stand there in a row in the room during the long sleepless nights. Through mimicry

showed that he was fine and didn't need a break. He could still stay by her side.

-Didn't you have an obligation to report to work? You've been staying here for three whole days without going out - his friend insisted again, feeling sorry for the state he had been in.

-I talked to the people at work. I informed them about everything and that I was here in the hospital. Don't worry, my friend. Thank you for your concern! - with a kind smile, he rubbed Besa's arms.

-Here, I brought you some food too, you certainly haven't eaten all day. I cooked them myself. Look at these cheese muffins and sweet ones with marmalade. Bekim really likes my cooking, but it seems to me the same... hahaha, - she laughed, looking at his plump and round body.

-Let's be more serious, because maybe Shpresa is listening to us and it doesn't make sense - said Dritoni. Besa's arrival filled the room with enthusiasm and a positivity in keeping with her always sparkling nature.

-She offered some pieces to Driton, who politely took them, tasted them, and with his hands playing with his fingers, indicated that they had become very good.

-Blessed are your hands! How delicious they are! - he said with his mouth full of chocolate.

-May they be good! But it seems that you are not that hungry... but thank you very much! - Besa replied, when suddenly a sigh was heard.

-Arrbëërrr, Arbëërrr... Both of them were stunned. A drowned voice came from the bed where Shpresa was. They turned to her. Driton left the remaining piece of cheese dough on the table and turned to his friend, who was giving signs that she was starting to wake up. She spoke incoherently for a few moments, blinking and raising her voice. Besa ran to call the doctor on duty, while Dritoni approached and held her hand until she was between sleep and wakefulness, a process that was transitory and from one state she slowly prepared to pass into another. Soon the same doctor from the previous days arrived

who was familiar with Shpresa's problem. He approached, noticed some changes and movements that the patient was now making and addressed the two of them:

- It seems that she is starting to wake up. We need to leave her alone, she might be having a psychic attack after she wakes up and sees you here and remembers the last circumstances that happened before she lost consciousness - the professional assured them to be aware of anything that might happen in the meantime.

- Where am I aaa, Driton, Besa, who are you sir? - Shpresa opened her eyes and began to address everyone inside. Driton's eyes sparkled with joy, Besa's as well when they saw their friend wake up.

- It seems that her cognitive state is okay, wait a minute, open your eyelids - the doctor said and with an additional light he looked at the pupils and iris inside.

-Everything seems fine, yes, yes, this too, - the doctor was talking to himself and in the meantime he was doing some additional tests in order to confirm the patient's situation, who now sobered up and followed her doctor's every move.

- Listen friends, you too Shpresa, the condition seems to have improved and we will monitor her throughout the day today and if we don't have any problems by tomorrow, which shouldn't have happened, but just in case, then we will release you home tomorrow, if everything remains in order. Do we understand? Now you can relax with your friend, - the doctor spoke in an orderly and hopeful tone. He greeted everyone present in the room and with a light supportive touch on the patient's arm that everything will be fine, he left the room.

Besa immediately ran to her friend in bed, hugged her tightly, while her eyes met those of Driton who was standing and looking down. Shpresa, when confronted with Driton's eyes, tears flowed.

- Shpresa, look, this friend of yours is worthy of every praise. Not a single moment has been left to you, for three days and three nights he has been by your side. Here, he

is our Dritoni, but it looks more like yours, Besa put her hands on the shoulders of her friend who couldn't take his eyes off Shpresa. For a moment, he leaned close to her, took her hand and, caressing it, said: It's good that you've come to our world, our dear Shpresa! We're all following your condition with attention, everyone is mobilized and waiting for you to get better, to return to us as you always have been. Greetings and congratulations from everyone. You also have some gifts that are close to you from the Danaj family. They were a very good, respectable couple. They were sad when they saw you, now they'll be happy when they find out that you're getting better, as if giving a light report to the beauty, waking up from a deep sleep, about the things that awaited her in the future.

I just talked to everyone and told you the good news. Freedom was on its way here, said the messenger Besa. I have to get back to work. Thank God you look good now. May it be over my sister! The others will come soon, don't worry, - she hugged her friend once more. She headed towards Dritoni, extended her hand and went out. On her way out, Shpresa kissed her with hands, while closing the door. Only Dritoni and Shpresa remained in the room. Shpresa wanted to say something, but Dritoni approached her, touched her lips with his finger as a sign that she didn't need to say anything. She read her friend's request well. He stood close to her face, kissed her on the forehead while standing half-lying next to her. Both of their eyes were up at the ceiling and it seemed that for a few moments all that silence spoke so much, that no words would fulfill the meaning of perfection, and no way of that defining moment that groaned in the idyll, an emotion that touched the steppes of the source of eternity. They stayed like that for a long time. They searched for infinity without being able to find the starting point. Their scattered dreams feared that they had lost their meaning when the feeling, desire, momentum and burning of being someone, belonging, such as maternal or paternal, was too long. They needed rest, for a handful of sea buckthorn, or morning dew, which comes immediately after a bright and beautiful moon that even the stars in the sky with their embroidered robes would envy. They did not need the sun because even the ice was now scorching them and from the shadow of the peak of the heat, a shelter of gurglings from the wake of joys that nourished the days for a better tomorrow, made them stay close to each other. But neither of them opened the door for the event to take its course.

They had the gate, but the key had been trapped between passion, morality, or fear of action. Neither had the weight to weigh down the past years, so that with a sword throw they could divide time where no one would remember the past. Both were stuck in the purgatory of enlightenment. They only prayed that they would not experience the pain at once… both or… together.

XXIX

While Liria was looking for the director of administration for signatures with some procurement reports, wandering up and down the corridors of the building, she saw John who immediately changed direction and headed towards Liria.

The short body like a snowball filled with a blond complexion and thick eyebrows like a chubby fur coat with its hair on its face and thick lips with a hawk's gaze directed his eyes towards Liria.

-We're going out for a drink tonight, today is Good Friday. I know a place where they have good food and they have happy hour, honey, can we make it happen, (they are happy hours, can we make it possible together) - he laughed with a flirtatious voice and eyes that wanted to have for himself even for a moment the extravagant Liria who, with her movements of her hips and short skirt kissing her body, made her music from her heels to her walk draw attention away from her, the decisive makeup on her indiscreet face showed that she was always ready for glamour.

- Let's see, I have some obligations with my friend who is in the hospital, but we will be heard, - she spoke without emotion, coldly to her work colleague and the head of an administration unit where they had to do with information technology and maintaining computer networks for the organization. He was leaning against the wall and with his wings spread out, he looked like a predatory eagle that is about to dominate its prey, after it has surrendered to his dominance.

When she was returning to the office, Liria almost ran into Andi. - What are you doing now, what is wrong with you, the male world? Are you awake on the left wing? - she would say with her hands and with a mockery, which encouraged the passers-by and the occasional colleagues to turn back to her.

- Look, I wanted to talk to you, I have a problem, Liria. - he addressed his work colleague in a moody and subdued manner. - It seems that my fiancée has left, she is not calling me, I suspect that female premonitions

have discovered something about us; I'm just saying, - Andi spoke shyly and with his eyes down.

After hearing these words, Liria grabbed his worried colleague and pulled him into a corner of the corridor where it was thought there was more privacy and their conversation would not be heard.

- Look, earlier John came right to me, to meet me tonight, I know what he wants... now you're in trouble. Why do you always meet with me in your whole world, why, I'm your crossroads? I don't believe we are the cause... it was of the moment, we have nothing, there is no promise or blessing between us, it was a rush of water that passes through the river, and who knows how many times such rushes will pass again. Calm down, maybe it will come back. Women always come where everything begins, regardless of their experiences, I say that I am a woman myself.

Holding his hands behind his back and moving constantly in a nervous sign, he seemed to be looking for rest.

-My girlfriend left me, work too... what's happening to my life...?

It seemed that all his ships had sunk, and he was playing the captain who was counting down to the decisive wave that would swallow him down there at the bottom, where he thought he belonged.

- I have to go to the hospital at Shpresa, but we'll see each other again. Tell me if your fiancée calls or comes back - Liria said. With these words, she stroked his arm and headed for her office with a bundle of papers. Andi just turned his head, followed the movements and headed out of the building. His silhouette, which looked like an out-of-tune metronome that doesn't even count the moment of chance, let alone the time that speaks in a muffled way for people like Andi.

Besimi met regularly with Vesna while she was in town. The meeting did him good to return to the days gone by. They started to get closer, they thought they were on the right track. But both of them seemed to have a different feeling than before, it wasn't that emotion, that spark like before. Maybe time, distance, or years with different events and circumstances had taken their toll and they were more strangers than usual. They sat, talked,

passed the time but that strange feeling seemed to bother them excessively. They did not tell each other but inside it made them stop all these meetings from time to time and stop communicating. Perhaps Besim's appearance, of an expository religious man, was creating an influence in not perceiving all this or Vesna was looking for the devilish, bohemian and lively Besim for all the tricks and deeds that she once wanted to try. Perhaps the political and circumstantial influence of Vesna's origin was also causing Besim to lose that former feeling. Perhaps the diametrically opposite definition of religious and ethnic concepts that once sparked war are a pretext for the deprivation of sincere love, if it exists somewhere, or is it just a deception, a momentary image that confuses you and keeps you only for a certain time. Like a drug that has its own temporal effect, depending on the dose of the drug, this feeling was also present. They had taken so many measures that the side effects seemed not to have appeared between them. Why is the influence of the social circle, or other irrelevant factors so great as to determine even the only intimate and very simple and necessary emotion such as love? How can it happen that something internal and very closed to others is influenced by the external world that should not have any contact with each other at all, wishing to keep it with untouchable jealousy, but here it was being touched. It is a deception, an illusion, a dream or a momentary fiction, to make you love the schizophrenic reality that only you know, see, touch and feel. They did not leave each other, they challenged the meaningless feeling that gripped them from time to time.

Hope had begun to feel stronger and better. Now sitting on the bed with her strength back, she looked at Driton who served her whatever she asked for. Now she had started to arrange some of her things.

- Why did you save me Driton, why don't you let me go where my brother is? - she spoke angrily, which made Driton drop some letters from his hands. He turned to her and sitting next to her, looking her in the eyes, he replied:

- I told you that I never want to be away from you. I love you, I adore you and whatever you go through, I will go through too, I will be by your side forever. Now you have given me one more chance to always be with you.

His words seemed to be very sincere. The voice, the melody, his eyes, his posture, the movements of his face were all in a divine harmony that created a feeling of a captivating halo where it seemed that the two of them were transported somewhere for a moment, where everything was nothing and nothing was whole.

-But you don't know how I became. I am a psychic case, a post-conflict trauma. I love you too much and for that reason I don't want you to suffer with me. I'm afraid that I won't make you happy as you deserve. I don't deserve you. You still don't know how much of my blood they drank, how much of themselves. The fiery bed that love sings to me is a cold grave that causes shivers in the body. I don't love, I can't imagine, a frigid psycho without feelings of lust unusual for a normal woman. Don't get lost in the mud-stained pool that holds you down, because I'm afraid you'll never drink clear water from me forever.

-Just the thought of you makes me want to be always by your side. It seems to me that we're meant to be together. Maybe even a thousand years or a hundred more lives if I lived, I would do anything, challenge every mountain, hill, sea, lake to reach you. Just being you, your existence makes me happy. Your presence near me makes me feel fulfilled. I know, you've been through the knife's edge, the pain hasn't been removed from your body's fabric, but you're here, my Shpresa that I've known since time immemorial. If they've crushed, raped your body, they've never managed to touch, contaminate, or bastardize your soul. It's exalted, untouched, and pure like a tear. I am in love not only with you but also with your soul. Your body is only a wrapper of your inner beauty. It will age, decay, and disappear, and what will remain of us after that is a memory of the moment, the smile, the spiritual intoxication that only the inner world that we possess allows. I make it permissible for all the sinners of war, only if they once fall to their knees and say that we took your body as a booty to wash away their dirty soul, which is lifting them up and they are not finding rest anywhere to leave their bones in peace, but are making them circle the earth that is vomiting them back. They will see death with the eyes of life. It seems that they are living death in their heads.

-But Arbër, what does he have to do with this, why him? - with a few tears on his face he finished the sentence.

-Arbër is nothing but a martyr of a sentimental perversion of a society in defining itself. We are afraid of ourselves, we thought we did not know who we are. With our face revealed, it seems that we expected to be saints. We are sinners like the whole world. If they think of imposing on us the divinity of arriving on earth with open eyes and on the way to the altar of eternity, they are wrong, because they say that we need the purgation of our souls from what we have done or what we have had to do by force, imposition, in the name of language, land, child, parent, brother to always have a door, a chair to sit on or a grave to rest our bones, it is a request of all supposedly normal people in the contemporary world. There is no greater sacrifice than the mud of your shoes that call out the name of your birthplace... never... never... there is no price to wash away the debt that our ancestors once started in this sky, that only rain, storm and only a little sun have blessed these centuries. There is no punishment for those who only want a blessed place in their sky. Sins are borne by those who disrupt the order and place of those to whom God granted life...

Shpresa remembered for a moment the bubbles that had so much resentment, anger, but now she did not have the same feeling for them. She remembered the eyes of the policeman who, while fleeing, asked for forgiveness, mercy for her like an executioner, on the road that she did not know where she was headed. Her eyes showed a brief and intermittent intensity that only the fire of hell and the teeth of Cerberus in front of the doors in the name of Mephisto would give meaning to their deeds. They were at their service, soldiers without an address, without a destination, they looked only like blind, sick creatures whose inertia of the carnivorous instinct in their veins had made them see for a moment their prey cooked with noble blood, their deeds to earn eternal damnation...Driton brought closer the things that Danaj couple had left for her. Shpresa opened the envelope, read the letter, took the necklace and, wiping the pages from the emotion of reading the letter, asked to help her put it around her neck. She looked beautiful with it on her throat, it had been made especially for the shape of her neck. When she saw herself in the mirror, she liked it very much but noticed something different in her appearance. Her image seemed different from the days before earlier, it wasn't from fatigue, health, it was something different, much different, she couldn't even decipher what it was....

- You look so beautiful with it on your neck! Thank you to the couple who seemed to love you so much! You should thank them, - said the friend, when suddenly the doctor entered the room. It was the same one who had taken over Shpresa's condition and followed her until the end.

- Just look at her! She got out of bed, she's walking around. These are signs that you're fine. Today we'll get the discharge form from the hospital and we hope that in a few hours you'll be back home, you'll be fine. All the tests have been successful, but now be careful. Don't play with your health and as I see you have a dear friend who never leaves you alone for a moment. I think that in his company you'll be fine, no, not good, but great, - he laughed with a smile that stung both of them like a newly in love couple. With these words, the doctor left the room, while Shpresa was still dealing with the necklace and the money they had left for her. Dritoni slowly gathered the patient's things and it seemed that he had everything ready to leave.

Liria met Besa near the hospital gate and the two of them entered the ward together and then into their friend's room.

They begged Dritoni to go and sober up and get clean while the friends would stay with Shpresa. He agreed after the insistence of all three, assuring him that she would be fine. After three days of staying in a room, he started to feel a little dizzy and his legs began to feel numb since he hadn't walked in days. As soon as he came out, a raindrop hit his head, making him raise his head and see the clouds that had made different shapes that resembled an old man with a white beard sitting on a rock. He lowered his eyes shyly, afraid that he might bump into something, knowing that he had not yet recovered from the fatigue of not sleeping and being in a closed environment, so he continued on his way home. All the way, he thought about Shpresa, about the state she was in. He promised himself that he would never leave her alone again. He thought that it was also his fault that he had not insisted more on being by her side. Maybe he would have spared her from the incident and would not have had time to think about raising a hand on himself. Hey! Arbër... he thought about her for a moment, his body completely shook when he remembered the face of his former friend who had now found eternity with the hope that he was resting peacefully in a better place. The thoughts that did not stop made him lose the sense of walking and when he saw himself in front of the neighborhood where he lived. He was surprised how he had reached there without realizing it, he had mechanically reached the desired destination.

Fitimi informed all his friends that the chances of bringing Arber's body were minimal or almost hopeless. They would have to agree with this, in the meantime it would be good for someone to inform Shpresa, but they had to find the moment that would cause the least suffering for him.

XXX

Shpresa left the hospital and the whole group came to accompany her on her way out. Besimi was the last to join the rest so it was an opportunity to be amazed by her.

-Where have you been until now, Don Juan! - Driton, who was holding all the bags with Shpresa's things in his hand, mockingly addressed him while they were waiting for the doctor's final report and to vacate the room. Everyone turned their eyes to the religious man and wanted to see any change in his appearance or appearance.

-I got stuck in traffic, I thought about walking all the way here, but I decided to use the local bus. But, with all this traffic congestion, it's faster to get there on foot than with these public cars. The horror, the horror of the roads! Look at who you're voting for mayor in the future. No, Driton, I wasn't where you think I am - he ironically returned the answer to his friend. He knew where he was thinking of hitting him.

-Shpresa, you look good. May it be over and may God help you and open the way for you in the coming days! We haven't seen each other before, condolences to your brother! Maybe I'm not one of the causes of your troubles. This is not the moment, but sometimes I'm afraid that I have some part of the blame for all this.

-No, Besim, you don't need to feel guilty at all. It seems that it was written to be like this... it was his choice to take the road.... - she said thoughtfully. It seemed that something was bothering him and Shpresa returned to her previous state again.

-I want to buy you a drink as a sign of gratitude right after we leave here, - she obliged the entire company to treat them for the care and dedication they had shown her during these days.

-We will, you don't need it. "Just let's hang out somewhere," said Fitimi, who seemed to be in trouble because the phone chirping was making him uncomfortable.

The media was still hunting him, so there was talk of a lawsuit against him for abuse of office. The accusation against him was now related to several contracts for work he had initiated in his digasteria where he managed this term. He seemed calm, but the many contacts he was receiving were starting to make him irritable.

- I have decided and don't spoil my mood, - Shpresa insisted. They agreed to leave it as she wanted. In the meantime, the letter they were waiting for arrived. It was a kind of diagnosis with a one-week follow-up therapy that had to be consumed. They were mainly sedatives and antidepressant vitamins to strengthen immunity and mental state. They all went out and soon found themselves near one of the city's cafes. While Besa and Fitim were walking, Besimi followed, Shpresa and Driton were left behind, while for a moment Liria, who was walking at the end, felt a hand behind her back touch her arm. It was Andi. Liria stopped, while the crowd in front of her entered the bar.

-I was looking for you at your apartment last night, you weren't there, - he spoke as if he wanted to ask for clarification about where she was at that time. She had the look of a detective who wanted to find some sign that would lead her to a long-awaited riddle.

I was out in the city, - Liria answered briefly and opened her eyes as a sign of what she wanted to do with this.

-At John, or with him? - he insisted repeatedly.

-It seems to me that you have had enough now, Andi. I have company and I have to get back to them. If you have something to tell me, order me and don't bother me anymore, - she spoke, trying to let him know that she wanted to leave and continue where she had started before was stopped by him.

-My fiancée still hasn't come back, it seems that everything is over between us. I'm not saying that you're to blame and that you influenced my relationship, but losing my job is also worrying me a lot now, while lately you've been on my mind all the time. It seems that now I need you, just as you once needed me... remember, you know what I mean.

-We'll talk later, I won't be late and I'll join my friends because there's no point. Shpresa just got out of the hospital, - she said and grabbed his hand and for a moment she left him and entered the narrow corridor that took her to the hall where the whole group was sitting, waving to her that "here we are." Andi remained stunned for a moment in front of the bar where his friend entered, whom he looked at until she disappeared from his sight. As he left, he pondered some thoughts about the problems he had. The nature of women is very interesting - he thought to himself. When I was in a relationship with my fiancée and we were having a good time, then she would chase me and make me her own. Strangely, it seemed like a competition between women to see who would be able to hold a man, a competition in which they push who is the most ladylike to achieve the goal. In this case, we men seem like a means to their achieved goal. Oh, no, it shouldn't be like this, my mind seems to be broken. There's no way. But why is she now standing cold, not like she used to, or does she look like me? There's no one to compete with now... that's the point. Now I know that my fiancée is no longer with me, so there's no one to show her what she's capable of, no one to challenge her or approve of her ability. No, no, I seem to be exaggerating. We men fall in love very quickly, sex plays a very big role in us. It seems to be the key and women have noticed this and know how to play their game, it seems that we will always be at their service, while they are tempted by the psychological sense. If you manage to master the spiritual world of a woman, then it's the key to her physical world. The connection lies in this direction and very few practice this among the rigid, harsh and senseless macho men in their sophisticated manners who lack the approach full of compliments that every woman wants to hear. The biggest liars are said to be the most skilled lovers in the world of women. Loaded with different thoughts to solve the understanding of his problem, he was lost in the crowd of the city center square like a shadow dazed by the drink that consequently has the injection of the nectar of love.

The atmosphere among the friends was quite good. They tried to forget for a moment the troubles and pain of Shpresa who sometimes lost her temper, but quickly returned from the mockery that was made in the name of Faith and Freedom. There was also no shortage of stings towards Driton who had been standing by her side for days and had become the object of healthy insults without offense.

-Thank goodness your sleep only lasted a few days, my beauty, because this prince of yours was turning into a Santa Claus, or a Robinson Crusoe without washing or shaving. In a few more days he would have a beard that would surpass Besim himself, - laughed Besa, everyone laughed with her.

- Tell us Shpresa how you woke up. It was just the two of you when you woke up. Did this kind of prince kiss you to wake you up, or did the poisoned apple fall from your mouth, my dark-haired Snow White, - gasped at the words of the spirited Besa who kept the mood at the table where the whole company was sitting.

- Now after several years of marriage, my Blessing, if I had remained poisoned and expected a kiss from him, maybe he would hesitate to do it. Of course it would keep me asleep for centuries, hahaha... they say that love is like a honey pot on top and the other half is slush. It seems that we have eaten the top part. The honey is gone now we have entered the bitter part. Oh, I'm kidding you, my friends, because you will think that is so, I say this only between you, as a matter of fact, - it seemed that she had overdone it a little and felt that she had offended her love. She regretted it for a moment and stopped speaking, giving the others the opportunity.

-Shpresa, I am thinking that for a few days you should not stay at home alone. You need some company and care until you get stronger. This is my opinion, - Besa gestured, addressing everyone, who unanimously approved. Everyone was ready to offer her help, take her or stay with her for the first few days after being released from the hospital. It was the friends who all came forward, while the men, due to the nature of the problem, gave her support in other ways.

-There's no need, I'll be fine. Even Danaj, the couple in question who live alone, offered me to stay with them for a few days, - she said while thinking and expressed this possible option to them.

-Very good, I like their suggestion, - Driton spoke, relieved because it seemed that she would be fine in their company, as long as she wasn't alone at home. He refrained from seeming pointless to offer her his own care, so as not to be misunderstood and offended by situation. It seemed like a good idea to stay with Aunt Myrvet and Uncle Bedri for a few days. He reminded her several times not to forget.

A phone call disturbed the whole party. Driton was asked by the journalism department to visit the editorial offices, so everyone had other commitments and they each got up to their work. Shpresa agreed that with Fitimi's help she would go to Danaj.

When they saw her in front of the door, they were very happy about the visit of the girl they loved like their own daughter. They hugged her and talked at length about all the events that had happened in these days. Their comfort made Shpresa feel stronger in their presence, but Driton could not get her out of his mind.

Driton, after making sure that his friend had gotten better, was now ready to return to work. The editor had assigned him a sensitive topic that he wanted to deal with himself. It was about several local and international officials who had been seen bringing in prostituted women from different countries in the region with the aim of trafficking them within our country. An investigative nose was needed, a seasoned watchdog, and that was Driton himself. He had dealt with similar and highly sensitive cases from experience. The case had to be confirmed and facts found to shed light on all phenomena that conflict with the law, even high-ranking international officials. After receiving all the reports in turn, Driton obtained some notes, names, and addresses that the editorial office had in its possession from an anonymous source who had previously contacted the media for information. He assured them that within seventy-two hours he would be able to compile an introductory report with all the relevant sources he would have in his possession and went out to collect facts, arguments or evidence that it was all true or a fabrication, fake news from different circles to compromise high public figures. He went out hunting like all journalists who follow the news. If the news or innovation has meaning and it is determined what is actually news, in the interest of daily politics or in the service of citizenship, society, the difference or its content in the definition encounters different interpretations. Besimi continued with the next meetings with Vesna. The days were approaching when she had to leave the city.

The seminar in which she was taking part ended the next day. Her impressions of everything she had seen in the country were quite positive. The only difference was the ending of the relationship with her friend, her former lover, how it would end or how everything would be organized from now on. They decided to continue their contacts in the future, now through the familiar modern virtual world, and not to rush until they both felt the moment together at the same time if they should take the initiative to strengthen the relationship or whatever was required. They had not communicated for years and all this had created a gap and disconnection in the emotions and changes they had encountered in each other, or the years that had made them such made it somewhat difficult for the strong relationship that now seemed to be somewhat broken somewhere in the middle. But there were things that gave hope that they could be healed if they were both of the same mind. They agreed that they would try to communicate with all the troubles or social problems that might arise in the meantime. Besa thought about going to visit her friend at Danaj during her lunch break, but a piece of news from the kindergarten made her change her mind. The teacher had announced that the older child had a fever and she had to go and pick up the child to take him to the doctor. She thought to herself: how can they call themselves a kindergarten or a preschool institution and not have a family doctor or pediatrician; now I have to run up and down, who knows what the child is in. We who work in the Ministry of Education also take part in the blame for this situation, since we do not address the problems properly, now the children suffer, the parents have to organize themselves, they have to be absent from work and so many other problems arise. It seemed that her mood was starting to deteriorate, but there was nothing she could do, she had to get to the teacher as soon as possible and take the child, find a solution for his cold. She remembered that she had heard him coughing several times in her sleep at night and tried to convince herself that it couldn't be anything serious. How lucky men are! They never disturb the peace. Mothers have to leave work, take care of the children, while the male world continues with work as if almost nothing has happened. The burden always falls on the mother and the wife. I think I'm exaggerating because I've seen many men, fathers who sometimes take care of them even more than their mothers.

You shouldn't generalize, I'm wrong, she said to herself. She remembered her neighbor Zana, who, unemployed, has managed to arrange her life with her husband's earnings. She has the child in the kindergarden, drives the car all day and spends the day from one cafe to another. They don't even cook at all since they order from different restaurants and the food comes to their house. All day long they are either driving the car or sitting on the phone browsing Facebook and seeing who has posted what on their profile or personal wall, what photo or who is where at this moment, since all the movements and actions of people are made public through these social networks and what is most important in the end the man finds time to deal with the children after work. With my own eyes I have seen how he changed the dirty diapers of the little baby while Zana communicated with the sister she had on the street. It seems that someone loves her, or not. This is not life either, staying like parasites. How do they pass the time, don't they get bored without feeling useful, valuable for themselves, their family, for even a moment. These thoughts brought her to the kindergarden gate, which made her run in. The child was not as bad as mothers usually foretell.

XXXI

It was their last meeting. Vesna would be leaving for home the next day. All official obligations were being completed, only a few things remained from her private aspect to take direction, what was still in question or at a crossroads and she sought a solution from her interlocutor, but also from her own confused head. Besim was still held hostage by that feeling that he did not know how to describe, but it was noticeable that the emotion was cold and did not give any good sign. He was afraid that it was some premonition that evoked evil, but his strong faith left no room for such superstitious things, that feeling still remained deep inside him, but that same emotion… it could also be a mistake. - Vesna, I understand that the years, circumstances have managed to influence us, in thinking, understanding life and many other things that keep us apart with or without our fault. I understand that whatever you decide, how we proceed… Your worldviews from the country you come from may be in some way an obstacle for you to continue communication or vice versa so that I am not misunderstood. In this country where we are, there are also still prejudices in relaxing inter-neighborly relations with neighboring countries in the region so that…. - he spoke, trying to choose his words and give direction to the conversation or ease the situation when Vesna stopped the religious man halfway:

-Listen Besim, I am now living alone, I left my family immediately after the conflict in Bosnia and Herzegovina. There were rumors that my uncle, a priest, we talked about earlier, was involved in a criminal case as a parish priest. It had gathered orphaned children as a result of the horrors, where during the separation of families brought by the war and various gruesome executions, many children were left on the streets without finding their parents, left to the mercy of God.

Several different international and local organizations had managed to shelter these children under their care, initially with the help of the church, then they had abandoned them somewhere across Europe, supposedly adopted by European families who had no children. There were also rumors that they had been subjected to improvised ordinances as a sign of trafficking in their organs, and some of them, while staying in the church premises, had been mistreated by priests who had abused all those orphaned children. There was a huge media frenzy and after my uncle's name was tarnished, I set off for Europe. I was educated there and for years I did not return to my homeland and lost contact with my family. So I have over time been cleansed of the identity purgatory and I have no problem with the circumstances, influences and prejudices or stereotypes that plague this part of the world. I am completely cleansed and unaffected by the political or identity circles that are strangling this region. While I see that time has left its mark on you, it seems that you are trying to achieve sublimation through sanctification, but to be honest with you, it does not suit you, - she said with a smile to herself, but very cautious.

- As far as I know, we are all sinners. I always liked the Devilish Besim, since we have something to be judged for when we reach the other side, and not to prepare ourselves now and go pure and untainted or holy in that world. Then where is the living of life left, through various predetermined templates with unbroken codes, - Vesna spoke in a tone of amazement, not hurting his friend's feelings.

-I have escaped from the clutches or shackles of identity, I am free, to act, to think as my entire intellect justifies, while you seem to have work to do to return to my former Besim that I loved so much.

Looking her in the eye with his mouth open and confused, he tried to join the conversation. -Are you talking like a feminist or am I wrong, my friend, - as if he wanted to hit where he thought the right target was. He waited for a reaction from Vesna.

-Ha, ha, you made me laugh, on the contrary I am not a feminist, I am offended by this word. We know that we live in a male world that very little space is attempted to be left to women, by the man himself who seeks to be at the center of everything, but I am against isms or ists.

I am not a feminist, because it seems to me that this ideology was not created to resolve gender relations, but to reposition women in a way that is opposed to the male world, in a conflictual position, with an emphasis on the feminine. The word feminism itself determines or emphasizes the categorization or hermetic closure of one gender to the exclusion of the other. I am against categorizations, identities that do not leave room for the universal, but are determined by the selection or radical change of an existing order that is, I admit, unjust at the moment. The creation of a new order is required, trying to make women take on the role, the dominance, that is, a change in positions, and not a rapprochement or state of a golden mean, where understanding, tolerance, compromise and exclusively the division of labor are more equal without discrimination or hatred of one gender.

Besimi was still surprised by her answers. She was saying to herself what she had missed.

-I have heard or even noticed that most feminists are homosexual, right? - the religious man interjected.

Vesna burst out laughing. - No, it doesn't mean that, it's not determinative. There may be cases in the type of radical feminists, but not generalizations. When they strictly devote themselves to themselves, their careers, their bodies and their inner world, not altruistically or alienating themselves in the name of the circle, the family, but preserving their ego and depriving themselves of the influences of the male world that they see as harsh and exploitative in relation to women from a biological or primordialist aspect, then there may be homophilic nuances. They hesitate to have children, create families and have some positions in relation to men, and it is true that they are closer to women, but it does not mean that they are exclusively sexually oriented as you say.

-I think that the middle is always golden, as Aristotle said. I am neither with the patriarchal world nor with the feminist one that is trying to turn our social life into a matriarchal order, that is, from one domination to another, only to exchange positions and still have someone who is above and dominates over the other. I do not like this at all.

Instead of both being free and cooperative, this creates an antagonism or contradictory situation that I do not approve of at all. Do you understand where I want to go? - he did with his hands and eyes convincingly that made the religious man nod his head in agreement without stopping in his movements that for a moment looked like a typical dervish performing the ziqr rituals after a spiritual interiorization.

-Now it remains for you to love with your heart or with your head, which one will you choose, or are you lucky that both are in synchronization and say amen to each other.

Saying goodbye, Vesna approached Besim, kissed her on the cheek and with a sigh said: - I finished my part, now you are on the move, it remains for you to finish things - she said and walked in the opposite direction, turning her eyes towards the religious man, who remained stunned and stunned by Vesna's gestures, the smell of which, a sweet, enchanting aroma among a spectrum of early spring fragrances, filled his nostrils that made him suddenly drugged between the breeze that released into his heart, the eyes that swallowed her fleeing appearance where the hair fluttering in the breeze tried to attract the attention of her long-legged body with a thin waist that seemed to be torn somewhere from the wide hips that determined the curvy body line like her long hair in harmony with the previous flirtatious conversation that made Besim get lost in her company. Only a few signs of breathing from time to time gave in her direction and for a moment he remained motionless, until she disappeared from his sight, the silhouette that made him intoxicated, just by looking at her physical form.

He didn't know what to do. His mind went to Liria, maybe she could clear his mind and give his situation meaning, direction. He called her and assured her to go to her in the apartment where she lived. On the way, Besimi thought about the whole conversation he had had with Vesna. It seems that she was determined and stoic in everything she said. She had self-confidence, she gave the impression that she was free from all the complexes that a person can have. She was always herself and unaffected by the social circle, it seemed that she had not changed yet. But me, I looked like a victim of this whole social order or propaganda influences of the mass culture, it seemed to me that her eyes were laughing, as if they were asking me where Besim's time went, my husband, what is this transformation in your worldviews and thinking. Different practices become habits, then they become ideas or thoughts, and finally, as a combination of all of them, attitudes are created that easily turn into actions. It seems to me that I am too busy and I am not thinking clearly. My mind is confused, I cannot solve them, maybe Liria can help me... He reached the door and went inside after Liria welcomed Besim, she instructed him to come in. The friend noticed that something was wrong with his friend, it was visible from his face.

Driton set out to meet one of the witnesses of the case for his journalistic research. It was person X who had to be interviewed and gather information about the sensitive event involving various public figures. Person X, a snotty-nosed man with curly hair, blue eyes and a medium build, gave the impression that he was very nervous and from time to time looked behind him, as if someone was following him. He gave the journalist a lot of information, names, phone numbers and addresses and professions of those involved in the case. For security reasons, he asked not to publish his source or name, he was afraid that he might get hurt. Fear had already seized him, it seemed that danger awaited him at any moment. After he parted ways with his interlocutor, on the way to the office, a message arrived on his phone. As soon as he opened it to read it, he looked at it two or three times with hesitation, not understanding or believing his eyes. We warn you in advance, to mind your own business, don't put your nose where it doesn't belong, curiousity killed the cat, it was written in the continuation.«The cat was killed by curiosity». It seems that someone is following me, they are following me. His mind went to Shpresa for a moment, who was still safe and sound at Danaj's. He looked through the names and notes he had once more and decided to contact them one by one.

Besim told his friend the whole story and everything he was thinking about it.

- Besim, do you still like Vesna? This is important, - said Liria as if she wanted to find the thread of the solution.

- She still attracts me, but I have doubts whether she still likes me. I

hope this new way of mine doesn't irritate her, - he thought and he expressed himself as if to himself, putting his hand on his head and moving around the room, which made his friend go crazy from the irregular look of the movements of the irritable interlocutor.

-You have to listen to your heart and act in accordance with it, without prejudice. Of course, she has the former Besmin in mind, just like we who are slowly getting used to you, since you have been one of the most lively among us. According to the conversation, she has been the same, unaffected by these events that have surrounded us these years, perhaps she also expected to find the same thing in you, but if she still feels something for you, secondary things will not affect the relationship at all, I don't believe it, - Liria spoke confidently, probably to give hope to her friend who was in trouble.

-We will continue the communication, but I don't know in what direction it will take shape. I'm afraid that all that enthusiasm we had at the beginning about meeting will fade away in time, and it's all my fault. I'm at a crossroads, so I don't know which way to go, - he tried to find the best way to put things in the right direction. He walked around the room constantly. While as a spectator without makeup and in sports clothes sitting at the kitchen table, his friend watched his shadow moving around and not taking up space. In that state, the player decided that getting some fresh air would probably help him solve the problem. - I'm leaving. Thank you for listening to me and offering me the opportunity to confess... I'm going out for a walk, see you later, - he greeted his friend and quickly went outside. Standing up, he just followed her with his eyes and left the apartment like a bolt of lightning. He went down the stairs and found himself in front of the building. He didn't notice that the rain had started.

Andi, wandering around the city, had approached the apartment of Liria, a colleague if we could call her that, and almost met Besim. He quickly took the direction and entered the building. He had no difficulty reaching her door. He rang the bell and waited for a while. Liria, after hearing that someone was at the door, thought it was the religious again, thinking that he had forgotten something in the meantime. With her mind on him, she approached the door, opened it and was left stunned by who she saw before her eyes. Andi, with a surprising tone, followed her gaze. As soon as the guest found a little space, he entered without the hostess's permission. He found himself in the corridor and headed for the living room. The colleague from work, closed the door in surprise and followed him.

-I can't do this, it seems I've lost everything, not a word or sign yet from my fiancée. This is what they call break up, there's nothing else, - he spoke in a fast cacophonous tone. - I don't know if I love you or hate you, you took everything I had, is that how you do it to men? I've heard of you, but never in this way. I needed you for a moment, but that moment is costing me... I wanted you, I wanted you, that, now, now I'm left... I'm left with nothing, - Andi spoke in a daze and in anxiety. It seemed as if it couldn't get any worse.

- Calm down, it'll be fine, there will be a solution, - Liria tried to calm him down, who was also starting to be afraid of the situation he was in. She had never seen him like this, like a rabid wolf looking for prey to force his teeth to release the resentment he had inside.

-How can I calm down when my life has been destroyed in one night? You know that now I don't even have a job. All of this happened to me from the moment I got involved with you, when I thought I would be there for you, to help you. You took me, used me and threw me away like a rag, because you needed me then, all of this is now costing me everything... and to lose everything just because of you, there is no other reason, - Andi couldn't calm down at all.

-It was all we both wanted, it wasn't just my imposition, Andi. It was just a flash of a moment, a spark, understand me, it shouldn't have been the reason for everything that's happening to you. Don't blame me for not having the idea to bring you to this state, trust me, - as if in the form of a confession she wanted to justify herself, but she stopped her speech in mid-sentence when Andi approached her face to face and, drooling, spoke absently: - Trust me, trust me, say heee…- she grabbed his head until he was standing in front of her and for a moment with both hands pushed Liria by the chest out of anger to the point that she lost her balance and began to take steps backward clumsily, trying to hold on and not fall. She didn't succeed. She fell headfirst onto the edge of the table and crashed to the floor. A trickle of blood covered a part of the floor that came from her neck. Liria didn't make a sound, she didn't move. For a moment she changed color and turned pale. Andi was left with his hands on his face, not knowing what he did. He sat down next to her, touched her face. It was ice cold. Rising like a hyena picking it up

what he came for and ran away, he also left the apartment, sighing with himself and like a deformed ball he rolled down the stairs. He disappeared like a heavy and evil shadow from the stench that he himself had prepared from his irrational blindness to judge things clearly.

The next day Liria did not show up at work. She had not informed either the office manager or her colleagues. Andi was confused and in a state of panic. He seemed worried.

Drita, her officemate, asked Andi if he knew anything about Liria, if she had informed him. Andi denied it, keeping his eyes on his desk. They arranged for a home visit by security personnel since she did not answer the phone either. Soon the organization's security patrol arrived at her apartment.

They approached the door and rang the bell. They were in pairs as usual. No one answered. They started knocking, but nothing. Accidentally, one of the security guards touched the door latch and, wanting to knock, the door suddenly opened. They looked at each other in surprise and gestured that they would go in and see what they would find. As soon as they entered the apartment or living room, they saw the body on the floor. They recognized it at first sight. They called the ambulance and the police immediately, reported it to their work office and took care not to leave fingerprints when entering the apartment, so as not to affect the investigation. Outside, in front of the apartment, the police and all the emergency units relevant to the case were waiting. Upon arrival, they notified Liria's family and the news spread. Her parents were among the first to arrive. They were the ones who had abandoned their daughter because of her lifestyle, they had not communicated for a long time. Her father was a stocky man with a mustache, a Parisian hat tipped to the side with a classic suit and a purse tied with a chain to his jacket vest that he played with mechanically. His eyes were wide open. Her mother, with a full body, traditional dress and a scarf on her head, wiped her tears with tissues and sighed. They stood in the room where her body was still being watched by medical personnel and the police. The tearful mother thought to herself, how she did not accept her daughter when she was alive and now in this dead state she came ... a paradox in herself that made her feel guilty. The father, managing to maintain his patriarchal honor and face in the eyes of the social circle, which seemed to be

more precious than his own daughter, from his yellowed corpse face he inhaled the poison that social pressure forgives in the absence of reason. The word of strangers more valuable than the life of his daughter... Social contexts sometimes if they do not dare to take and control life or take it all. He sat slumped, taking the form of a bubble that does not rest anywhere, which stands alone in the air without legs but waits to be dissolved in the meantime by the social winds that blow elsewhere.

According to some police investigations and recordings of a neighbor's cameras, they had detected the religious man and his recent visit to the victim. There was also a face, a stately body that had rolled down the stairs, but they had not yet managed to identify it.

The society of Liria also gathered. Everyone was shocked, especially the friends, the surprised and upset friends looked at each other. Besimi approached, gave a statement and told what had happened the previous day at the meeting with the deceased. After being informed of the case, Drita asked that she and Andi go to the scene of the incident. Andi hesitated, but at the insistence of her colleague who managed to convince her, they went together. On the way, he didn't speak at all, he was distracted, he seemed lost. At first, he stopped on the road a few meters near the entrance to the apartment, but Drita begged him to go in together.

-You go, I'll come now, I get worried when there are these kinds of cases. I'll stay here for a while, you go…- he tried to separate from Drita. He needed to be alone, to think, to make the right move.

XXXII

After leaving the scene, Driton hesitated to tell Shpresa. He would have agreed, but he would have found a more suitable occasion to tell her the bitter news. In memory of Liria, he walked and tried to decipher what could have happened to her. Besimi didn't think he would go that far...

Suddenly, even though he was distracted, a car caught his attention, walking parallel to him, the car on the highway while Driton on the sidewalk. Their speed seemed to be synchronized. He turned his head to see how the speed matched his walking. As soon as he looked at the car, which with its long black windows, resembled a luxury limousine. Without a second, a rear window opened, from which a face dressed in a black suit emerged, sitting in the back.

-You seem tired of walking. Will you come and join us in the car? - the tone of the words resembled a commanding sophistication, with eyes that were visible after the glasses were taken down to see better. From the wrinkles on his face, he seemed to be middle-aged. A mark on one cheek spoke volumes about the knife blade that had left a stain on it from the turbulent past.

-I'm fine, no need, thank you, I prefer to walk - before he could finish his words when suddenly the front window opened, where the driver and the person next to him were. Both were nicely dressed, younger in age and with a well-groomed and physically built, muscular head. The person next to the driver took out a revolver that seemed to have a silencer, rubbed his face and nose, and in a drowning voice, he looked down at the boy walking on foot:

- The boss says come inside! The words were in sync with the movements of his revolver, aimed at himself and at the pedestrian, who made him come inside after the back door opened.

- It's great that you joined us,- said the man with a sign on his face after Driton sat down next to him in the back seat. - Do we know each other? - Driton replied. He smiled once and looked ahead at his two friends while the car

didn't stop. It seemed that now he had also increased his speed while they were talking.

-I've heard that lately you've been sniffing around a lot, poking your nose into other people's business. Just know one thing, everyone has a hook in their mouth, they have someone who is on them, even your employers. Don't let your paths cross with me later... because everyone will come to me one day. As he spoke, he scratched the mark on his face, as if it contained in itself the most terrifying stories, tales, and events of life.

-Be careful with your actions because these friends of mine, later on, will not only remind you of my words, but also your dearest ones, - he said, looking at his friends in front of him. They made gestures with the revolver, only the trigger was missing. With such gestures, it seemed that they wanted to scare him or let Driton know what he was getting into with his new writing if he tried to do it.

- Condolences to your friend! - he said ironically, as if he knew who you were and who you were with, until the car door opened to let Driton out.

- Now you can get out of the car. It was a pleasure talking to you, - The Sign looked at him. Driton hadn't even said two words to him. He let go of the car and a bad feeling covered his head, a shudder from the top of his head then followed him to the bottom of his feet. He looked at the car until it was lost in the crowd of other cars in the city. His mind went to Shpresa. It seemed that he had missed her.

Besimi carried within her a kind of guilt and bad feeling for everything that had happened to Liria. He was considered one of the suspects in his friend's murder until the case was solved. The neighbor, who had accidentally hit Andi while he was going down the stairs from Liria's apartment, had been a classmate of Andi's from elementary school, whom he had not noticed due to his confusion. The neighbor had stated during the investigation that he had met him. During the cameras that had recorded, they had investigated to see some of the selected people in the detection, help in the case like Drita. She had immediately recognized the shadow and clothing of her office colleague. She was shocked when she saw him on the recording.

His fingerprints in Liria's apartment had also matched. He had become one of the main suspects in her murder. Fortunately, Besimi escaped and all investigations led to Andi, who was imprisoned and charged. Liria's funeral took place the next day. Many family members and friends attended her funeral to her last home. Everyone was sad and at the same time upset about her early departure from life. As soon as Besimi felt freed from suspicion, he felt an emptiness inside him that he could not explain at all. It seemed that he had already begun to miss his friend.

The preparations for the graduation party failed with the new trends and events that shocked the generation. They agreed that in memory of their friend, they would postpone it for another year. The departure of Liria left everyone wondering how such an extravagant, moderate and well-organized woman could end up in this situation. It is known that most tragedies are related to the difficult socio-economic life, but in cases where everything seems to be in order... but such things also happen. It seems that when there is a lack of balance between pain and joy, being deprived of pain, dominated only by the state of happiness attracts or brings sadness more in any form, since this state is also part of life. It finds a way to appear sooner or later, since the sun does not always warm, even rain has its own value, to better recognize the value of the sun's warming rays. The lack of rain or pain to create a vital balance between the individual and social life causes in most cases to hate the sun and seek rain in its absence, which will then make it come, but in a more severe and perhaps more unbearable way. The imbalance of things and relationships in life in any form, whether for good or bad, will be radicalized and will cause one to dominate the other to the extreme. If we constantly have pain, sadness, then we will seek happiness unconditionally and the dominance of happiness infinitely in relation to pain will create suffering, since its excess in itself will bring sadness that cannot be articulated in its absence.

Just as evils also know how to kill, since many good things find their way to evil if they are not balanced.

Driton continued his journalistic investigations into the case. He had previously scheduled a meeting with one of the missionaries of an international charity organization that was working for several individuals who were incriminated and part of that illegal act. He was supposed to meet with Gabi, the head of a department that dealt with law and order within the mission. He welcomed the guest very warmly.

As soon as he entered his office, there was a work desk with all the modern equipment that an office has and an auxiliary desk near a secretary who was on a break. He deliberately chose the time to have privacy during the interview, while looking at the flowers in the pot that he loved so much and motioning to Driton if he wanted to be served something from the restaurant that was located one floor below the office where they were. Driton denied the desire to be served.

-(speak in English) "Listen my friend; you know everything is war, life, death, fortune, even the jobs are some kind of war, they are created in that way that who first comes first serves, or everything is business and it seems that this kind of business is good " He approached the flowers and began to smell them. -"Scent flies me in the past, didn't arrive to smell the future through beautifull flowers, strange is it? "

Driton informed him about what he had come to see him for. A plump, medium-sized, bald man, Gabi, with a thick lip and a sad expression on his face, told him not to rush, to take things easy.

-I have heard that there are cases where your holy mission is being misused and with the help of some local workers, illegal trafficking is being carried out in collaboration with some international individuals. Is it true? Do you know anything about this? There are informal reports about the case, - he fired off a barrage of questions, like an experienced journalist, without any expression on his face and with a consistent tone.

-"Most of internationals are here to help, they have been sacrificed for this saint mission leaving their families and staying in years to assist and rebuild your institutions and society to the democratic levels, even we are well paid, have a good life and very good accepted by the locals here, including young females who are seeking for modernism," - he started laughing to himself, which made his thick lips foam for a moment and continued - "Sacriface must be paid, as I said, war is business and it seems business is good, It got employed many locals as well… is according to the law and no activity by the mission or by the employed occurred so far which might be misconduct or facing with violation of the regular law requirements. So please leave the office cause I have so much work to do."

Thick lips asked Driton to vacate his office and it seemed that the interview with him had ended. But there were still many issues to be discussed. There was nothing he could do. He thanked him and left the office. Escorted by the security guards, he reached the main door and was quickly outside. On the way, as he walked, he thought about the meeting he had, about the way the thick-lipped man felt superior to him, behaving dominantly over the local man who made him feel bad and submissive. He thought of visiting some nightclubs, about which little was known and which were said to be kept in great discretion by various circles. Only a narrow circle knew about them. He had received information from person X about some. He wanted to see them. He also had a letter of introduction thanks to the enigmatic person. Initially, he wanted to meet Shpresa and then continue with his work. Shpresa had begun to recover, spending time sometimes at Danaj's and sometimes Besa kept her company. Driton was less available due to the many jobs he had in recent days. Fitimi was having problems with successive court processes, with accusations of the usual kind of mismanagement, while Besimi was visiting his circle of friends less than usual. It was said that he was in a somewhat bad mood after the recent events, especially the case of Liria.

Driton had received the address at one of the night clubs. He decided to go and see what was going on there. It was a narrow alley that did not give the impression that at the end of it one could find a metal door that did not look promising from the outside. He rang the bell and held the entrance card in his hand. Someone came out to the door. He was completely masked, his face could not be seen. Tall, with the weight of an athlete, he asked the guest for the password. Driton knew through person X, after he said "incognito", the masked man opened the way for him. As soon as he passed the entrance, he found himself in a long, narrow, well-lit corridor full of surveillance cameras. After about ten meters, he was faced with a door. The attendant swiped his card through an access code and the second metal door opened. The distance to the third door was only two meters. If the security had any doubts, you would have been trapped between the two doors like in a two-by-two prison cell. The security was impressive and the impression from the outside did not give the impression that you would encounter anything of the sort. The third door also opened and for a moment a large space was seen, a hall that was filled with many people. Some at tables, some at the counter and some were near the podium where half-naked girls were dancing and entertaining the guests. For a while, Dritoni looked at the environment where he was and was more than surprised. While he was standing at the entrance door, his appearance as a handsome brunette attracted attention. This did not escape Gabi either, who surprisingly

the guest was sitting at the counter and following one of the girls who kept dancing near him, who seemed to him like a writhing snake that would attack and take him for itself with its deadly poison at any moment. Gabi motioned for Driton to join him. The handsome brunette moved from his place and headed towards his acquaintance who was constantly inviting him with his hand.

-See what a fragrance the flowers bring, my friend, -he said and gestured to one of the many women who were dancing and entertaining the half-drunk guests, most of whom had hungry, drooling wolfish looks. One of the beauties approached, spoke in a language that resembled Slavic. Gabi pulled her towards him, kissed her hard on the face until he managed to hold her for a moment and sniffed deeply, turning her face towards his friend.

-Look at the piece, smell it if you want, the scent of behar or a cocktail of flowers, your brain will explode if you smell it, -he said. It seemed that the drink he was drinking had thickened his tongue. Driton restrained himself, made a defense with his hand, preserving his intimate space that was almost broken by the woman's face pushed by Gabi's hand by the neck. Driton looked at the woman with a greeting and flattering look, giving an expression to his face that he doesn't need it, she can withdraw. She was surprised by the guest's dismissive behavior.

-Why don't you like, what you have, my friend? - Gabi spoke again, feeling embarrassed by the journalist's reaction.

-Tell me how you came here, how did you find the place?

-Words fly very quickly and good things, according to you, are given away, right? - he threw the journalist in his face with a sharp look. Gabi felt his gesture well.

-Don't be sexually oriented my friend, because there is no one who can resist these chicks, hehe, - the missionary spoke with a flood of laughter, terrifying, cacophonous.

-Listen, these are women who come from different countries of the former communist bloc. They have existential problems and here they feel safe and employed performing various services. Women are spared, your local girls my friend. You should thank us. There are many missionaries, workers who come from different countries of Europe. They have left their families there, the women, so everyone needs a little entertainment, or to forget their troubles or homesickness for their own country…. these enable them. Yes, more than true, they make you lose your mind, they are professionals, - he spoke while intermittently swallowing from time to time from his nearby glass, a sip that made him distort his face from time to time.

-Is this type of business permitted by law? Something seems very discreet to me, -Dritoni asked sensitively without confusing things with Gabi.

-Look my friend, here in your country there are many things that do not have permits, they function very normally and there is no fuss at all. This business has benefited your locals a lot, from the employment of many young men and women, the food we buy, the drinks, the rent of the bar and many other things that you benefit from this work, do you understand me now?

- Okay, okay, but this activity, these girls, are they reported to the local authorities? There could also be signs of prostitution, trafficking here… - Driton's words stopped after Gabi raised his hands in displeasure and waved at the guards who stood across in key positions in the hall. One of them approached Gabi, always at his service, waiting for the request from the orderly.

- Please escort our guest, he is leaving, - he said to the guard, looking at Driton to make him understand that he was no longer wanted there. Driton stood up and looked Gabi in the eye. He didn't say anything to him except to give him a letter with the inscription "Never play a saint when you are a trained sinner" and accompanied by the guard left the room. The cloaks with masks quickly led the guest out of the bar into the narrow alley, making you wonder that this place could exist right there. Gabi took the letter the guest had left on his way out and read it. He pursed his lips, frowned and tore the letter into pieces. He emptied the entire glass he had in one,

go next to him and as if his mood changed. He started flirting with one of the girls dancing on the podium. The noise of people around the tables and the girls' attendance made this place very lively from the early hours of the morning.

Driton asked for a radio taxi since it was late and he didn't want to bother Shpresa in those hours that left midnight and when the first signs of dawn had begun. He thought about meeting Gabi. He began to doubt him, in his way and approach to the commitment to be useful, helpful or missionary, which is more than sacred. The international community has brought a lot of good to our country, freedom as well, but it seems that there are individuals who are spoiling the opinion about them. It seems that these are people like us, sinners, beneficiaries. No, I don't say criminals because I have a very good opinion of everyone, but this Gabi, I find somewhat suspicious. He has a hand in this kind of illegal business. With this intra-personal conversation he noticed from the car window that he had reached his apartment. He greeted the taxi driver, paid for the service and jumped into the entrance and went up the stairs. He soon found himself in bed. He felt tired, more mentally than from having done any heavy physical activity.

XXXIII

People had gathered in the city center in protest of all the daily evils that burdened the citizen. There was an increase in the price of electricity for the umpteenth time, it had become an unaffordable cost, especially in the winter season when energy consumption was greatest. In a country rich in coal, the enormous electricity bills were one of the many paradoxical evils that pushed people to show their dissatisfaction. Traffic fatalities had become another black mark, public safety was in question, the murders of young people in the cities from various deviations, schools from uncontrolled delinquents who lost their lives for trivial reasons had made citizens mobilize and take to the streets. Driton was breaking the road to reach the desired destination to take notes on the social event and to listen to the articulation of people's dissatisfaction, when for a moment a hand from the crowd pulled him away from him. He turned his body in relation to the force of attraction and barely deciphered his friend Besim. He opened his eyes in surprise and remained motionless for a moment. Besim, with a convincing attitude, looked at Driton with eyes that spoke quite clearly. He had shaved his beard, changed his style of dress and no longer held his hands in his pockets. Driton immediately noticed this change at first glance and it seemed that he saw his friend as if he were seeing him for the first time. He hugged him tightly and held him by the arm.

-Please don't laugh. It's not that I can't find myself, even Vesna didn't affect me. I had the idea to do it this morning and I did it. I'm feeling comfortable. What I have inside I will jealously keep to myself, I will not expose myself to the outside to know who I am, or to be read from a distance. I will try to be an unread book for others, not to know the essence from the cover. They will only know me if they stay with me, like you my friend. I am really very comfortable feeling myself like this for the moment, believe me… - he spoke and moved his hands along his body and rubbed his face.

-I'm glad my friend! No matter what you look like, you will always be my friend, it doesn't matter how you dress or how you look on the outside, but what's inside you. I know that world in you very well, so I agree with you, one of the rare agreements between you and me lately, - he said with a laugh and hugged his friend once again.

-A phone call stopped the conversation of the two friends. A murder had occurred, it could be related to the journalist's research case and the editorial office asked him to go to the morgue to find out more about the identity of the murdered person. Besimi told the journalist that he would stand around the protesters to listen to the words of the organizers, while Driton took another direction from the crowd. He started to leave, when cheers and slogans of dissatisfaction began to be heard from those gathered, or from someone who had taken the megaphone and led the protesting chorus. What the person who had found a place upstairs where everyone could see him was being repeated by the entire crowd: Come on, come on! - the entire city center was shouting, and sometimes it was shouting: - Criminal, criminal!

-Driton arrived at the UCCK morgue unit. He tried to enter, but there were police and civilians nearby who stopped him. They asked him why he had come. The journalist said that he was there on duty in his capacity as a reporter for the event, and while someone from the entrance to the morgue went to get permission to enter or not, Driton took advantage of the opportunity and quickly entered, since the door had been left open. Upon entering, he saw a female body on a table nearby, lying lifeless, and several doctors examining her. He immediately recognized the dead woman; she was the same one who had danced the previous night in that bar when he had been present near Gabi. He noticed that there were signs of violence on the body. His head felt very heavy for a moment. The eyes of the forensic team stared at him, asking what he wanted, why he was there. He noticed their piercing, reproachful gaze and went out the door. Meanwhile, he heard the voice of the guard who had gone to consult earlier, who was returning. He positioned himself as before, so as not to arouse suspicion about his previous act, as if nothing had happened.

- This is the supervisor. I'm sorry, but according to the regulations and the investigators' requests, you are not allowed to enter the morgue premises Please leave the building, - he said, looking at the colleague he had with him, while addressing the journalist. -I'm sorry, - he said, raising his hands as a sign of regret. Driton just nodded in approval and headed for the exit without saying a word. All the way he remembered the dead girl and her exotic dance that she had done the night before and how she had been wooing him while standing in the company of Gabi by the counter.

On the way, he noticed that his mouth was dry and he felt thirsty. He stopped near a grocery store and asked for a bottle of water. It was news time and the seller was surprised to hear on the portable TV that he had positioned on a high shelf.

The moderator briefly announces the news: "Today, early in the morning, a murder occurred in the city. The identity of the female person and the motives for the murder are still unknown. The investigations are ongoing and as soon as the details are gathered we will announce the most detailed report so as not to affect the progress of the investigation process."

-Yes, yes, "the investigations continue." Are you listening, as far as I know, they never managed to uncover any murder after the war. The investigations, the investigations continue… our security institutions have become like parrots, - the disheveled salesman spoke in extreme anger with a stick between his teeth until he went to the refrigerator to bring the glass bottle of water.

Driton just clapped his hands in approval that this was so and after paying for the water, he left the store with a thank you for the service. He returned to the office and did nothing for a few hours, just thinking. He thought about calling Shpresa but left it for later.

He told the editor the news and the report on the events related to the murder, but he remembered the limousine and the sign that warned him of many things, for everyone who would later meet him. All roads lead to the sign. This prevented him from revealing everything to the editor about what he had seen.

Putting his hands in his pockets, he saw Gabi's business card with his contact number. He turned it over several times, looking at it thoughtfully, decided to meet him. He called him on the phone, they agreed to meet in one of the quiet cafes in the city away from the noise and many eyes.

They saw each other quickly and found themselves as they had agreed at a cafe table with a few guests, in a quiet environment to talk without anyone disturbing them.

-I saw the murdered girl, - Driton immediately interrupted. Gabi's face fell, he began to scratch it with his hand and looked at his interlocutor.

-There are many things that come out without planning, sometimes they happen without thinking. Such things are normal for the time we are living in, - he spoke slowly, calmly without any burden.

-I'm talking about the girl who was dancing at the counter next to you. She seemed to know you well, she didn't leave you. I saw her today in the morgue, there were signs of violence, while the police and media reports are trumpeting nonsense. They are hiding something, or someone, - he said the last words, raising his voice a little more than usual, which made Gabi look around to see if anyone was listening to what they were saying. This also affected Driton, who turned his head left and right in a suggestive way.

- I told you that unpredictable things happen, you have to understand me, the girl had no future, the past was no worse. You are pushing me to express myself in terms of collateral damage, capiche.

- She must have a name, identity, past and future. Who are you to play with people's fate? She certainly ended up there due to circumstances, so that you can suck her young soul alive. Don't you have a hand in all this? Something is being hidden here, international gentleman, you have no legal, moral, human right to behave like that.

A terrifying laugh stopped the journalist's speech.

-Do you think you journalists know everything? You stick your noses everywhere. Be careful, you'll get dirty before you even smell it! You have the wrong beliefs, my friend, you think I'm upset about the girl, about you, about this place?

Hahaha!…. No, not at all! I'm here to take my loot and run away somewhere in peace to a life full of prosperity. Summer comes knocking on the door, my friend, do you understand me? I left my children, my wife, my country, my parents. Do you think what price I pay to stay here with you now, heh… How many times a day do I think about who my wife shares a bed with now far away, who my son or daughter is with, in the company of drug addicts or criminals. I sacrificed everything to be humane with you, with my daughter, with all of you who need help, and I, do I need help? I wasted my wealth, my money, when my whole family goes down, dissolves. This is the price I pay, the price you will never understand by staying in this miserable, rotten place, where it will never get better. This place is not only bad for you, but also for us…

He foamed until he wiped his mouth with a paper napkin and gave Driton a sharp look that made him understand that the meeting with him was over.

The journalist got up from the table without making a sound. Gabi, frowning, swallowed the grape brandy to the end and kept his eyes down in thought. Driton, slowly, not disturbing him more than he really was, moved away from Gabi without ever taking his eyes off him. He soon found himself outside. From the window, he noticed that he was still in misery with the same depressing attitude.

He had not yet stepped out of the cafe when a car he recognized very well approached him from the parking lot of the place. The first door near the driver's side opened furiously. A tall, balding man forcibly grabbed him by the arm and, after opening the back door of the car, pushed him inside. Driton found himself again facing The Sign sitting in the back seat. He waved at the two bald heads and the car started.

-I can't stand those who don't listen, especially if they despise my words. You seem like a good boy, quite intelligent, you understand, I have no doubt.

His words were accompanied by a sharp blade that came out of his seat and ran along Driton's face. Sometimes he pressed it harder on the journalist's forehead, which made him feel pain or sometimes he bled from The Sign's slight cut.

-I warned you to mind your own business. It seems you didn't listen at all, you're entering where you don't belong, - The Sign shouted and waved. The car stopped and Driton found himself lying on the ground in a suburban area of the city. The two muscular men grabbed him by the waist, which prevented him from touching the ground. They started punching and kicking him as hard as they could, until he started bleeding from all sides and lost consciousness. The stopped car had opened the rear doors and with one foot on the ground since half of his body was outside the car, The Sign sat down and watched as the journalist was beaten terribly, like in a boxing match in which the difference between the rivals was obvious. It was a fight without a referee, without the words knockdown or knockout, it was a cage fight, a killer fight. For a moment, The Sign stood up and waved in the direction of his men. Both of them stopped immediately. He approached the prey, which seemed ready to flee if they continued at this pace. He knelt on the lying body of Driton, who had lost consciousness. He gave him two or three slaps, which brought the journalist to his senses. The sign grabbed him by the hair from behind, lifted his head with a bloody face and whispered in his ear:

-This is my last warning!

He slammed his head on the ground and stood up. He took a handkerchief from the pocket of his expensive suit and wiped his bloody hands after touching the journalist. As usual, with a gesture, he made the colossus get back in the car and continue on, leaving the journalist on the ground beaten. He remained in that state of euphoria for several hours until he woke up and gathered his strength. He noticed that it was already dark, he could hear the barking of stray dogs. He did not have the strength to get up. Doubled over, he managed to sit down once, and with all the strength he had bent over, he stood up, but immediately fell to the ground. His legs could not support him. He stood in that position for a few moments, tried again, gritted his teeth, and stood up again. As if drunk on brandy, he began to walk to a corroded structure of a car. He held on to it for a while, looked around, and deciphered where he was. It was several kilometers from the city, out of sight of anyone. He walked for a while in that state to a gas station. He went into the bathroom, wiped the blood from his face, and noticed that his ribs were hurting a lot. He somehow wiped his dusty clothes. After straightening himself up as best he could, he headed out the door-in themain road. He stopped several times, but no one stopped the car. A large trailer noticed the passerby who was barely walking, sometimes falling and sometimes getting up by holding his hands. The driver opened his arm and stopped, trying to talk to the passerby in distress. From the car window he approached his head while the random passerby turned his face in his direction. The driver saw signs of violence on his face. He was surprised by the sight. The journalist recorded such a look very well.

--Where are you going, my friend, - said the bald driver with a round face with a cigarette that was not lit in his mouth.

--In the city, city, - the passerby barely spoke.

-The driver opened the door, escorting him with the words: "Come on, get in the car in that direction, I'm going too." The passerby, with half-strength, managed to somehow climb onto the truck seat, his face contorted from the pain that was running through his entire body. The driver helped as much as he could from his seat. He closed the door and did not take his eyes off him.

-What happened to you, you had an accident, what good did it do you? -the curious driver greeted him immediately after the guest had settled into the car seat.

-I was hit by a train, - the passerby said, looking the driver deep in the eyes and both of them burst into tears, so much so that the driver could not stop laughing, while the passerby laughed carefully because he felt pain every time his body moved or shook from the tremors of laughter.

-Here I can stop because I will take the road to the outskirts of the city,

- the driver said after a few minutes of driving together calmly.

-Thank you very much! I need to get off right here, - said Driton, slowly getting out of the car.

-Be careful my friend…! Did the train hit you or... hahaha, - the driver laughed and continued on his way, while the journalist found himself back in the city.

XXXIV

Driton thought about what to do the whole way as he walked. He didn't want to meet Shpresa. He thought that if she saw him in that state… No. He spared her. He talked on the phone and made sure that she was fine and was slowly recovering. He didn't even want to go home, so his parents could see. He decided to go to the office to get ready a bit and then go to the apartment later, when everyone was asleep, so as not to disturb them with his appearance. He passed by the bar where he usually had his morning coffee or lunch with his work colleagues. No, didn't want to stop, even though he had a coffee to sober up a bit. Looking out the bar's window, he noticed the tables with guests, but there weren't that many.

From the lights reflecting outside and the view he had, from where he was standing, he could see people's faces and the drinks they were drinking. Suddenly he stopped, increased the focus of his eyes and ... yes indeed, saw his editor at a table with several people. He also noticed Gabi, positioned from the back on the chair, but he could not decipher the third person. He took a few steps to face the person who could not be seen from the outside due to the lighting of the place. The dark external environment that prevented the internal reflection of the lights, gave the journalist the opportunity to wander around as much as he wanted without being noticed at all.

Yes, yes this is it, -Driton shouted, without noticing that he was talking to himself. It is The Sign, I'm sure. Aww, this game seems to be deeper than I thought.

Why is the editor there in the company of them? He was the initiator of the investigation of the case... The Sign, Gabi, are they all a group of criminals? - he thought to himself. He grabbed his head with his hands and rolled over on the spot several times, sometimes to the left and sometimes to the right. It was clear that he was worried and did not know what he had gotten himself into. He touched his face. He was still in pain, he looked at his clothes, which were stained with blood in places. I will call Fitim, - he thought and his eyes lit up for a moment. He immediately called his friend, asked to meet him in a more discreet place to discuss. Fitim did not delay and they met in one of the less frequented bars not far from the city center. Meanwhile, the journalist had been in his office and had somewhat adjusted his appearance and the miserable state he was in.

-What happened to you, my friend, are you okay? - he noticed the light hitting the journalist's face before he even sat down properly. Fitim was horrified by what he saw.

-Calm down, Fitim, I'll tell you everything now, I'm fine, don't get upset.

The journalist began to tell him everything that had happened: about the report, the meetings with Gabi, The Sign, the alleged incident, as well as the table at the bar where he had seen them all together.

-You've seen hell these days, my friend. If it's Sign that you call the person accompanied by two large cars and a black limousine that roams the streets, I think you're talking about Uncle Tony. He got his nickname from the famous movie Scarface, The Sign - Tony Montana, or Uncle Tony, is very dangerous, he deals with dirty work that he carries out under contract from politics, internationals or the state. He does all the dirty work with professionalism. Because you were lucky how you escaped alive from their hands. I know from my colleagues at work that he has collaborated with several ministries, when they needed him, when he threatened villagers for their lands, where they were bought for a small amount of money by the group with his influence, while in conversion, expropriation with the state, the clan has turned them into big money. I know the case when a person who wanted to run for the decision-making position of chief prosecutor, had his child killed in order to resign from the candidacy, otherwise he would continue with the other children... not even the state has anything to do with him, it is the state itself.

-Yes, Gabi, what could he have to do with it? - the journalist asked in surprise.

-Yes, he clears all the obstacles that Gabi and his friends have. If any heavenly dust is needed, Uncle Toni brings it. He provides the poor girls from the countries that emerged from communism with everything through trafficking channels, weapons, or whatever. There is a lot of talk about him, but no one dares to go after him, he has strong connections with all the decision-making structures.

-One thing I can't understand or connect, why my editor, when he was the initiator for me to investigate the case, why did he push me, - Driton said, wringing his hands and moving his head with speculation.

-This group also controls the media, some of them, which channels opinion or misinforms the public with fake news, trying to confuse everyone. It controls TV, radio and some of the most widely read portals. Where exactly did you meet with them, - Fitim raised his glass up without realizing it, not letting it go from his hand, which made the journalist follow it with his eyes until he understood and put it back on the table.

-So the editor supposedly wanted me to start dealing with the topic in question, but he knew exactly how this work would go. I wouldn't be able to finish the report at all, it would be done in the "ordered" way, or according to their wishes. So, a kind of professional mistake on my part in all this, risking my life in the face of them, if they notice that they are being threatened by me. But who am I, in relation to them? Phew, to endanger them, - the journalist was talking to himself and sometimes he looked at Fitim, trying to connect things in his head.

-You have to be careful with them. I speak from my experiences during the war and my brothers in the company of some of the war commanders, they know them well. They are a product of the war in the worst possible way, they have exploited everything in the name of the sacred "liberation war." It is said that Uncle Toni did not participate in the war for a single day, but with fake certificates and booklets he imposed himself in various circles and began to extend authority with the support of politics and the state. I had advised you not to mix anything with them - said Fitim.

-I have numerous testimonies, I have photographs, recordings of conversations, morgue footage of the girl who has never been reported, neither by the police nor by the media. Many girls who are being smuggled without documents and are ending up in prostitution, none of them seem to have legal documents. I have photographic evidence of the bar, they are there all night, while they remain closed all day so that they are not detected by the neighborhood, - Driton spoke angrily. It seemed that he had a more personal fight with the group in question.

-Think with your head, let go of your emotions because you might get hurt. They don't forgive, they are very dangerous, be careful, - he tried to calm and clear his friend Fitimi's head a little.

-Okay, I understand you, I am very aware, but I will not leave things unaddressed. You will not be able to get away with it for the rest of your life. If this type of people have power or authority, then we are stimulating and promoting crime, there is nothing from our state or country. We will become an underground state. And who will this country be useful to? No one. Let's all get out of this mess then. No, no! We must find a way to stop this disaster that is devouring this country. There will be a future, because we have had a bitter past. We will find a way to get things back on track, there is no other way, - Driton exploded, convinced of what he was saying.

-Can you arrange passports for me and Shpresa? I have an idea how to get out of this mess. – Driton spoke.

-I have contacts with all the ministries, as well as the Ministry of Internal Affairs, I think this can be arranged. But why Shpresa? Where are you going? - Fitim muttered through his teeth.

-Look, if I leave, I have to take Shpresa with me. You know about her, they mentioned her in the threat, I don't want to take any risks, but first I have some things to finish, while we're going to disappear for a while, and then we'll come back when the situation calms down.

- Driton, I know what you have in mind. My intuition tells me something dangerous. Be careful! Stop it, it's not worth it, please! I'm worried about you. You still don't know what they're capable of doing. Don't mess with them, my friend, he begged the journalist to change his mind about getting into a fight with them.

They greeted each other, looked each other in the eye, almost wanting to give the journalist courage and luck so that nothing would happen to him. They each went their separate ways. Driton noticed that it was getting late and he could go home without being noticed at all and without disturbing his family. He took a shower, cleaned himself up, and made some rubbing alcohol on the places where there was dirt and blood. Several burns covered his body, accompanied by a few snorts, but he soon got ready to sleep.

He couldn't sleep all night. He was dreaming about what he had experienced during the day. The sign, Gabi, wouldn't leave him alone at night either, they had become anxiety for him. He woke up, sat up, held his forehead and noticed that he was drenched in sweat. He looked at the clock. It was still early, just beginning to dawn. It was a few minutes past five in the morning. Something occurred to him. He got up, approached his computer on the desk, sat down and started working on compiling the report. Sometimes he would turn on the dictaphone with the recordings he had made. He made sure that his voice was low so as not to wake the others in the house. He worked without moving for hours, a good four hours, until his mother knocked on his door and asked him for breakfast. He only ordered coffee from his mother, saying that he had work and wasn't up for breakfast. The mother, with a medium-sized body, leaning against the door with a sweet face and curly hair that crossed her forehead, wearing a light dress that fit her well, looked at her son, deep in work. She stood for a while, smiled and left him alone. Driton had turned his back on his mother so that she would not see the marks on his face.

He put all the recordings from the dictaphone that he had secretly made in conversations with dangerous people on CDs and made several copies. He also compiled reports with several copies. He did the same with the photos. He had provided each of them with a separate envelope. They were specially made for all the main embassies of the quintet in the country, five of them, plus a copy of a reliable TV medium, also written. He was only waiting for the travel document to enter the action. After drinking his morning coffee away from his parents, he left the apartment and met with Besim.

Besimi was confused when he saw him. There were still some small marks on his face. He only calmed down when he explained the situation to him in a few words, but not in so much detail that he wouldn't worry the religious man.

-I still can't get used to your new look, so don't forget, - they both burst out laughing in sync, "what counts is what's inside, not what's on the outside", - they both laughed. - It's not who you are, but what you know, - the journalist continued. - You started to overdo it, - laughed Besimi, who was dressed in a frock with the most prominent brands of the time and smelled of one of the most respected perfumes. Besimi of high school had returned.

-I'm going to visit Vesna these days. We agreed to spend a weekend together in Sarajevo. I hope to see you again soon, my friend, -said the priest, now modern. Driton hugged the religious tightly. -I'm glad to see you happy. We'll see you anyway - the journalist greeted him.

It was time to meet with Shpresa. He began to explain everything he wanted to tell her.

-Listen, you and I are going to leave here for a while, you understand,

-Driton spoke.

-I can't calm down. Who are the people who did this to you? I'm worried about you, Driton, -Shpresa spoke and her eyes immediately started to redden.

-Come on, don't worry, everything will be okay, you understand?

- If you say so, so be it, -Shpresa answered with full of doubts every time she looked at the now bruised face of the man she loved.

-Let's go somewhere and have a drink.

-Okay, let's go- Shpresa agreed.

The two walked hugging. From behind it seemed that the journalist's movements were a bit disorganized from the blows he had suffered earlier. Luckily for him, there was nothing broken, only bruises on his body. Reason for not seeking medical help, indicated in the medical register that is related to the police when there are such cases and to make it known what he had found, from whom, more reason to take revenge. If the sign spoke...

The farther the couple walked, the smaller they looked. They were tied together so that from a distance their silhouette and shape gave the appearance of a heart shining from the rays of the sun that hit everywhere, and from them came reflection and brilliance that was enough to kill the eyes.

The next day Fitimi announced that he had the documents ready for the trip. He could pick them up whenever he wanted after they met.

Driton asked to meet all his friends one more time before leaving with Shpresa.

They chose the city park where they would meet. Driton talked to everyone about what had happened to him. Besa bit her nails while the journalist spoke; Shpresa heard about some events for the first time and was just stunned, she was lost; the religious man just prayed, sang duas and thanked God that he had escaped alive. From time to time, Fitimi would fill in, when he was distracted or lost in thought.

-The plan is that at the same time as my report, we will make it public to the most well-known embassies in the country, the respectable television medium, the printed newspaper and the reliable portal, the chief state prosecutor, as well as the international one, and leave while the news gets out, taking into account our safety. Then we will see what will be done, how things will go.

-We will help you distribute the reports while you are traveling. Don't take any risks, whether you have friends or not, - Besa spoke, determined to help her friend in trouble.

-This is for the good of our country, we must come together to remove evil from this country once and for all, - Besa stood up excitedly.

-I will deal with the distribution to the embassies - Besim spoke, determined.

-I will deal with the media - Besa added, while Fitimi said:

-I have no choice but to the chief state prosecutor and the international one.

-You, my friends, don't need to get involved in these matters, to take risks too, but at the same time thank you very much for the support and help you are offering me, - the journalist spoke.

-You should listen to us! You do your best work and we will deal with other things, until you are safe somewhere. We will publish them

your reports. Try to make them good and strong so we can get these bastards inside - Besimi moved excitedly as he spoke.

-Here are your passports, my friend. Good luck to both of you, - Fitimi greeted them, handing the documents to the journalist.

-I have one more unfinished business, I have to go to the office and meet with the editor of the newspaper. Tomorrow I think we will leave and you will distribute the reports. Do you agree, Shpresa, to prepare your suitcases in the meantime? - Driton addressed Shpresa.

-Okay, let it be as planned. Good luck! - Shpresa supported her journalist.

As he approached the office, she met the editor on the stairs coming out of the building.

- What happened to you, Driton? -asked the editor, gesturing around his face to show that he understood what he was talking about, trying not to burden him.

-I had an accident, I'm fine now, I'm working on that report you asked for, I'm taking it seriously and professionally, - the journalist replied.

-I'm going to a meeting, but of course I'll see you in a bit,

- the editor said as he left.

-I hope so -said Driton, climbing the stairs and turning his head towards the editor.

For a moment, the two of them stopped and looked into each other's eyes. The look was more than words. It seems that at that moment, each of them told the other everything through their gaze; they understood each other quite well and each continued on his own way. He entered the office, took some things he needed that he had left there. He opened the drawer, saw a photograph of him together with his friends. Liria was there too. He looked at her, smiled sweetly and put it in his jacket. He checked his work computer, deleted some documents that shouldn't be seen, some emails, and released

office. He looked at his desk once more and closed the door. As soon as he went out into the hallway, he saw his colleagues gathered and listening to the news. They looked worried.

-What happened, any news? - Driton asked.

-A dead body has been found, suspected of murder, a young man.

- Genta, responsible for the graphics and design of the news, spoke. Driton approached the television and saw the face of the boy who had been found dead. He recognized that face well. It was person X. Yes, it was him. A strong tremor shook his entire body. They found him, they killed him, - he said to himself. The sign, Uncle Tony, or whoever is, is doing the job as best he can. But no, with me, not anymore, he had the chance then, now we'll see how it goes, - he fought with himself. He thought he was being noticed by the others, greeted them and went down the stairs to the exit of the facility. Before he was even outside the building, he suddenly saw the black limousine parked in front of him near the main gate. The two colossuses were next to the car, looking around, at the clock, with their eyes on the gate. It seemed that they were waiting for someone. Driton hid immediately, he knew that they were looking for him. He used the back door and ran away from the office, entering a narrow alley on two sides with house yards diametrically opposite the main road at the gate where The Sign's dogs were waiting. While running, he thought that they had to leave the city as soon as possible. He felt that he was in danger, there was no time to waste. Somehow he reached home to get ready for the road the next day. It was afternoon, he had just left after three o'clock. There was still time for the trip, the next day seemed like a century. He informed his parents about the route he would take, but not in the way it actually was.

-You're saying you have a work trip, a seminar that will last a few days, right? Why didn't you tell us earlier? - asked the father who was holding the newspaper in his hands and didn't put it away at all, but lowered the open pages and lowered his eyes below his glasses so that he could communicate more freely with his son, but he didn't take the newspaper out of his hands.

-That's right, and I think I'll go sleep at my work colleague's tonight so we can leave early together. I just came to say goodbye with you and take some things and leave, - he tried to convince his parents while standing.

- God bless you, my son! - congratulated his mother who was standing near the sink with some dishes that she was washing and they seemed to have no end. She weighed one foot and the other while not taking her eyes off her son.

- Okay son, let it be so. - said the father and changed his leg. They still pressed but did not remove it from their hands, the extended foot between the slippers looked like a finger of reprimand pointing at the circumstances in which his son was and they did not know anything. He slightly ruffled the sparse hair on his head and gave Driton a sign of approval with a benevolent smile until now one side of the leaflet was hanging in one hand while he scratched his head with the other.

As soon as he left the apartment, he noticed his followers at the main entrance. They had found his house and were waiting in front of the neighborhood. He mobilized, took a deep breath and started running. His pursuers saw him.

-There, there he is! Right behind him, - shouted The Sign to the two colossi who were close to him. They quickly got into the car and furiously set off in the direction of the fugitive.

The journalist ran and from time to time turned his head to see if he was being followed. It seemed that they would catch him, but the fugitive wisely used the narrow parts and stairs where the cars could not follow him, but they found alternative routes and were always close to him.

-Give it, give it to us, we caught the dog! He will play tail with me, - shouted The Sign and with his hand he hit the front seats where his colossi were sitting. It seemed as if he was beating the horses to increase their speed.

Driton saw a one-way street and decided to enter it so that the cars coming in the opposite direction to the pursuers would stop their movement. But they did not stop. They found space by moving on the sidewalk, the road face to face with the cars that were coming at them but did not give in.

-What are you doing, get caught in this dirt, come on you weaklings,

look how you are getting away!- he continued to hit the driver's seats from behind and tried to give him courage and pressure while driving the car, and that he had to be very careful not to roll over somewhere, or encounter a frontal obstacle. The horses had entered a gallop.

Seeing that the pursuers were not giving up, the fugitive entered a narrow alley that turned out to be a dead end. He decided to overcome the metal fences of the yards that were there and entered the properties of the houses. Passing from one gate to another, he somehow managed to penetrate into a completely different road. The pursuers saw him, someone ran after him, while the car took a different direction to get ahead of them. They did not manage to notice that the journalist somehow managed to avoid them and was in a safe area. He took out a vest with a hat and put it on to disguise himself and set off. But where to? He took out his phone and contacted Fitim.

-I'm in trouble, my friend, they're after me. Tonight I have to spend the night at your place, - he spoke, panting and full of breath and with one hand wiping the sweat from running. He waited for his friend's answer. Fitimi offered him shelter and asked him to immediately head to him, discreetly and without being noticed.

On the way, he mixed with the crowd. From afar, his eye caught the car that was following him, he stopped, entered a store and looked where it was headed, it seemed that it was moving around, looking for prey. Driton changed direction, chose a longer route to his friend's and always disguised and included in the crowd, he walked at the same pace as them.

-You idiot, loser, look how you ran away! Didn't you manage to catch him running, I never saw him, -shouted The Sign and took out his revolver. He shot him several times and opened the door while the car was moving and threw the body out.

-What are you looking at, do you want the same fate to await you? Open your eyes, you might be seeing the handsome man somewhere, -he said, cleaning the barrel of the floodgate and the blood with which it had been sprayed by the victim who had been near it during the execution.

-Yes, boss, as you say, - the driver replied timidly, pretending not to have seen anything and ignoring the previous act.

The journalist reached his friend without being noticed at all. He called Shpresa and asked her to be careful to spend the night at Danaj's and to meet him at the airport early in the morning, accompanied by Uncle Bedri. He told her briefly what had happened and what protective measures were being taken for the safety of both of them.

-Driton, are you okay? You sound very worried. Have they done something bad to you again, tell me - said Shpresa, whose voice showed that she had been overcome by worry from the conversation she had with her lover.

-Honey, I'm fine, a little tired, we can't last long but be careful, decide whether to come to Fitimi's tonight or meet tomorrow morning before the flight. I secured the tickets for both of us while I was in the office, via the Internet. Rest and see you early tomorrow morning.

His mind went to his brother in Sweden, but he still thought to himself that it was better not to bother him in this situation. It was a good thing I chose another destination, - he was trying to find a way to rest and calm down.

Fitim offered all the necessary comfort to his friend.

- Tomorrow I will accompany you to the airport, - he spoke to the guest with complete conviction.

- No Fitim, there is no need, don't risk more. I will call a taxi or better for both of us, it seems safer to me, - said Driton, holding his friend's arm. With grateful eyes he released him from the obligation.

The next morning, early in the morning, he very easily found himself at the airport. There were no surprises from the pursuers. It seemed that they had lost track of the pursuit. Shpresa arrived soon, accompanied by Uncle Bedri.

- Driton, we have Shpresa as our daughter. Take care of her, we know you are a young man and you do a lot for her. May you be lucky and live long! Have a good journey! - he did not let go of Shpresa's hand yet. He hugged her tightly and a few tears of emotion overtook the elderly hunter. He extended his hand to Driton as if he were a man and they dispersed into the crowd of the airport.

They hurried to check their tickets and luggage. As they were going up the escalator towards the security checkpoints for the passport control, from above they recognized two people who hurriedly entered, looking around. It was those pursuers again: the Sign and his remaining colossus.

-Shpresa, lower your head and quickly get to the second floor!- he said and covered his girlfriend's hair with his hands while he remained hunched over, hiding like a shield from the people around him.

-We escaped, they didn't see us. Now let's continue with the other routine checks. Once we cross the border, we'll be safe, -he said hurriedly, pulling her hand to hurry, and they headed towards the guards standing in front of the luggage and body detectors. They passed through security without incident and approached the border and passport control. Now it was time for Fitimi to show himself with the documents he had prepared for them.

-Where are you headed? To tour Europe or to visit family? - asked the border guard as he checked the passports and visas on the documents to make sure they weren't fake. He put them in the camera and turned his eyes to the passengers.

-We just got engaged, we want to pay a visit to our family, a surprise if we can say so, but we'll stay at the hotel, - replied the journalist, who in the meantime turned his head to see if the pursuers had reached there too. The border guard did the same with Shpresa's document, looked her in the eye and validated the passport in the corresponding camera. After a while, he stamped both of them, offered them the documents and wished them a safe journey.

-Thank you, my friend! - shouted the journalist loudly, kissing the passports, immediately after crossing the border. He hugged Shpresa tightly and they headed to the appropriate gate to prepare for the flight.

In front of them stood a family waiting for the same destination of their journey. They were a man and a woman, well-dressed, good-looking, and looked like they were brother and sister. They had a daughter, about three years old or so, as beautiful as an angel, but also lively. She had a tube of soap bubbles, she ran, wandered, she was scolded by her parents if

something happened to her. They had bought it for her in the middle of the zone after they had passed passport control in the shops nearby. They told her that she would not be allowed to board the plane with it. For the first time, Shpresa did not feel anything bad as she watched the bubbles flying high, wandering, and from time to time hitting each other and bursting, creating sprays of water for those nearby. She began to like these kinds of bubbles. She had Driton nearby, she was no longer afraid of anything. She followed one of the balls that were waving up, it went quite high, the other followed it as if after it, they connected and became together like a larger bubble ball, but surprisingly they did not burst, they flew together, wandering without worries, full of dreams. It seemed to her that she saw herself and her life, which she identified with the bubbles that sometimes rose and sometimes fell to the ground, but there were always bubbles, they never stopped moving, each one had something special in it, it could even have a name, it could be me, you…

-Now we are safe, - Driton kissed Shpresa on the lips, put his hand on her neck and pulled her close to him. The door opened after a while. They got on the plane and flew.

-It seems that they escaped us. They did not inform us in time that they would be at the airport.

The editor at the journalist's desk seemed to have found out about the tickets purchased from the work computer late.

-Too late, my friend... now mice like birds are migrating elsewhere.

With one hand, the Sign took his hat off his head, looked at it a few times in a daze, patted it on his expensive suit, took his pocket watch out of his vest, nodded slowly to say that he had no more business here. He headed outside, followed by the colossus, his driver.

XXXV

At ten thirty the next day, everyone who was in favor of the action of sending the journalist's report to the designated destinations gathered. It was agreed that around eleven o'clock all the copies would be distributed at the same time. Besimi took the first step towards his part of the task for five destinations. He tried to be as expeditious as possible in their distribution and not to take up time. He had made the plan and itinerary of the movement. He thought that within ten minutes he would go through the embassies of the fifth in the country. He would start a few minutes before the appointed time so that at the promised time they would all be distributed. Besa was ready for the designated media outlets that she would frequent. She had also brought her husband, Bekim, to help her during the delivery. Fitim would go to the areas that he usually passed by every day. He was not too worried about the work that had to be done.

-Good luck to us! We will leave in a few minutes, each one will finish their part and we will meet again at this same place at noon. Okay? - Fitim addressed Besim and Besa.

- We will see each other at twelve, - Besa said, looking at her husband who was waiting for her in the car to leave.

- May God help us, open the way for us! We will see each other later and see how the work went, - Besim conveyed her last words with prayer.

After a while, they scattered like bees from their hives, selecting pollen from the best flowers to produce the required nectar.

They gathered again after an hour, at the same place. Each one reported on the work they had done.

- It went very well, Alhamdililah! - Besim said, - Just as I had planned, - the religious man finished his report.

"I didn't have a problem at all either, I asked for the general directors, telling them it was too sensitive, but they welcomed me very well," Besa replied happily.

-And you, Fitim, do you have anything to tell us, how did you do? - Besimi pressed him, looking at his friend, deep in thought and worried.

- Excuse me! I distributed our friend's reports very well, but I was surprised by the chief state prosecutor, who during the delivery said to me: "You have a sensitive report to hand over to me, don't you?" The fact is tormenting me, where he found out, where he could have learned what I had in my hand, - the ministerial official spoke, still surprised. - But luckily I first sent the document to the internationals and then to the locals, - he finished his words, convincing himself that he had done the right thing in choosing who to serve first.

- Does this one of ours have a hand too, do you think Fitim? If so, then we hope that the internationals will deal with him too, or, - trying to provide a solution to Fitim's concern, Besa declared.

Winning with a nod of approval only sealed what his friend said.

Somewhere in Europe, Shpresa had woken up earlier than her boyfriend and was making her morning coffee. The sunlight had taken over the room, the entire apartment, and it was clear that Driton had slept enough. He still felt tired and ached somewhere in his body from the events of the last few days.

Shpresa's phone rang, since Driton didn't carry his number with him for security reasons and it was his friends from his hometown who were calling. Shpresa ran to Driton, who was trying to wake up from his sleep. His eyes had been closed from the glare of the light that was entering the room since Shpresa had opened the curtains earlier.

-It's his friends, they've all gathered together. They're calling from Viber, they've turned on the camera. Wake up so we can see them, - said Shpresa, trying to help her boyfriend get up, holding the phone in other hand.

A voice from the phone that was deciphered as being familiar spoke: - Turn on the TV and watch today's news, it's live now! It was Besimi excited.

-Yes, you are listening to the news from our country, - they all spoke almost in unison.

Driton ran into the living room, turned on the TV and searched for local channels to see what had happened. Shpresa followed him with her phone, while Driton, still in his pajamas, immediately came to his senses after hearing the moderator's first words, who was going straight to the point.

"Today, in the early hours of the morning, during a police operation by the anti-crime unit, they found a bar full of girls forced into prostitution who were in poor health and without basic hygiene conditions...

The two of them looked at each other while the cheerful voices from their friends on the other end of the phone did not stop. The moderator continued: "the organized network also includes several well-known public figures from political and social life who have also been involved in murders, eliminations...." - she continued to mention various names with photos of the suspects.

-Driton, does this person resemble your colleague from Liria? His name is John, aww! -Shpresa was surprised.

Driton had opened his eyes and now he had lost sleep watching the faces that emerged one by one from the operation that the country had undertaken, without the help of internationals, that had received support from various European circles that were fighting crime and corruption with their own forces. The Sign, the colossus, the editor, Gabi, and many others that the journalist had not even seen before also passed through the screen. The accusations were of the most diverse, from human trafficking to various murderous crimes with corrupt backgrounds involved in various clans that were also institutional parts.

-Yes, it was John, -Driton replied coldly as if in repentance. Shpresa followed the enthusiasm of her friends through the camera and sometimes followed the news and sometimes looked at Driton's face, which changed every time a well-known name was highlighted on the list of criminalized people.

It seemed that this work was over, for the best, as if a heavy burden and weight had been lifted from Driton's body. He looked at Shpresa, took her in his lap. He was still in his pajamas and his curly hair was messy.

Shpresa had a short dress that reached her knees, clinging to her body. As soon as put her on his lap, a part of her silk slipped and rose up, revealing her beautiful, soft legs and thighs. He lovingly hugged her slender waist, held her face with both hands and pulled her closer to him. He kissed her forehead and caressed her for a while on his chest. Huddled next to him, she looked like a baby a few weeks old in the womb. This position gave Shpresa security and a sense of fulfillment like never before. A flash of thought about her brother crossed her mind, making her eyes watering.

- What's wrong, is something bothering you? - the journalist noticed what had seized him.

- Nothing.

He didn't want to ruin the moment they were in. It was a perfect moment of intertwining feelings that created a halo of exaltation that was not exaggerated but reasonable and down to earth. It was more than an emotion, it was a feeling, a feeling of love, that only appeared when Driton was near.

Enjoying his morning coffee and the beautiful moments that the sunlight of that very significant dawn for the couple in question allowed, this tranquility or spiritual idyll of fulfillment was broken by a phone message that came to Shpresa. The phone was on the table near them, accompanied by that same sound with additional vibrations.

-Take it, it's not for you, honey, -she brought the phone closer to Driton, getting up from her lover's lap with the finished coffee cups towards the sink to wash them.

The journalist opened the message and for a moment his face turned pale, changed in appearance and mood. It was as if he had seen a ghost with his own eyes, not a phone message. It read: "It seems you were lucky, he respected you a lot, it seems he loved you even more, one of the main local players in this whole game is your precious friend Fitimi, anonymous.

He remained motionless for a few moments. The phone fell from his hand, Shpresa turned her head to see what was happening while washing the few dishes that were left.

Driton waved his hand from the phone. The two sadly looked at each other eye to eye. The sun's rays disappeared for a moment, almost as if they were sympathizing with the couple, who were suddenly covered by a cloud. A bird stopped at the window, wanted to sing, but was frightened by the faces he saw inside and migrated to another roof. He needed spiritual optimism, for hope, for all those things that often seem petty and that beings need for a sweeter tomorrow of awakening. The photograph of the view in the room with the frozen faces remained static for a few moments. There was no energy, no movement, no spirit… they were drunk on the deeds and the undone in that whole torn sack that, like a trickle or a pile of nails in the marrow of memories, generated uncertainty, where neither a glass of brandy nor a stalk of trifles helps at all. The moment brings the moment, the moment the opportunity, while the opportunity is framed in the venture, and all this has a narrative…a lie…in which we either believe or declare heresy.

End

Cataloging in publication – (CIP)

National Library of Kosovo "Pjetër Bogdani"